An Amazon Editors' Pick for Best Romance

One of the 22 Best Erotic Novels to Read from
Marie Claire **magazine**

"Hardt spins erotic gold."
—*Publishers Weekly*

"Intensely erotic and wildly emotional."
—*New York Times* **bestselling author Lisa Renee Jones**

"With an edgy, enigmatic hero and loads of sexual tension, Helen Hardt's fast-paced *Follow Me Darkly* had me turning pages late into the night!"
—*New York Times* **bestselling author J. Kenner**

"A tour de force where the reader will be pulled in as if they're being seduced by Braden Black, taken for a wild ride, and left wanting more."
—*USA Today* **bestselling author Julie Morgan**

"Hot. Sexy. Intriguing. Page-turner."
—**International bestselling author Victoria Blue**

"Helen Hardt's gift for engaging storytelling and unforgettable characters is at its full shine."
—*USA Today* **bestselling author Angel Payne**

"Christian, Gideon, and now…Braden Black."
—**Books, Wine, and Besties**

"This book is off-the-charts hot, very near scalding."
—**Books Best**

"It completely consumed me and I'm in love with the mysterious Braden. I want and need to know more about this man."
—**The Sassy Nerd Blog**

FOLLOW ME
ALWAYS

A NOVEL

#1 *NEW YORK TIMES* BESTSELLING AUTHOR

HELEN
HARDT

Entangled Publishing, LLC
10940 S Parker Road
Suite 327
Parker, CO 80134
rights@entangledpublishing.com

Amara is an imprint of Entangled Publishing, LLC.

Visit our website at www.entangledpublishing.com.

Edited by Liz Pelletier
Cover design by Bree Archer
Cover images Gorlov/GettyImages-1292424729,
OGphoto/GettyImages.157588714,
Anna Kim/GettyImages-1156926694,
MRS.Siwaporn/Shutterstock-1018213306
Interior design by Toni Kerr

ISBN 978-1-68281-556-4
Ebook ISBN 978-1-68281-557-1

Manufactured in the United States of America

First Edition August 2021

10 9 8 7 6 5 4 3 2 1

Also by Helen Hardt

For everyone on this journey called life.

Prologue

Oh? What are your hard limits?
I only have one.
What is it?
I don't talk about it.
Don't you think I should know? So I don't bring it up?
Trust me, Skye. You will never bring it up.

Braden was wrong. I brought it up. Why did he think I wouldn't? Control. It's the ultimate loss of control, and he assumed I'd never go there.

"Why?" I ask. "Why won't you do it?"

"Why? Perhaps I'll tell you why…as soon as you tell me why you feel you need it."

"I…don't know."

He inhales. Exhales. Inhales again. Is he thinking about how to reply to me? Is he angry? Sad? Does he feel anything at all?

Because I can't tell.

"For God's sake, Braden," I finally say. "Can you show me some emotion for *once* in your life?"

He cocks his head as his nostrils flare. "You think I don't show you emotion?" He stands. "How can you say that? I've shown you more emotion than I've ever shown anyone. *Anyone*, Skye. If you don't know that, you should."

He's right. I'm not being fair. He showed me a ton of emotion last night when my dinner burned, and I lost it. "Braden—"

"No. You don't talk. Not until I'm done. I told you who I was. I told you I wasn't wired for relationships. But I made an exception for you. I made that exception because I love you, Skye. I wasn't looking to fall in love. I knew it would put a dent in my life—"

I can't help responding. I'm torn in half, and I'm angry. "A dent, Braden? I'm a fucking dent?"

"Shut up! Just shut the fuck up, Skye. I will have my say, and then you can have yours. If you're brave enough."

"Brave enough? What's that supposed to mean?"

"You know exactly what it means, and if you interrupt me again, this discussion is over."

My lips tremble as I nod.

He clears his throat. "I made an exception for you. I decided to have a relationship—or try, at least—but I fear this little experiment of mine has failed."

Little experiment? I'm a damned experiment? I want to yell, scream, tear out his hair. Punch his smug face until it's bruised and battered.

I want to cry, sob in his arms, and tell him I'll do anything to please him.

I want to beg him to take me back underground, tie me up, choke me.

I want to bare my soul, confess my love, tell him I'll do anything... Anything...

But I sit quietly. I sit quietly because I'm afraid. I'm very afraid of where this is leading.

If you're brave enough...

I've lost so much already.

And now I'm about to lose the man I love.

Chapter One

Seconds pass like hours.
Tick.

Tock.

Tick.

Tock.

I wait.

I wait while emotion hurricanes through me in a mass of anger, sadness, and fear.

I wait for Braden to continue. To say what he has to say.

To end our relationship—a relationship that perhaps should never have begun.

I could be content right now. Who needs Susanne Cosmetics? I could still be working for Addison Ames. She paid me pretty well, and yeah, she's a narcissistic bitch, but I was making contacts.

And Tessa. I'd still have Tessa. My best friend forever, except that forever apparently has an end after all. Maybe I'd be dating that Peter guy. He's not a billionaire, but he's an architect at a major firm. He does all right. Who needs a private jet anyway?

Or a private driver? I'll settle for a guy with a decent car. Who needs to be tied up? Spanked? Choked?

I never did.

I was content before.

Except that I wasn't.

I was never challenged.

And Braden?

He challenges me. Not just in everyday, run-of-the-mill ways, either. He challenges my very way of thinking. He challenges my concept of myself. He dares me to try new things. Things I never even conceptualized before.

Things I never knew existed.

And I'm not just talking about the bondage.

I'm talking about life. About my photography. About seeing a bigger picture. About becoming what I'm meant to be.

Braden did all that for me.

And now he's going to take it away.

"Well?" he finally asks.

I lift my eyebrows, fearing that if I speak, he'll walk away that much sooner.

"You may speak," he says.

I nod. "Well, what?"

"Fuck it all, Skye. Don't you have anything to say?"

What? Did he say something after the experiment comment? Shit. He may have. I was busy having a little pity party for myself inside my head.

"I'm sorry. I'm a little…distracted."

"Distracted? Really? So you don't give a shit that we're breaking up?"

My heart sinks to my belly. His words aren't unexpected. No. In fact, I predicted them. But actually hearing them? In his voice?

They hit me like a tornado, crashing into me and shattering every glass window inside my soul.

It's an implosion of thought and emotion. Of reality and identity.

"I'm sorry." I choke back a sob. I made a fool of myself last night, crying over my ruined dinner. I won't do it again.

Not for Braden.

Not for anyone.

"This was a mistake," he says, "and I take full responsibility."

"My contract…" The words come out independent of thought.

"Yes, I've thought of that. If Susanne cancels the contract because you're no longer my girlfriend, I'll remunerate you until you find work."

I tilt my head, my body numb. "You'll *remunerate* me?"

"Yes. I feel it's only fair. Your association with me cost you the job with Addie, and your association with me also got you started as an influencer. If you're no longer associated—"

"No. Remunerate means to pay for services rendered. Why would you use that word? Do you think I've been *servicing* you, Braden? That I was letting you—"

"For fuck's sake. Of course not. But I'm very aware that women will let me do what I want to do in exchange for the privilege of being with me."

Heartbroken as I am, I can't let him get away with this crap. "Privilege? Are you kidding me? You really think I let you tie me up just to be your arm candy?"

"No. I said I didn't. But it's happened in the past."

"With Addie?"

"Christ! This is serious, Skye. We're having a significant conversation, and you bring up Addie and me again?"

"*You* brought it up. You said it's happened in the past."

"I wasn't talking about Addie."

Right. He wasn't. His… What was it anyway? His…dalliance? Anyway, whatever it was, his time with Addie took place before he made his millions. Way before he made his billions.

"I'm not like anyone else," I say.

My heart seems to fragment, exploding into little pieces inside my body and then sinking to my feet.

Rock bottom.

This must be what rock bottom feels like.

Does it matter anymore? Addie and Braden?

No. Not if Braden and I are no longer together.

"I don't regret my time with you," he says.

I scoff softly. "Great. I don't regret my time with you, either."

"I'm glad."

Silence for a few moments. Until—

"Skye…"

"What?" My tone is less nice than I anticipate.

"I don't want to end things. Please understand that."

"If you don't want to end things, don't end things," I say adamantly.

"It's not that simple."

"Seems to me it is. You end things or you don't. Simple choice, Braden, and you're the one making it."

"There are things you don't know." He holds his chin high.

"Only because you won't tell me!" Anger flares within me. I've already hit rock bottom, so what the hell? I can't sink any lower, so I may as well have my say.

"Some things I don't talk about," he says, "with anyone."

"Then this relationship was doomed from the start, Braden. We never really had a chance, did we?"

He sighs and rubs at his temples. "Maybe we didn't."

I can't help it then. I let a tear fall. One. Two. Three. Then several more, until sobs erupt from my throat and the tears become gushers. "You're wrong! We always had a chance. Yes, I made some mistakes, but so did you. You should have been honest with me. About Addie. About your mother. About everything!"

His jawline tenses. I can almost see his teeth grinding together, as if his skin and muscles are translucent.

"I'll be honest with you the day you're honest with me," he says.

"I've been honest with you from the beginning. That's not fair."

"You *think* you've been honest with me, but you haven't. You can't even tell me why you wanted me to choke you tonight. *You*. Skye Manning. Queen of control. *You* wanted a man to put rope around your neck, to cut off your air. Do you have any idea what that means?"

"I just…" I wheeze as another sob erupts from my throat. "I just…"

Braden clenches his jaw. "Say it, Skye! Fucking say it!"

All the emotion deep in my belly coils outward like a snake. "I wanted to sink! Sink into nothingness! Give you the ultimate control over my life, okay? Is that what you want to hear? Does it make you feel like a big man to get me to admit that? Does it?"

"It's dangerous," he says solemnly. "You're an intelligent woman. I shouldn't have to tell you that."

I gasp back another sob. "I trust you."

"I know you do. This is no longer about trust, Skye."

"Then what is it about?"

"What if something went wrong? What if you…"

"I said I *trust* you," I say, willing myself to gain control over my body and my emotions. "But if it's so dangerous, why do you let other people at your club do it?"

"Does it matter?"

"Of course it matters!"

He pauses a moment, rubbing his chin. "I'm insured. The club is insured. People go there to live out their ultimate fantasies, and I give them the latitude to do that."

"Well, then?" I meet his gaze, his blue eyes not fiery but still adamant.

HELEN HARDT 9

"It doesn't mean I *share* all their fantasies. And breath control of any kind is my hard limit."

I whip my hands to my hips. "Even if I want it?"

"*Especially* if you want it, Skye. I will *not* put you in danger. What if you had a fetish of being thrown in front of a moving vehicle. Do you want me to indulge that?"

I resist rolling my eyes. It won't go over well. "It's different, and you know it."

"Is it?"

"Of course it is. I don't want to harm myself."

"What do you want, then?"

"To—"

I stop abruptly, my mouth hanging open.

I drop my gaze to Braden's bed, and I smooth out a wrinkle on his navy comforter.

He's going to push me. He's going to insist that I answer. And the truth is…

I don't *know* the answer.

I mean, I know the answer that's the frosting on the cake. I want to lose control. I want to lose myself, especially now when I've already lost so much of my life. My job. My best friend. The contract with New England Adventures.

And now…Braden.

But that's a surface answer, and Braden knows it.

He wants the real answer. The deep answer. Not just the cake beneath the frosting but the filling, too.

And honestly?

I'm not sure I'm ready to face the real answer.

Chapter Two

"I want to...find myself?"

Damn. Already I berate myself for adding inflection to my response. He'll know I'm not sure of my answer, and he'll call me out.

"Really?" he says, doubt lacing his tone.

I inhale a deep breath, drawing as much courage as I can muster—which isn't a lot at this point. See? When you lose so much, you lose your courage as well.

"To challenge myself," I say, keeping my tone as even as I can.

"And you think me choking you will challenge you?"

His tone isn't mocking, but his words are. I choose to take him at face value. And at face value, his question is valid.

He deserves an answer, a truthful one.

"Honestly? I don't know. All I know is that I saw it in the scene, and I wanted it."

"And do you still want it now?"

I could lie to him. Tell him I'm over it. Anything to keep him in my life. But I love him too much to lie. He'll know anyway.

"Y-Yes. I still want it now."

"I see."

He stands and paces across the deep red Turkish rug. He rakes his fingers through his already disheveled hair.

Fear slides through me. I already know we're over, but as I watch him, look at him, *see* him, I realize how deeply I've fallen.

He's beautiful, yes. His ass tight in those black pants, his broad and muscular shoulders apparent in his black button down. A masterpiece.

But I didn't fall in love with his masculine beauty.

And he's rich. So ungodly rich. I've dined in the best restaurants, sampled the finest wines, flown in a private jet, for God's sake.

But I didn't fall in love with his money or his things.

I fell in love with the man who volunteers at a food pantry when he could get by with writing a gigantic check.

I fell in love with the man who rescued two dogs—one for me.

I fell in love with the man who cut his business trip short because he couldn't wait to get back to me.

I fell in love with Braden Black the man, not Braden Black the icon.

And I need to tell him.

"I love you, Braden."

He turns, his eyes heavy-lidded and a little glazed over. "I love you too. I wish I didn't, but I do."

His words both warm me and cut me. He *loves* me. But he wishes he *didn't* love me.

My lips tremble. "Then can't we work this out?"

He shakes his head slowly. "No. Not when you can't be honest with me."

"But I—"

"Skye, you're not. And what's more, you know you're not. Look inside yourself. Figure yourself out, because until you do, you'll always yearn for something I can't give you. And I'm not just talking about the neck bondage."

. . .

He let me sleep in his bedroom. I don't know where he slept. After I was all cried out, maybe I got some sleep. Truthfully, I don't know.

I know only that I rose in the morning and accompanied Braden in silence to the airport. We boarded the jet, also in silence. Thank God it was a short flight. Christopher met us and dropped me off at my place. Braden, ever the gentleman, walked me to the door.

He touched my cheek lightly. "Goodbye, Skye."

I nodded. No words got past the lump in my throat.

This all happened mere hours ago, and it feels like a lifetime.

I lie on my bed, unable to move.

Unable to—

I jerk upward. My contract. My damned contract!

I'm still under contract to create content for Susie Girl Cosmetics, and my last post sucked big-time.

No more tears. I'm all cried out. I run into the bathroom and—

Oh my God. I look like a hag. A red-eyed, swollen-faced, snot-nosed hag.

And I have to do an Instagram post today.

Three posts per week pursuant to my contract.

My contract that I have only because I'm Braden's girlfriend.

Somehow, I have to get myself together. I have to do the post, and it has to be great after the last disaster.

If only I had someone to talk to.

Tessa could help me, but we're not speaking.

Penny would snuggle with me, lick my face, and make me feel loved enough to maybe get my creative juices flowing. But she's still at Braden's, and she will be until I move into a place that allows dogs.

That's it! I'll go over to Braden's to see Penny. She's my dog, after all. I should be able to visit my own dog.

I bite my lower lip.

That's not the answer, and I know it. Though I long to see my puppy, I'm really hoping I'll see Braden. I'm hoping he'll change his mind when he sees me, remembers how much he loves me.

He'll accuse me of manipulating him.

And he'll be right.

I'll visit Penny tomorrow, then, when Braden's at his office. He already told Christopher during our tense drive home earlier that I'm allowed to see Penny as often as I want, as long as he's not home. I even have Christopher's number to text him personally.

My phone is like a magnetic beacon in my pocket.

Just one text… Maybe Braden isn't home? Maybe he went into his office? Maybe…

But I can't.

I'm a mess, and as much as I want my puppy, I can't be that woman.

It's manipulative. Needy and manipulative.

I draw in a deep breath and stare at my disgusting reflection. First things first. A shower. A cold one to help ease the swelling in my face. It won't be pleasant, but I don't want anything pleasant at the moment. I want the blast of cold water on my body. Maybe it will fuel the creative part of my brain, because, damn, I need a post to end all posts today.

I have to give Eugenie and the rest of the team a reason to keep me on the payroll even if I'm not Braden Black's significant other.

I'll show them that Skye Manning is worth their confidence just because she's Skye Manning.

Now… If only I can convince myself.

Chapter Three

The cold shower helps a little, but I still look like I've been to hell and back. I hastily pull the contract out of my briefcase. Does each post have to be a selfie? I hope not.

I read through the instructions for each post, and... "Yes!" I shout. Nothing in the language says I must appear in every post.

What can I do, then?

What can I do with this new pile of Susie products without actually using them on my face? I sift through them, looking each one over, hoping one of them will speak to me in words. Of course, that would mean I'm hearing voices, which wouldn't be a good thing.

Come on, Skye. Time to get creative. Think, brain. Think.

And when it finally comes to me, my heart thuds.

Susie Girl Mood Lip Gloss and Plumper.

It changes color according to skin tone and to mood, or so it says.

Let's prove it, then. I'll show the world how it looks on someone other than me today, and tomorrow, I'll wear it. But who?

This is a new line, and it's all about the everyday woman, right? So why not find an everyday woman to model one of the lip colors? It doesn't have to be me, especially when I look like a fright.

Tessa, of course, is my first choice, but she's not an option. Too bad, because her darker skin tone and lip color would be the perfect contrast to my fairness.

So...Betsy.

She's perfect. Very pretty but not glam like Tessa. Her skin is pretty light, but not as pale as mine, and her lips are more an orange flesh tone compared to my pink. Her hair's slightly darker, as well, and her boho frocks will show her as a carefree soul.

Of course...she may turn me down because of her relationship with Addie. Addie can still get her a lot more business with her Bark Boutique than I can, especially if I don't have Braden backing me up.

Damn.

I can go out, find someone at a local shop or café, introduce myself, and ask them to help me out.

Except I look like a hag from hell.

I have no choice. It has to be Betsy.

I punch in her number.

"Hello?" she says.

"Hi, Betsy. It's Skye."

"Hey, Skye," she says hesitantly. "What's up?"

"How would you like to star in one of my Instagram posts?" I say, willing my voice to sound excited and not nasal from all the crying earlier.

"You mean here at the shop?"

Crap. Of course she thought I meant the shop. She thinks I'm calling to help her. Instead, I'm calling to get her to help me.

Talk about self-centered.

"Never mind, Bets. Sorry to bother you."

"You okay?" she asks.

"Sure," I lie. "How are you?"

"Good. I mean, yeah. Good."

"Are you sure?" I ask. "You sound…off."

"No, I'm good. It's a good day at the shop. Things are good with Peter. You know, good."

Just how many times can she say good and still think I don't know something's up?

"How about Tess? Is she good?" I swallow.

No response for a minute. Then, "She's a mess, Skye. She'd kick my butt if she knew I told you, but she's still a mess."

"About Garrett?"

"About Garrett, yeah. And about you."

I'm a mess too. I can't do this without her. I can't do this without Braden. Without Penny. Without you, Betsy. Without all of you. I'm a fraud, through and through. I don't even know my own mind.

Those words never make it past my lips, of course. To say them would hurt too much.

"I'm sorry," is all I say.

"You should call her."

"I… I can't."

"Why not?"

"Because I've hit rock bottom, Betsy. Below rock bottom."

Another pause. Then, "You just said you were okay."

"I lied. I fucking lied."

"Wow. I'm so sorry. What happened?"

I can't tell her Braden called it quits. If I say it, it becomes real.

But it *is* real, and I can't hide from reality. I simply can't.

"I'm a mess. I'm such a damned mess that I bet Tessa looks amazing next to me." I resist the urge to break into tears again. Barely.

"Skye, I've got some customers…"

"Yeah. I get it. Sorry."

"I'll call you back as soon as I can."

"Okay. Thanks. Bye, Betsy." I end the call, and within seconds, my phone buzzes again, a number I don't recognize. "Hello, this is Skye."

"Skye, hi. It's Kathy Harmon."

Kathy Harmon. Bobby Black's girlfriend. "Hi, Kathy."

"I was wondering if you were free for dinner tonight."

Dinner? Not while I'm at rock bottom.

For a hot minute I consider asking her to take Betsy's place in my post but decide against it. I need to figure this out for myself. I like Kathy, but I'm not fit to hang with anyone at the moment.

"I can't tonight, Kathy. But I'll call you soon, okay?"

"That'd be great. Can't wait to see you again."

"Same. Talk to you soon." Again, I end the call.

I heave an exasperated sigh. Now what? No Braden. No Tessa. No Penny. And no Betsy and no Kathy, by my own doing.

I have to come up with a new idea for a post. Today. Fucking *today*.

Not only that, I also need to post other stuff. If I'm going to be an influencer, my posts can't be just about sponsorships. They have to be about life. About *my* life.

Will anyone care about my life if it doesn't involve Braden?

You have to make them care.

The words land in my mind so quickly that I'm unaware of where they came from.

I have to make them care. I do.

And they'll care if they relate to me.

Today I'm sad. I'm so, so sad. I've lost everything that matters, but I still have this contract. *It* still matters.

I still matter.

Even if I don't paste on a happy face.

What's wrong with posting that I'm having a bad day? Who the hell can't relate to that? It's not done a lot, of course. Most profiles are constantly touting how good everything is. That's great, but what does it inspire?

Sure, some people will feel good to know an influencer is feeling good, to know an influencer is on top of the world, to know an influencer like Addie was born into money.

But others? To others, posts like that only inspire envy.

I don't want to inspire envy. Really, there's nothing to envy about me, especially now that Braden's gone.

I'm just a regular woman.

And I *still* fucking matter. Even if I don't feel that way at the moment. My feelings aren't important right now. The feelings I invoke in my audience *are*.

I walk back into my bathroom and gaze at my reflection. Oddly, I look a little better. My eyes are still slightly bloodshot and slightly swollen, and my nose is still red around the edges as well. I'm no longer sniffling, and the tears have dried up.

I brush my hair out and let it flounce over my shoulders. The color is basic brown, not much luster to it, but it's a nice and even color and it's thick. My eyes are brown as well, nothing special. But you know what? They're still my eyes, and they're a lot less red than they were only an hour ago.

I wash my face quickly with cold water, getting rid of the last traces of mascara from last night.

That makes all the difference.

Then I sift through the pile of Susie cosmetics once more, looking for something that stands out to me.

The mood lip plumper? Maybe. If it indeed will show mood, but right now, my lips don't need any extra plumping. They're still swollen from my sobbing fit.

Blush? God, no. I'm already redder than I want to be.

Mascara? And draw attention to my swollen eyes? I don't think so.

Eye shadow? Yeah, that's a no.

Nail polish.

Bingo!

Why didn't I think of that before? No one has to see my face if I do my nails. Eugenie sent me two colors—Make Things Happen, a flashy neon pink, and Night on the Town, a reddish black.

The pink. I can put this to good use. I'll take a selfie and say I haven't had the best day, and it's okay not to have a good day once in a while.

Then I'll do the Susie post—a photo of my hand with the pink polish. Pink makes everyone feel better, right? Now to figure out the copy.

I muse over what to say while I paint my nails. I have to admit, the polish is nice. It's not too thick and it dries quickly. They didn't send me base and top coat, so I use what I have on hand. Doesn't matter anyway. All the followers will see is the pink.

I regard my finished nails and smile.

I actually do feel better.

The power of pink—

And then I laugh out loud.

That's my copy! The power of pink!

I grab my phone.

Chapter Four

The posts go live, and I fall into bed. Just a nap, except when I wake up, the sun is rising.

I slept for over twelve hours?

Shit. My posts!

I grab my phone…and it's dead, of course. I hastily plug it into the charger and check my two posts from yesterday.

And my mouth drops open.

The "likes" are off the charts for both, and I see more comments than I've ever had.

We all have bad days. Sending hugs!

Easy does it. You got this!

That pink is fabulous!

Pink power!

Girl power!

Don't let life drag you down!

You rock, Skye!

Gorgeous color!

You're still beautiful!

What happened? Sending lots of love.

That color rocks on you.

You should be a hand model.

Don't let the bastards get you down!

I skim through all of them—it takes a while—tears welling in my eyes. These people care. Maybe not about me so much as the idea of me, but they care that I had a bad day, and that's something amazing.

They don't need me to be Braden's arm candy to relate to me. They just need me to be *human*.

They need me to be relatable.

I scoff softly. Addie has hundreds of thousands more followers than I do, and she's hardly relatable.

But she gives the illusion of being relatable. That's the key.

I'll be relatable without using illusion, without using sleight of hand.

I'll be relatable because I'm me.

I'm a woman who just lost the man she loves.

Am I giving up on Braden? Hell, no. But everyone can relate to losing a love. I won't post about it, of course, but the news will get out eventually, and I'll have to address it.

In the meantime?

Maybe I need to get to know *myself* a little better, not just for Braden, but for me. If I couldn't give him more than an "icing on the cake" answer to his question, perhaps it's time to look in the mirror. Put Skye under the magnifying glass.

But where to start?

Therapy?

Not a bad idea, and I'll look into it. I have COBRA benefits from my employment with Addison, and I may as well put them to good use. I'll find a therapist.

But first…

I need to go back to where I began.

Kansas.

I have to go home.

Before I make any further plans, though…how about a bedhead selfie? Just a personal post to show followers the real me, because that's my new focus. The real Skye. Not Braden Black's girlfriend. Simply Skye.

And another Bingo! I just created a new hashtag. #simplyskye

I rise and walk to my window, letting the sun stream onto me. I hold my phone and train the camera on my face, moving until the rays hit me just right, making my skin glow. My eyelids and lips have returned to their normal size, and in the sunlight I look…good. Not gorgeous or anything, but good, as if the dawn of a new day has healed me.

Am I healed?

No.

But I do feel better. Morning has that effect on me.

I snap a selfie, do a few minor edits, and post.

Bedhead! Nothing better than the dawn of a new day. #feelingbetter #embracethenewday #simplyskye

Time for coffee. I head to the kitchen, start a pot, and then fire up my laptop at the table to check email.

My stomach plummets.

A message from Eugenie sits in bold print in the middle of my screen. It seems to pulse, making it stand out from the other new messages.

I brace myself and click on it.

Good morning Skye,

Congratulations! Your post showcasing our nail polish yesterday got us a record number of comments on the Susanne Corporate Instagram account. What a great idea to use it as a way to feel better when you're having a down day. We've been inundated with requests to change the name of the color to The Power of Pink. While that's not feasible, given the fact that we've already manufactured an abundance of the shade with the original packaging, we'd like to bring you back to New York to discuss the creation of a new shade. Your background in art and photography makes you an expert in color, and we really want your input. Please let me know your availability. The sooner the better!

Fondly,

Eugenie

My mouth drops open.

Nothing about my shitty post from two days ago? And already, within sixteen hours, people are clamoring to change the name of the nail polish?

And this all happened in the time since Braden broke up with me?

Of course, that's not common knowledge yet.

Maybe...

Just maybe...it won't matter.

I need to get my bearings. I'm poised to respond to Eugenie right away, but I stop myself. The coffee's done, and I need to think about how to approach this. My first instinct is to write her back and tell her how excited I am, which is true. But I need to think it all through.

I sigh.

I should tell her about Braden and me.

It's a risk, yes.

But she needs to know.

I'm under contract, and I'll be paid for four months regardless. I can find alternate employment in that time if they choose to drop me.

I must be honest and up front, and I shouldn't do it in an email.

I need to call Eugenie.

I take a sip of coffee and stare at my laptop screen. I flip through the rest of my emails, hoping I'll find one from Braden.

I don't.

It's really over.

I stop the tears that threaten to well in my eyes. I can't become a slobbering mass of emotions again. Not today. Not when I'm trying to prove I don't need Braden to do my job.

I rise and head to the bathroom, where I turn on my shower. I enter, and as the warm water pelts over my body, I close my eyes and inhale the fragrant steam. I'm still slightly congested from my power sobbing yesterday, and the steam therapy helps.

After my shower, I towel off and don a robe.

Then back to my email.

Still nothing from Braden.

Not that I expected anything. Just hoped.

Hope is a good thing, right?

So…two things require my consideration. First, Eugenie. This is my livelihood, and it requires my attention.

Second…*me*. I must ask myself the question Braden asked me, which means beginning with a trip home.

I switch to my phone.

Already my bedhead post is blowing up!

My post that has nothing to do with Susanne Cosmetics and Eugenie.

Which makes me realize where my attention must be focused.

I can't do my best job if I'm floundering, and right now, I'm lost. Sure, I'm creative enough that I figured out a way around my swollen eyes and lips yesterday, but none of that helped me to get where I need to be.

I pull up my travel app and book a flight home to Kansas that leaves two days from now.

Home is where I'll begin this journey.

Chapter Five

Next...Eugenie.

I inhale a deep breath. I have to tell her my circumstances have changed. It's only fair. I quickly punch in her number.

"Susanne Corporate," a woman answers.

"Eugenie Blake, please. This is Skye Manning."

"Just a moment, Ms. Manning. I'll see if she's in."

More seconds that seem like hours. Time standing still seems to have become part of my life now, and it pretty much sucks.

"Good morning, Skye!"

I gather what little courage I can find. "Hi, Eugenie."

"I assume you got my email."

"I did. I'm so glad the post is doing well."

"Much better than we'd hoped, considering it's only your second post."

The first one sucked.

She doesn't say it, but I hear it in her tone. Should I mention it?

Hell, no.

The words are in Braden's voice, and he's right. Why should

I bring up something negative if she's not going to? That'd be ridiculous.

"Thank you," I say simply.

"What's your schedule? Can you fly back to New York next week?"

"I just booked a trip home to Kansas for Sunday," I tell her. "I suppose I could fly to New York tonight and meet with you tomorrow. But tomorrow's Saturday."

"That's no problem," she says. "We work around the clock here. I haven't worked less than a sixty-hour week in years."

I clear my throat. "All right. I can rearrange my flight home and fly from New York to Wichita on Sunday."

"I'd be happy to have my assistant make the arrangements for you," she said. "Especially since it's so last minute."

"That's kind of you," I say, "but there's something else we should discuss first."

"What's that?"

"It's… Well, my circumstances have changed."

"How so?"

"I'm no longer…" I sigh. *God, Skye, just spit it out.* "I'm no longer seeing Braden Black."

Silence.

Again those seconds that pass like hours. Do I enter some kind of time warp when I'm waiting for bad news?

Finally, Eugenie says, "I'll have to run this by the VP of marketing, but I'm not sure it changes anything."

"How can it not?"

"Your following has grown exponentially since you started influencing. Yes, it took Braden to get you going, but you have huge potential to grow on your own."

"I do?"

"You do. You know what? I'm not going to bother Elaine with this. She's the VP of marketing. The company is bound for the first four months under your contract, so let's give it a try. If your growth taps out and we're not generating sales, we won't exercise our option under the contract. It's that simple."

Admittedly, it does sound simple enough. Four grand per week is peanuts to a company like Susanne. If Braden were here, he'd tell me to jump on that wagon and never look back.

But Braden's not here.

Eugenie is giving me a shot—a shot I should welcome. I may fail, but it's not set in stone. It's only a given if I don't try.

"Skye? You still there?"

"Yeah, I'm here."

"You have to know we took this into consideration before we offered you the deal. Braden Black has never been in a serious relationship that anyone's aware of, so of course your breakup was a possibility that we considered."

"And still you chose to work with me?" Damn. That inflection again.

"We did. You're the ideal face for this new line. You're beautiful, but you're also approachable. You're the perfect Susie Girl. Plus, your photos are wonderful. You're quite a talent, Skye."

I warm all over. Ha! Who needs Braden Black?

I scoff silently. I do. I need him. I need my puppy. I need...

Another silent scoff. Such self-indulgence. He's gone, and I still have a contract. Eugenie is giving me a chance, and I need to take it and run.

"You still want me to come to New York, then?" *Damn! Stop it with the inflection already!*

"Of course. Shaylie is already putting together a presentation, and our design team is fleshing out the color. I'll get you booked on a flight tonight. Will that work for you?"

"Yeah, that will be great. Thank you, Eugenie."

"You're very welcome. I'll take care of your flights and I'll email you the details as soon as we get everything scheduled."

"Wonderful. Thank you."

After ending the call, I walk to the bathroom and gaze at my reflection. Bedhead. Such bedhead. And still, Susanne wants me. Is it because they're stuck with me for four months under the contract? Or is it because they truly want me?

And a light shines in me.

Because it doesn't matter. The answer to that question *doesn't matter*, because the result is the same.

I have four months to prove myself. Four months to become the best influencer out there. To take photographs. To show the world my art. To show the world who I am.

I'll do it, damn it.

And while I'm doing it, maybe I'll show myself.

No private jet this time, but Eugenie booked me in first class. The larger seats are nice, and the flight attendants are obsequious. I actually get offered a drink before we even take off. Seems silly, as I'll have all of ten minutes to drink it before I have to give it back, so I decline.

After the short flight, I grab my luggage at baggage claim and spy a driver dressed in black, holding a sign that says Manning.

I approach him. "I'm Skye Manning."

"Good evening, Ms. Manning. I'll be driving you to your hotel."

My hotel. The Marriott Marquis in Times Square. Funny. I've been to New York twice now, and I haven't done any of the tourist things. No Empire State Building. No Ground Zero. No Statue of Liberty. No Met. No buying a hot dog from a street vendor.

I won't have time for any of that this time around, either, as I'll be meeting with Eugenie tomorrow and then flying home to

Kansas the next day, which is Sunday.

Oh, well.

My driver drops me off and hands my bag to me. Do I tip him? I have no idea. I don't have any cash on me anyway, so it's a moot point. I simply thank him profusely, hope Eugenie's assistant added a generous tip, and then I make a mental note never to travel without stopping at the ATM first.

It's already dark outside, and I'm tired. One good thing about this spur of the moment trip to New York, I haven't had a lot of time to ruminate on Braden and how things went so terribly wrong.

Once I'm in my room, though, the thoughts come roaring in like a tidal wave. He invades me, and I know I'll never be free of him.

Why?

Because I don't *want* to be free of him.

I love him.

What's more? He loves me. He admits it. How do you give up someone you love who loves you back?

Clearly, it's easier for him than it is for me.

But is it?

I sigh.

I don't know. He hides so many of his emotions. I honestly don't know *what* he's feeling about our breakup.

What I do know, though, is that Braden is a doer. He translates thoughts into action, so maybe that's what I need to do as well.

Tomorrow, I'll wow Eugenie and her team, make them realize they're right to take a chance on me.

Then, on Sunday, I'll go home. Back to where it all began for me.

And somehow, I'll find the answer to Braden's question.

Chapter Six

The same driver who picked me up from the airport drives me to Susanne Corporate. I'm dressed to the nines—in clothes I purchased myself this time. As I packed yesterday, I yearned for Tessa's input. I couldn't wear the same thing I wore at the last meeting with Eugenie and her staff, so I had to make do. I finally decided on simple black pants and pumps with a burgundy silk top that shows a tiny amount of cleavage. My makeup is pure Susie Girl of course, including the mood lip plumper I considered using for a previous post.

Turns out it's a simple, dark dusty-rose, which will look good on almost any complexion. Nicely done, Susanne.

"Thanks," I tell the driver when he drops me off at the building in Manhattan. *Shit*, I add to myself. I forgot to hit the ATM for tip money.

I'm on edge as I walk into the building.

Addison is here. I can feel her. She's going to be in the office, like she always is. And she'll give me some snide comment about nipple clamps or a butt plug.

Ha! The joke's on her.

Braden and I are over, and there's nothing new she can taunt me with.

Except the breakup itself, of course.

I breathe in deeply. Exhale. *Get with it, Skye. Eugenie believes in you. Now you need to believe in yourself.*

I check in with security, head to the elevators, and press the up button. I brush my hands over my arms, trying to ease the chills that erupt on my flesh.

She's going to be in my face when the elevator opens.

The bell rings and the doors open, and I know she'll be there. I just know—

The inside of the elevator is empty as I walk in and exhale slowly in relief.

Chills erupt again as I ascend.

The doors open—

No Addie.

Okay. Two down. A hundred bucks says she's talking to Lisa at reception again.

But as I glance through the clear glass doors, I see no sign of her.

Still the chills. She's probably in the back with Eugenie.

I approach the reception desk. "Hi, Lisa."

Lisa's eyes glow with recognition. "Ms. Manning, nice to see you again."

"Please, call me Skye."

"Of course. Do you have an appointment with Eugenie today?"

"I do." I look up at the clock above Lisa's desk. "In five minutes."

"Great. I'll let her know you're here. Can I get you anything? Coffee?"

God, no, I might barf. "I'm fine. Thanks." I take a seat on one of the chairs in the reception area, and then I dart my gaze toward every corner, waiting for Addie to emerge.

Instead, Eugenie appears, looking sleek and professional as always in a light green suit, her short gray hair styled to perfection. I rise.

"Skye!" She takes my hand in a firm grip. "So great to see you! Come on back."

She leads me to the same conference room where Shaylie, Brian, and Louisa wait. They all smile when I walk in.

"Hi," I say, trying not to sound nervous.

"This won't take long," Eugenie says. "Shaylie has put together a PowerPoint on our social media marketing plan for the new Power of Pink Susie Girl nail polish. Brian will take you through the numbers. But what we're really here for is to decide on the actual color."

I smile. "I appreciate you allowing me to have input on the shade."

"Absolutely. You came up with the name, and you have a keen understanding of color. We definitely want your opinion."

Shaylie and Brian make their presentations, and as Eugenie promised, they're quick and entertaining.

Louisa, the intern, speaks up, her voice commanding but slightly wavering. "I've put together some samples of colors that are different from what Susie Girl is currently offering. I hope you like them."

"I'm sure they're all lovely," I say.

Louisa distributes color swatches to all of us. "I thought about putting these into a PowerPoint, but you just don't get the vibrancy of the colors that way."

"I totally agree." I flip through the ten swatches. "They're all beautiful."

"I agree," Eugenie says. "Skye, which one do you like best?"

"It's still hard to say without seeing how the polish looks on an actual nail. It might change a little. Color can be funny."

Shaylie nods. "You're so right. I've bought nail color and lip color in the past that looks amazing in the package, but when I get home it looks terrible on me."

I nod. "There are certain shades, though, that flatter almost everyone."

"Definitely," Eugenie says. She flips through the swatches, throwing three into the center of the table. "For me, it's these three."

Her choices are on point. "You have an excellent eye for color."

She smiles. "Coming from you, that's a compliment. Thank you."

I throw one more into the pile. "I'd add this one. It's a little more neutral but still quite vibrant."

"Shaylie?" Eugenie asks.

"I'd throw in this one." She tosses a neon pink into the mix.

It's a beautiful color, but it won't work on all skin tones. I don't say anything, though. It's not really my place.

"Brian?" Eugenie asks.

Brian's cheeks flush. "I'm just a numbers guy."

We all laugh.

"Louisa," Eugenie says, "you put these together, but do you have any favorites that we haven't put into the pile?"

Louisa chooses one more, a soft, pale pink. "This one is lighter than the others, but it's such a beautiful hue."

I nod. It is beautiful, but it's way too light to be called The Power of Pink. Again, though, I don't feel it's my place to say this.

"All right. Nice job, everyone," Eugenie says. "I'll give these six to the art department, and they'll put some samples together for us. Skye, I'll be in touch when they're ready. We want you here when we choose the final color."

"I'm honored," I say, my skin warming. "Thank you."

A sense of triumph settles through me. I did this. And I did it without being Braden Black's girlfriend.

Eugenie walks me back out and we say some quick goodbyes. I still expect Addie to crawl out of the woodwork, but so far so good.

I step into the elevator, descend, step out, walk to the revolving doors where my driver waits.

Still no Addie.

I smile, feeling the sense of triumph once more.

For a woman who managed to lose the love of her life, I feel like I just won a battle.

Not a war, but a battle.

Addison isn't here at Susanne today, but she's not gone.

She lurks around some corner.

I can feel it.

Chapter Seven

I'm flying coach, of course.

No more private jets for me, and you know what? It feels kind of good. So good that I do a selfie on the plane from my window seat. I don't mention coach, but I do mention that I'm heading to my hometown. *#simplyskye*

And yes, I know Braden will see it, but that doesn't matter. If he's interested, he has the resources to find me wherever I am.

Besides, he's not interested.

I miss him, though. I truly do love him, and I know he loves me, too. Somehow, we'll figure this out. But before that, I'll figure myself out.

I have a three-hour plane ride ahead of me, so as soon as the flight attendants announce that we can use our large devices, I whip out my laptop to write to Eugenie.

Dear Eugenie,

Thank you again for your hospitality yesterday. I enjoyed working with your team again, and I love the marketing you've come up with for The Power of Pink. I won't let you down!

I'll be in Liberty, Kansas with my family for the next week, as

you know, but I have my computer and phone and will be doing
all my posts as scheduled.

Have a great day!

Skye

I hit send with more force than I mean to.

I was honest with Eugenie, and it paid off. I did the right thing. Influencing was never my dream job, but I stumbled into it and it's paying the bills.

And damn, it feels good to be honest.

But the influencing game is full of dishonesty. Look at Addie, for example. She hates coffee, but Bean There Done That pays her a fortune to hawk their drinks.

I'm heading home to get real with myself, so why not start now?

Influencing can be lucrative, and it allows me the chance to take photographs. So far, though, I haven't really flexed my creative photography muscles.

Tomorrow, I'll start getting more creative. I was creative three days ago with the nail polish and my copy. Nice start, but I'm a photographer, not a writer. That's where I can shine.

I glance down at my computer screen.

The flight attendants come around with drinks and pretzels. I take a bottle of water but forgo the carbs. I'll be carbing it up big-time at home. My mom's an award-winning baker. Her pies are legendary at the county fair each year.

I put away my laptop and check my Instagram posts from the past couple days.

Oh… I have a private message from @realaddisonames.

My gut churns. I knew she was lurking somewhere.

I can delete it without looking at it. Would probably be for the best. Who needs her negativity?

But I'm a glutton for self-flagellation, it seems. I click to open the message.

Sorry about your bad day, but I tried to warn you.

That's it.

She knows.

She knows Braden and I are over.

My only consolation is the message came three days after the post in question, which means she's not checking my feed daily. Is that good? Not necessarily. In her eyes, it means she doesn't consider me a huge threat to her audience.

And in truth, I'm not. At least not yet.

I sigh. Will she make Braden's and my breakup public? Probably not. First, she doesn't have any concrete proof. Second, it wouldn't look good to her followers for her to be gossiping about another influencer. Besides, her relationship—for lack of a better word—with Braden has never been public. For all she knows, he might have told me everything. Which brings me to the third reason why she won't share our breakup. To do so would bring attention to her past with Braden—something neither of them has been willing to talk about.

In reality, Braden hasn't told me anything.

All I know I learned from Betsy.

But Betsy said he broke up with Addie when she wouldn't go dark with him again.

Seems he broke up with me for the opposite reason.

Oh? What are your hard limits?

I only have one.

What is it?

I don't talk about it.

Don't you think I should know? So I don't bring it up?

Trust me, Skye. You will never bring it up.

Except I did.

Why is it his hard limit?

Unless…

Breath control. Neck bondage. It must have something to

do with Braden and Addison.

My fingers are poised over my keyboard to respond to Addie's message. Something like, "You've got me all choked up." Surely, she'll recognize the double entendre.

But I stop.

I'm not Addison. I don't hurt people simply to make myself feel better.

I take a screen shot of the message and then delete it. Never hurts to keep records.

My plane lands, and I catch a cab home. I didn't tell my parents I was coming. They're always asking me to visit, so I figured why not surprise them?

During the sixty-minute cab ride, my phone rings. A Boston number that I don't recognize. It could be new work, so I answer it.

"This is Skye."

"Hello, Skye. It's Ben Black."

I drop my jaw. "Braden's brother?"

"The one and only."

Why is Ben calling me? Not even a week has passed since Braden broke up with me. Maybe he doesn't know.

"Okay. Hi."

"I suppose you're wondering why I'm calling."

"Yeah, it crossed my mind."

"You need to throw my brother a bone."

My heart thumps. "I need to…what?"

"He's miserable. What the hell happened?"

He's miserable? A wide grin splits my face. I shouldn't be happy that Braden's miserable, but it means he's miserable without me. So yeah, I'm a little giddy.

Make that a *lot* giddy.

"I… I think that's between him and me," I say.

"God, you sound just like him. He's in full asshole mode,

Skye. He's out of control."

Out of *control.*

So unlike Braden.

"And that's abnormal for him?" I can't help asking.

Ben chuckles. "Man, you two are made for each other. Let's just say he's being nastier than usual. When I asked about you, all I got was a growl."

"A growl?"

"Yeah. And I'm not exaggerating. I'm being literal. He fucking growled like a wolf, and then he said you were over."

"Then you know as much as I know," I say.

"No offense, Skye, but that's crap, and we both know it."

I can't fault his observation, but no way in hell am I telling Ben that his brother dumped me because I wanted him to tie a rope around my neck. That's a little too personal.

Actually, all of this is a little too personal.

But…I have forty-five minutes until I get to my rural home. Maybe I can learn something.

"Ben, what happened between Braden and Addison Ames?"

He pauses a moment. Did the call drop?

Finally, he says, "Addie? That's ancient history."

"It's not that ancient."

"I can't tell you anything that Braden hasn't already."

"He hasn't told me anything."

"Nothing at all?" His inflection makes him sound genuinely surprised.

"Only that they were both young and didn't know what they were getting into."

"That's a big part of it."

"But I've heard other stuff…"

"From whom?"

I swallow. I won't violate Betsy's trust. "I can't say."

"Fair enough, but if I don't know the source, I won't be able to tell you if it's true or fabricated. So you have to tell me."

"I don't have to do anything. I won't tell you."

"Then why would you bring it up?"

He has me there. I pause for several seconds.

"You still there?" Ben asks.

"Yeah."

"The connection seems weird. Where are you?"

"In a cab."

"Oh."

"Driving into rural Kansas."

"What?"

"I'm on my way to visit my parents."

"When will you be back?"

"My return ticket is for Saturday. I'll be here a week."

"Hmm. Okay. But another week of Asshole Braden is going to wear on all of us."

"I can't help you, okay? Braden is the one who ended it. It wasn't me."

His turn to be silent. Then, "Seriously?"

I keep my jaw from dropping again. "Yeah, seriously. Do you think I'd lie about that? Didn't he tell you the same thing?"

"He just said it was over, so I assumed—"

"You assumed *I* did the dumping?" I shake my head to the phone. "Unbelievable."

"He seriously broke up with you." His words aren't a question. They're more of a flabbergasted statement.

"Yes. He seriously broke up with me. Why would you assume it was the other way around?"

"Because of the way he's acting. He's miserable, and anyone that miserable wouldn't have caused the misery himself."

"Apparently he did."

"But Braden doesn't..."

Doesn't what? Make himself miserable? No, he doesn't. I

can't help chuckling to myself. That time he flew back from New York early because he wanted to see me, and I came clean about stealing the piece of mail from his place, he made his stance clear.

I could end things with you, but I didn't fly two hundred miles today to punish myself.

No, Braden doesn't make himself miserable.

"Braden doesn't what?" I ask.

Again, more silence for a few seconds. Then, "He left early this morning."

"What? Why?" I ask

"Said he was going back to New York for an extended period of time. Possibly indefinitely."

New York. Black Rose Underground. Does Ben know about Braden's club?

Boston is Braden's home. He made that clear many times. So clear, that he keeps part of himself only in New York.

And now he's thinking about going there indefinitely.

Which means the club.

Which means scenes.

And if I'm not there to do scenes with him, someone else will be. Women will be lining up to make Braden Black's fetishes come true.

Women who won't ask him to do something that's unthinkable for him.

Women who…

Women who aren't *me*.

Chapter Eight

"You still there, Skye?" Ben says.

I swallow down the vomit that threatens to crawl up from my stomach. "Yeah. I'm here."

"You've got to talk to him."

I clear my throat. "Why? If he's gone to New York, you won't have to put up with his asshole behavior."

"Ha! Of course I will, and so will everyone else. A virtual asshole is still an asshole."

He has me there. "I wish I could help you, but—"

"Then call him. Tell him you're sorry."

"I'm *not* sorry, Ben. I'm not the one who ended things."

"So you'd be with him if he hadn't ended it, right?"

"Well...yeah."

"Tell him that."

I shake my head, well aware that only the cabbie can see me from his rearview mirror, if he's even looking. "No way. I still have my self-respect. I'm not going to go crawling back to a guy who dumped me."

"This has nothing to do with self-respect, Skye. The man

is miserable."

"That's his own fault, then, isn't it?"

"Yeah. Of course it is. But Braden isn't used to things not going his way. He finds solutions, and whatever went on between the two of you has got him confused."

I let out an exasperated huff. "Confused? He knows *exactly* why he ended it."

"That's not what I mean."

"Oh? What do you mean, then?"

"Braden finds solutions. That's how he made it so big. His original idea was a solution to a problem in construction. And every success he's had since then, from innovations to investments, has been the result of finding a solution. This has him flummoxed, Skye."

"And?"

"And what?"

"Sorry, Ben, but I'm not following. Relationships are not problems to be solved. They're relationships."

"That's not how Braden sees it."

"I can't help that. That's how it *is*."

"Maybe," he says.

"You're probably just like him, aren't you? You don't want a relationship, either."

"What? Where did that come from?"

"Just a hunch."

He sighs. "I'm not looking, it's true. But I'm not averse to a relationship if I find the right person."

"Braden told me, at the beginning, that he and I couldn't have a relationship. Apparently he was right."

"Not surprising. Neither one of us is wired for long-term love."

"Why do you say that?"

Silence.

Seriously, silence so thick over a cell phone line that I swear

I can hear its density.

"You still there?" I ask.

"Yeah."

"Are you going to answer the question you know I'm about to ask?"

More silence. Then, "I can't."

"Why not?" I ask.

"There are things Braden and I don't talk about. Not to anyone."

My breath hitches. "And one of those things is why you're not wired for relationships?"

No response.

"I'll take your silence as a yes," I say.

"It's not what you think," he says.

"I'm not *thinking* anything."

"Sure you are. You're thinking it has something to do with Braden and Addison."

"Why would I think that? Is she a reason why *you're* not wired for relationships?"

More dead air.

"This is getting tedious, Ben," I finally say.

"I can't speak for Braden," he says, "but Addie certainly has no bearing on *my* situation."

"I see."

Yet more silence. Then, "I think you can make Braden happy, Skye."

Despite myself, my heart leaps a little. "Obviously not."

"You can. He was different with you. Different than with any other woman he's ever brought home."

"What if he can't make *me* happy?"

"I just…"

"You just assumed anyone would be thrilled to be with your brother. Or with you. I get it."

"No, that's not what I meant." His tone is huffy and resolute.

"That's *exactly* what you meant. It just so happens that my happiness is important here, too."

"I never said it wasn't. But, Skye, you just told me if he hadn't broken up with you—"

"Cool it with your euphemisms, Ben. He *dumped* me. Call it what it is."

"Fine. If he hadn't dumped you, you'd still be with him. So clearly he made *you* happy."

Ben isn't wrong. Braden made me ecstatic. He showed me a world I never knew existed—a world of pleasure and love and loss of control. A world I could only face in the dark.

Maybe I took it too far. Maybe this *is* all my fault. Maybe I need to face it all in the daylight to understand.

But how can I be at fault simply for asking for what I want?

"What do you want me to do?" I finally ask.

"Reach out to him."

"What makes you think he'll even talk to me?"

"I don't know if he will." Ben sighs. "But he's hurting, and you're the only one who can help him."

"Fine," I finally relent. "I'll…email him. Or text him. I won't call him."

"That's a start. Thanks, Skye."

"If this turns into something worse, I'm coming after you," I say.

"Got it. You can punch me in the nose or something."

I can't help a short laugh. What the heck can I ever do to Ben Black? A big fat lot of nothing. "Don't think I won't."

"I absolutely think you will. I knew from the first time we met that Braden had met his match. I think that might be part of the problem here."

"Problem?"

"You're too much alike. That's what attracted him to you in

the first place."

Again, he's not wrong. Braden admitted he was drawn to my need for control. Almost as if he wanted to break me. And I allowed it. I gave him my control, which led to the most amazing things I'd ever experienced.

But maybe…

Maybe he doesn't actually *want* ultimate control over me.

Maybe that part of him is an illusion.

And maybe he's finding that out for himself now. Maybe that's what has him confused.

I'm near home. Even as the cabbie drives, I sit on the edge of my seat as my rural home comes into view. Green. Kansas is so green compared to Boston. Cornfields line each side of the county road.

"This has been interesting, Ben," I say, "but I have to go. I'm almost home."

"Got it. Just think about what I said, okay?"

"Sure. I said I'd text him." Of course, I didn't say when.

I'll think about it. Could I *do* anything about it? Not really. I'm not about to go begging to Braden for him to take me back. As much as I want to be with him, as much as I love him, I'll never beg for anything.

"Good. Have a nice time at home, Skye."

"I will. And Ben?"

"Yeah?"

"If you get a chance, tell Braden…"

"Yeah? Tell him what?"

"Just tell him I said hi."

"Okay. Will do. Bye."

I shove my phone back in my purse as the cab parks. Will Ben tell Braden I said hi? If he does, he'll also have to tell him he called me, which may not go over well.

"Thanks so much." I pay the cab driver and take the luggage

he pulled out of the trunk for me.

Then I draw in a deep breath.

I'm home. My birthplace.

Time to figure out who I truly am.

Time to figure out why that neck binding is so important to me.

I smile and turn the knob on the front door. I know it's open, as we've never locked our doors. We live in the safest place on the planet.

I walk in.

And my jaw nearly drops to the floor.

Chapter Nine

M y mother sits on the blue sofa in our small living room. My father sits in his old leather recliner.

They have a visitor.

In the faded brocade armchair sits Braden Black.

My flesh freezes, and my fingers release my suitcase. It drops to the floor with a loud *thud* and topples onto its side.

"Honey!" Mom rises and pulls me into a hug. "What are you doing here?"

A few seconds lapse before my voice works. "I live here. At least I used to. What's his excuse?"

"Mr. Black… Er…Braden called earlier today and asked if he could come by."

"Why didn't you tell us you were in a relationship, Skye?" my father queries.

"Because I'm *not* in one," I say.

Braden clears his throat then, rises, and walks toward me. "I realize how this may look."

How this may look? My feelings are a whirlwind inside me. Am I happy to see him? Angry at his presumptuousness? A little of both. Mostly I'm perplexed. That word he loves so much.

Not much perplexes me, Skye.

"It looks like you're spying on me," I reply.

"Why would your boyfriend spy on you?" Mom asks.

"He's not my boyfriend," I say adamantly. "He's a thirty-five-year-old man, and I don't have a clue what he's doing here."

"He came to meet us," Dad says.

"Without bothering to tell me," I say.

"I was in the area," Braden says, "so naturally, I thought I'd stop by to say hello to your parents."

"Braden, what the—"

"Come with me." He ushers me back out the front door. Then, "What are *you* doing here?"

"Uh…I think I already made that clear. I live here."

"You don't. Your home is in Boston."

"My parents' home is my home. That's what they've always told me. I sure as hell have a lot more right to be here than you do. What the fuck, Braden?"

"I didn't mean for you to find out. Why are you here?"

I whip my hands to my hips. "I don't have to explain that to you, but you sure have to explain it to me. What are you doing in my parents' house?"

He sears me with that sapphire-blue gaze. That gaze that says, "Don't test me, Skye." Well, too late for any of that. He can no longer punish me.

"I'm waiting…"

"I was in the area."

"Bullshit. What the hell kind of business do you have in Liberty, Kansas?"

"All kinds. My company manufactures products used in construction, or have you forgotten?"

"Yeah, and I'm sure you have a lot to do in such a thriving metropolis. We don't exactly have skyscrapers here. Besides, Ben said you were in New York."

Shit. Fatal error. Now he knows I talked to Ben.

Oddly, he doesn't press me on it. Instead, "I have a meeting in Kansas City tomorrow, so I flew in early, called your parents, and they invited me over."

"Of course they did. My parents are very hospitable people. But why? We're not together."

"Because I wanted…." He rakes his fingers through his dark hair. "I wanted to meet them. I guess I…"

"What, Braden? For the love of God, what?"

"I wanted to meet them because they're part of you."

"Why?"

"Because… For fuck's sake, Skye, you know why."

"I'm afraid I don't."

"Because I love you, all right? I fucking love you, and I want to figure out what's going on with you. That's why. Satisfied?"

I raise my eyebrows. Do I believe him? If I do, I have to accept that we both came here for the same reason.

I came to find myself. To figure out why control—and more recently, losing control—is such a big part of my life.

Is he here to help me?

"I call bullshit."

"Call it whatever you like," he says. "I don't have to explain myself to you."

"Oh, you sure as hell do when you show up unannounced at my parents' house."

"I wasn't unannounced. I called them first."

"It was unannounced to *me*."

"I had no idea you'd show up today."

"Didn't you? I call bullshit again."

"You think I'm having you watched?" He stalks closer to me, that look in his eyes I know so well.

Have I gone too far?

His eyes are on fire, his jawline tense. I've seen this look before. He's angry. Angry and full of lust.

He wants to grab me. Kiss me. Tie me up and fuck me, just like he did that day in his office when I came rushing in, throwing accusations at him.

"Y-Yes." My lips tremble. "I wouldn't put it past you."

"Why would I have you watched if we're not together?"

"Why would you show up at my parents' home if we're not together?"

"Damn it, Skye!" He grips my shoulder. Hard. "Damn it all to hell!" His lips come down on mine.

My parents are still inside the house, only yards away. They may very well be watching.

I don't care.

Braden is impossible for me to resist. When his tongue demands entrance, I part my lips and let him in. We kiss angrily for a minute, until he breaks the kiss abruptly.

"Damn it!" he says again.

"You don't have any business here, do you?" I say.

He doesn't reply.

God, he and Ben are cut from the same cloth. If they don't like the answer they just don't reply.

"So why are you here, then?" I ask.

"I'm worried about you," he says.

"I'm a grown woman."

"I know that."

"Why worry, then?"

"Just because I can't be with you doesn't mean I no longer love you." He trails one finger over my cheek.

I tingle all over. "I love you too. Why can't we make this work?"

"You know why."

"Why do you think I came here?" I ask. "I came here to start at the beginning. To figure myself out."

He nods, though I'm not sure what he's nodding to.

"So why are you here?" I ask again. "And don't tell me you're worried about me. You know I can take care of myself. Tell me why, Braden."

"Maybe I came here to try to figure you out, too."

"Is it me you want to figure out, Braden?" I inhale a deep breath, gathering courage for what I'm about to say. "Or is it yourself?"

Chapter Ten

Again, he doesn't answer.

I'm getting real sick of this silence game he and his brother like to play. It's old news.

"I think I have my answer," I say.

Still, he says nothing.

"You've looked in the mirror, haven't you?" I continue. "Just as I have. And you're not exactly sure what you see."

"To the contrary, Skye, I know exactly what I see."

"Do you? Or do you only *think* you know? What are you hiding, Braden?"

He pushes his hands into his pants pockets. "I could ask you the same question."

"You could, but I don't have an answer. I came here to find one."

"And you can't believe that maybe I came here for the same reason?"

"You have no history here. That belongs to me. You want to find yourself? Start in South Boston." I gather more courage. "Start with Addie."

"Damn it, Skye—"

"Scratch that. Addie came much later. Start with your father, Braden. Start with your *mother*."

His jaw tenses again, and his eyes are alight with wildfire. "Damn you," he says between clenched teeth.

"Damn you, too," I counter. "Fucking damn you."

Then his lips are on mine again, without even a semblance of gentleness. It's harsh. It's painful, even.

And it's magnificent.

We stand in my parents' front yard, our mouths fused together, and I'm ready. So ready. Ready to strip for him and make love right here, in front of the house where I grew up. Where I played with toys. Where I got lost in the cornfield.

I break the kiss and push him away. "Stop it."

"No."

"Yes, you will. Have your forgotten my parents are inside? Easily watching us through the window? My dad is probably loading his shotgun about now."

He draws in a breath. "This was a mistake."

"You bet it was. You crossed a line, Braden."

He scoffs. "*I* crossed a line? Have you forgotten how many lines you've crossed? Stealing a piece of mail from my house? Barging into my office and demanding information?"

Yeah, neither of those were my finest moments, but, "We're not talking about me. We're talking about you. But since you brought me into it, the last time I checked, I never showed up at your father's home unannounced. That's a *major* line."

He doesn't reply. I'm not surprised. He can't argue my point, and he knows it.

"What are you really doing here?" I ask for the umpteenth time. I'm determined to get an answer before he leaves.

He shakes his head. "I don't honestly know, Skye. All I know is I was on the plane, ready to go to New York, and I told the pilot to change the flight plan."

"You didn't know I was coming here?"

"No. I swear I didn't."

"Then why? Seriously. And don't tell me you were worried about me, or you were trying to understand me."

"That's actually the truth."

"No, that's the truth you told yourself so you could live with yourself for making this decision. I want the real truth."

"I'm telling the truth. Or at least, the partial truth."

"What's the rest of it, then?"

"I don't know. I just know…" He rakes his fingers through his hair once more. "I've never felt this way before. It's…unnerving."

"Felt *what* way?" I hold my breath.

Emotions play across his face as he wrinkles his forehead, purses his lips. He's angry, regretful, imposing. Maybe even slightly amused.

Then he looks away from me. "When did you talk to my brother?"

"Interesting pivot," I say. "It's not even slightly related to my question. But I'll play along. He called me an hour ago, while I was in the cab coming here."

"I see."

"He says you're miserable without me."

"This is why relationships aren't in the cards for me. I have a problem with misery of any kind."

I can't help a laugh. "You think that makes you unique? No one likes to be miserable."

"I like it less than most."

"You do? Because you, the great Braden Black, know how misery affects everyone else on the planet?"

"Damn it!" He's tense again, so tense his body is trembling slightly from the rigidness.

"This is getting nowhere," I say. "I'm going back in."

Braden offers me a half smile. "Your mother invited me to stay for dinner."

He meets my gaze. It's almost a glare. He's challenging me — challenging me to make the decision for him. He wants my response. But I refuse to play.

"It's a free country. Stay."

"Do *you* want me to stay?"

I let out a huff and chuckle. "Since when do you care what *I* want? Suit yourself." I walk toward the door.

Though he poses an interesting question. *Do* I want him to stay? I've met his father and brother. If we were still together, I would have eventually brought him home to meet my parents. Maybe not quite this soon, but it would have happened.

I grin to myself when his footfalls follow me. I pull open the screen door and then the main door. My parents are no longer in the small living room. I find my mother in the kitchen. My father is probably down in the basement in front of the television. It's his man cave.

"Hi, honey. Are you okay?" Mom asks.

"Yeah, I'm fine."

"Will your friend be staying for dinner?"

"My friend? Mom, this isn't some guy I brought home from school. This is a billionaire."

She smiles. "I know that, dear. Everyone knows who Braden Black is. What we didn't know is that you and he were…"

"Together? We're not."

"But you were."

"Only for a few weeks."

Braden walks in behind me and clears his throat. "Is the invitation to dinner still open, Mrs. Manning?"

"Of course it is. And please call me Maggie."

He nods.

"Why don't you join Steve in the basement? He'll be happy

to pour you a drink."

"I'd enjoy that. Does he have Wild Turkey?"

Mom laughs. "It's only his favorite."

Braden nods and walks toward the stairs to the basement. "Can I get either of you anything?"

"Sure," I say. "I'll have a Wild Turkey, too. Bring Mom a vodka and seltzer."

He nods again and walks down the stairs.

Mom turns to me. "I see we have a lot to talk about."

Chapter Eleven

Mom's right. I do want to talk to her, but not about Braden. I came home for a reason—to start at the beginning and figure myself out. Not just so I can answer Braden's question about what I want, but also to know myself better. To understand why I am who I am.

I have to start at the beginning.

I'm just not sure I can do that with Braden here.

Yet, I still want him here. I want him with me so badly I can taste it—that irresistible flavor of smoky mint and cinnamon and man.

Braden.

"What can I help you with in here?" I ask Mom.

"I'm pretty much done." She smiles. "I guess you're not ready to talk about you and…"

I inhale and decide to pull a Braden and ignore her question. "Pot roast. It's almost like you knew I'd be home."

"Dad and I have pot roast about once a week, and I always make a lot so he can have a sandwich the next couple days. So we have plenty for you and your guest."

He's not my guest.

I take the cover off the pot on the stove. "Succotash?"

"Yup."

Another staple. We live on a corn farm, after all. Will Braden like it? It's so...rural.

"Plus carrots and new potatoes," Mom continues, "cooked in with the roast, of course." She takes a wrapped loaf of bread out of the refrigerator and places half of it on a plate. "Could you put this on the table for me, Skye?"

"Sure." Sliced grocery store bread on the table. Another staple from my childhood. Mom's a baker, but only desserts. She doesn't bake her own bread.

A wave of embarrassment sweeps through me.

Store-bought sliced bread on the table. What will Braden think?

An image floats into my mind.

It's Benji, the little boy who came into the food pantry with his mother the day Braden and I volunteered there. As his mother dragged him away in his little red wagon, he pulled out a loaf of bread from one of the bags and squeezed it.

Just like I did so many times.

I glance at the bread on the plate, the nearly perfect squares of white with light brown crusts. When I was a kid, the slices were always mangled from my squeezing the bags of fresh bread from the grocery.

Yeah, I'm home.

Bread on the table and all, I'm home.

Mom is scooping the carrots and potatoes into a bowl. "Will you put out the succotash?" she asks.

"Sure thing." I find a serving bowl and lift the lid on the pot. The buttery corn goodness wafts toward me. Another wonderful scent of home. I scoop the corn and lima beans into the serving bowl, add a large spoon, and set it on the kitchen table next to the bread.

Mom glances up. "Oh, I'm sorry. I thought, since we have a guest and all, we'd eat in the good dining room."

"Oh. Okay." I pick up the bowl of succotash and the plate of bread and walk out of the kitchen toward the formal dining room.

It's hardly formal. When I was a kid, Mom's sewing machine usually sat on the oak table. Now? The table is set for four with the good china Mom inherited from her grandmother when I was little.

The day I broke one of those plates was not a good day for me.

In fact…

More images rush into my head. Memories.

That was the day I got lost in the cornfield. Wasn't it? I was running… Running away…

No time to think about that now. I place the bread and succotash on the table and glance at the white-and-gold wallpaper. It's old now and slightly yellowed with age, but still elegant. I always wondered why we never used this room. Or the good china.

"It's just for company," Mom always said.

The only company we ever had was family, and they didn't rate. We ate in the kitchen or served ourselves and ate outside.

Braden Black, apparently, *does* rate.

I whisk myself back into the kitchen.

"Go tell your father and Braden that dinner's ready," Mom says.

"Okay." I head down into the man cave.

To my surprise, Braden is laughing. Laughing with my father while they both drink Wild Turkey. Apparently he forgot he was supposed to bring drinks back to the kitchen for my mother and me.

I can count on one hand the times I've witnessed Braden laugh like this. It's a wonderful sound, like bells during the holidays.

I clear my throat. "Mom says dinner's ready."

"Okay, sweetie. Tell her we'll be right up." Dad turns to Braden. "I have a little wine cellar in the corner. I'm sure it's nothing compared to what you're used to, but let's pick a wine for dinner."

"My pleasure," Braden says, rising.

My pleasure? It's his pleasure to pick out some cheap wine my father keeps in his wooden rack that he calls a wine cellar?

I have to admit, Braden is charming the dungarees off my dad, and I can't help loving him for it.

It's more than that, though.

Braden is enjoying himself. Actually *enjoying himself* with my father in his man cave. Drinking Wild Turkey and watching *Jeopardy*.

And it dawns on me... Braden is at home in this modest existence—this modest existence that may be more luxurious than how he grew up. My family never visited a food pantry. In fact, we donated what was left of our crop at the end of the year, after all contracts had been fulfilled, to help feed the hungry.

No, we weren't rich. We never had more than one car, and we didn't take fancy vacations. I didn't go to Disneyland until I was nineteen, when Tessa and I pooled our money and took a redeye to LA during spring break. We could only afford two days in the park, so we spent the rest of the time on a public beach.

But my family never went hungry. We were never cold. I always had plenty of clothes, and since I was an only child, I never wore hand-me-downs. My mom was crafty and sewed a lot of my clothes, but there was always enough money for me to have a few of the latest fashions once I hit high school.

Funny how I never appreciated this until now, after I've seen the luxury of a private jet.

I wait while Braden peruses the few bottles of wine in my father's rack. He chooses one. "This one, I think. It should go well with the pot roast your wife made, which smells amazing, by the way."

"Agreed." My dad pats Braden on the back.

I have to stop myself from laughing. My father just patted Braden Black on the back! I can't imagine Braden's own father ever doing that. Of course, I only met Bobby Black once. He was charming…and dating someone my age…

I can't imagine my dad doing *that*, either.

"After you, sweetie," Dad says.

I nod and walk up the stairs to the dining room. Braden and Dad follow me.

"Dinner's all ready," Mom calls from the kitchen. "I'll be right in with the meat."

"Sounds good, Mags."

Dad shows Braden where to sit, but first he holds my chair out for me.

Braden's always done that. He's a gentleman. But I can see Dad is suitably impressed. Braden and Dad both wait until Mom comes in. Dad holds the chair out for Mom, and once she's seated, both he and Dad finally sit.

Dad says a quick grace, and then the silence ensues.

At least five minutes pass in this unbearable quiet. I take a serving of each dish that's offered to me, my gaze focused on the plate of store-bought bread.

Until Braden grabs two slices. "This takes me back," he says. "Sliced bread on the table every night. I grew accustomed to it."

"Really? In Boston?" Dad says. "I thought it was a Mid-western thing."

"It's definitely a Boston thing, too," he says. "Sometimes, bread was the only thing on our table."

My eyes widen into circles. Did Braden just offer another clue to himself? First the food pantry. Now this?

Silence again. Neither of my parents seem to know how to respond to Braden's revelation, and in truth, neither do I. His cheeks redden a bit, and I wonder if he regrets his words.

And then I get it.

Why he's here.

Maybe he's doing the same thing I am. Going back to his roots to figure things out. Only his roots don't exist anymore. His family no longer lives in South Boston. He can't "go home again" to start at the beginning like I did.

I was right.

He didn't come here to figure me out.

He came here to figure *himself* out.

My father begins a conversation about the stock market, something my mother and I have no interest in, but it keeps Braden occupied. In the meantime, I devour my mom's pot roast. Next to her stew, it's my favorite home-cooked meal. The succotash is delicious, too. Nothing better than fresh corn and butter to make lima beans palatable.

When all the plates are empty, I stand to clear the table.

Mom stops me. "Sit down, Skye. I'll take care of this."

"That's okay, Mom. I'm happy to help." And happy to get out of the dining room for a few minutes. With my father and Braden discussing stock options, I feel like I've just landed in another galaxy.

My dad knows a fair amount about the market. He's done well over the years, choosing stocks to invest in and making a modest profit. But his knowledge is nothing compared to Braden's. Still, Braden listens intently, as if my father has something valuable to offer. I'm impressed.

I help Mom bring in her homemade elderberry pie. It's one of my favorites and something I can't find in Boston. Dad and I love it. The elderberries are about the size of BBs, and the seed takes up most of the berry. They're delightfully tart and tannic, though, and the seeds aren't any worse than eating blackberries or raspberries. Will Braden like it?

Even if he doesn't, he'll be polite.

I, for one, can't wait. Mom also has homemade whipped cream flavored with vanilla and bourbon—the perfect complement.

"I hope you have room for dessert, Braden," Mom says as she hands him a giant slice of pie topped with a large dollop of whipped cream.

"I always have room for dessert, Maggie."

Though he's addressing Mom, his gaze locks with mine.

Dessert, indeed.

Many times, Braden and I have indulged in dessert.

But if I think too much about that right now, I won't be able to stop squirming against the tickle between my legs.

"Mom's elderberry pie," I say. "My favorite."

"I don't think I've ever had elderberry pie before," he says, "though my mother made gooseberry pie once. I remember thinking it was kind of sour."

Mom smiles. "Now that takes me back. I haven't had gooseberry pie in years."

"What's a gooseberry?" I ask.

"It's a green berry," Mom says.

"Green? A berry?"

"Yeah. You can still find them in stores with the canned fruit sometimes, but I haven't seen a fresh gooseberry since I was your age, Skye." She turns to Braden. "Elderberries are tart as well, but don't you worry. I use a fair amount of sugar in this pie, plus the whipped cream will add sweetness as well."

"I'm sure it's delicious. Something doesn't have to be sweet for me to like it." Braden smiles.

He's smiling at my mother. That smile that I hardly ever get to see!

Calm down, Skye. Being jealous of your mother is all-out ridiculous.

He quickly maneuvers his gaze to mine, though. His words echo inside me.

Something doesn't have to be sweet for me to like it.

He's not talking about the elderberry pie. He's not talking about my pussy, either, as he's spoken soliloquies on how good I taste.

No. He's talking about me.

My personality.

I'm not sweet.

Fine. Neither is he.

Braden takes a bite of the pie, chews, and swallows, never taking his eyes off me. "Delicious."

"I'm glad you like it." My mother grins.

But he's really not talking about the pie.

I squirm. I'm tingling all over, and my heart is thundering. I take a piece of pie, hoping I can get it to my mouth without it landing in my lap. My hands are shaking.

The pie makes it past my lips, but it has no flavor. The only flavor on my tastebuds at the moment is Braden.

The texture of his full lips touching mine.

The spicy taste of his tongue entwining with mine.

The salty and musky flavor of his cock inside my mouth.

I'm as horny as I've ever been, almost near orgasm…and I'm sitting at dinner with my parents.

This isn't going to work. Braden has to leave. How am I supposed to figure myself out when all my body does is respond to him? He's not even touching me, and still I want him. Still my body cries out for him.

I cry out for him.

I finish my pie, still not tasting it. I help my mother clear the table, and when everything's in the kitchen, she turns to me.

"Go have fun with your friend," she says. "I'll take care of this."

I nod.

Fun with your friend.

If she only knew.

Chapter Twelve

When I return to the dining room, Braden and my father are walking out.

"Where are you staying?" my father asks.

"The hotel in town," he says, grabbing his phone. "I'll call a cab."

"Don't be silly." Dad smiles. "You can stay here. We have the room."

"Thank you, but I don't want to put you out."

"If you insist," Dad says, "but you don't need a cab. Skye can drive you."

Both of them glance at me.

"Uh…yeah, sure. I'll drive you."

If Dad knew what my body was doing at the mention of driving Braden to a hotel, he'd take back his words.

"Thank you, Skye," Braden says. "I'd appreciate that."

"Keys are on the hook," Dad says.

Our days of only one car were over by the time I hit high school. Dad and Mom each have a car now, and then of course there's Dad's pickup, but I never counted that.

But those are the keys that are on the hook.

"I'll see if I can take Mom's car," I say. "I don't like driving the truck."

"Suit yourself. My car's in the shop for a tune-up." Dad holds out his hand. "Great to meet you, Braden. I hope we'll see you again."

"I hope so, too." Braden shakes my father's hand and then turns to me. "Whenever you're ready."

I head to the kitchen to get the keys to Mom's hatchback. Has Braden ever ridden in a hatchback?

Maybe. When he was a kid.

I suck in a breath and jingle the keys. "Ready?"

"I am. Thank you again for dinner," he says to Dad, "and please tell your wife thank you as well."

"I absolutely will. Good night."

"Good night, sir."

Sir? I've never heard Braden refer to anyone as sir.

Interesting.

We walk out, and I lead him to Mom's light blue hatch. "No luggage?"

"I dropped everything off at the hotel and took a cab here."

"Not a limo?" I can't help asking.

He doesn't respond, and I don't blame him. I'm being a brat, and I know it.

I unlock the car and get into the driver's side. Braden slides in beside me, his long legs scrunched up. He fiddles with the knobs on the side of his chair until it slides back into a more comfortable position.

"Since we only have one hotel in the tiny downtown area of Liberty, I assume you're staying there."

"You assume correctly."

I start the engine and pull out of the long driveway. It's a twenty-minute drive into town. "Why didn't you rent a car?"

"I don't know. I just wanted to get here. I'll rent one tomorrow."
I nod.

"Tell me something about your childhood," he says.

"Is this a two-way street?" I ask.

"Sure. You tell me something, and I'll tell you something. Except I get to choose what I tell you."

"Is it a two-way street?" I ask again.

"Sure. You choose what to tell me. I know about the cornfield. You know about my trips to the food pantry. That's all we know about each other's childhoods."

"Fair enough." I clear my throat. "My mom used to make my clothes when I was little. I never wore anything store-bought until I was in high school."

"I see."

"Now, you go."

"I did get to wear store-bought clothes," he says, "but they were never new. We got them from thrift stores, and when I grew out of them, Ben wore them. He got the shorter end of the stick. While they were never brand-new, at least they were new to me."

My heart wells up. I never wore anything used. My clothes may have been hand-sewn, but they were always new.

"Your turn," he says.

"I… I did well in school."

"I assume that. Dig deeper, Skye."

"That's deep. I was one of the brainy kids. The brainy kid in handmade clothes." I'm not being fair. A lot of the kids I grew up with wore handsewn clothes. It's a rural thing. It wasn't a big deal, and I was never bullied for it.

"Skye—"

"Your turn."

"Fine." He draws in a breath. "My father drank. A lot."

I raise my eyebrows. "He did? He seems fine now."

"He's a recovering alcoholic. Did you notice he didn't drink that night at dinner?"

"No, I didn't." Because I was more concerned with making a good impression on Bobby and Ben and watching Kathy.

"Your turn," he says.

"Wait, wait, wait… You can't just throw that one out there and then say it's my turn. You need to elaborate."

"That wasn't part of the deal."

I roll my eyes. "Fine. My parents aren't alcoholics. They've been pretty happily married since…"

"Since when?"

A lump forms in my stomach. I never think about that awful time. I've put it in the past. But maybe…just maybe… Braden threw out something and then didn't explain it. I could easily do the same, but I came home for a reason. To figure things out.

And maybe what I'm about to say is part of the key.

"When I was little, about seven or eight, my father went away for a while right before harvest. My mother spent a lot of time crying, and I spent a lot of time trying to get her attention. He came back around Christmastime. Mom stopped crying then, but things were weird for a while."

"Where did he go?" Braden asks.

I sigh. "I don't know. They never talked about it. I have my suspicions, of course. He was probably having an affair."

"But you don't know for sure."

"Why else would a husband leave and a wife cry all the time?"

"Have you asked your mom?"

"Yeah. I asked both of them. All they say is it's in the past and it's nothing for me to worry about."

"When was the last time you asked?"

I wrinkle my forehead. "The year I started high school, I think. They had a big fight about… I can't even remember what. My dad stormed out, and I relived that day when my dad had left before. I asked my mom about it, and again she just said everything was fine and I didn't need to worry."

"And you haven't asked since then?"

"Nope. Why continue asking when they won't tell me?"

"That doesn't sound like the Skye I know."

I cock my head. No, it doesn't. I've been hammering Braden for the truth about Addie and him since we met.

Why *did* I stop asking my mom about that time? Since I have no answer, I say, "Your turn."

He chuckles. "I kept you going for longer than I thought I would."

"Your turn," I say again.

"All right. My father set our house on fire when he was drunk once. My mother…"

Shit. His mother. The mother he won't talk about. "What? What about your mother?"

"She was badly burned."

"Oh my God. Did she…"

"No, she didn't die. Not at that time, anyway."

His response puzzles me. "Your father… He didn't…do it on purpose, did he?"

He shakes his head. "It was an accident. A drunken accident. But insurance wouldn't pay because they called it arson, and my father couldn't prove he hadn't set the fire on purpose, so he lost the house. Then, my mother's medical bills were so outrageous…"

"And that's how you ended up going to the food pantry."

He nods. "My mother always wore a scarf over her face to hide the scarring."

I swallow, choking back tears. Poor Braden. Poor Ben. Poor Mrs. Black. She must have been beautiful to produce such beautiful children.

I stop at a red light. "How did you ever forgive your father?"

He turns toward me, his sapphire gaze burning. "What makes you think I have?"

Chapter Thirteen

"He works for you," I say. "I just assumed—"

"He got sober. He's smart. He works hard. He's my father. I wouldn't exist if not for him. So I let him ride on my coattails, and he's good at his job. Doesn't mean I've forgiven him."

"And Ben?"

He chuckles. "Your turn."

How is this not public knowledge? Dozens of publications have written extensively about Braden and his family, and of course, I've read them all.

"Braden…"

"Nope. Your turn."

I can't top that. My father isn't a drunk. My mother isn't scarred. Sure, they separated for a few months when I was young. I still don't know why, but we never lost our home, and we always had food on the table.

Things I took for granted all those years. Things I still take for granted now.

I turn onto the main road, and our small town comes into view. "Welcome to Liberty. Don't blink or you'll miss it."

"It's charming," he says.

"It has a bit of charm," I agree, "but the charm goes to shit when you're looking for a good cup of coffee and all that's available is Mrs. Temper's black water at the Sunrise Café."

He chuckles.

Funny. I've seen him laugh more since I got home than I have in the weeks we were together in Boston.

I drive to the tiny hotel. "Only four rooms. You were lucky to get one."

"Are they usually booked?"

"I was being sarcastic, Braden. No one comes here." I pull into an open spot on the street. "Here you go."

"Want to come up?"

"Don't you think my father will notice if I don't come straight home?"

"I'm not asking you to have sex, Skye. I'm just asking…" He sighs. "Hell, I don't have a fucking clue what I'm asking."

"Aren't they expecting you in New York?" I ask.

"They are. But they'll wait. Not like they have a choice."

"I suppose not."

He grabs the car door handle but holds onto it, not opening the passenger door. "Skye…"

"Yes?"

"I can't stop thinking about you."

"I can't stop thinking about you, either."

"At the dinner table, watching you… God, I want you so much."

He's anguished. Not unnerved—or perplexed, as he likes to put it—as I've seen him many times before, but truly anguished.

"Braden, what's wrong?"

"Nothing. Nothing's wrong."

That's a lie, and we both know it. "Thank you," I say.

"For what?"

"For telling me about your mother. It means a lot to me."

"Oh, Skye... In the grand scheme of things, I've told you nothing."

He doesn't grab me or try to kiss me.

I'm disappointed, but part of me understands. He's in a weird headspace. He told me things he probably doesn't let himself think about often. In fact, I know that to be true, as neither he nor Ben talk about their mother.

"When are you flying to New York?" I ask.

"Sometime tomorrow."

I clear my throat. "Would you like to—"

"Take you with me?"

I gasp in astonishment. "No! Where did *that* come from?"

"You begged me to take you to New York last week."

"Yeah, and we all know how that turned out."

"Yes, we do."

Is he having regrets?

"Why is everything black-and-white with you, Braden?"

"What makes you say that?"

"I asked you for something you didn't want to give me. Instead of working it out, finding a compromise, you ended our relationship."

"I wouldn't have ended it if you could have answered my question."

"Maybe I need your help to find the answer."

"Do you?" he asks.

"I...don't know. Maybe."

He shakes his head. "You don't. If you needed me, you wouldn't have come *here*. To your hometown. You would have come to me."

And it dawns on me then.

Maybe I *don't* need him to find my answers.

But he needs *me*.

And he hates that he needs me. It *disturbs* him. It *perplexes* him.

"Stop fighting yourself, Braden," I say.

"I don't know how to."

I lift my brow. Not the response I expected. I was thinking more along the lines of, *You don't know what you're talking about, Skye.*

Apparently I do know what I'm talking about.

As much as my own psyche confuses me sometimes, perhaps I know *my*self better than Braden knows *him*self.

"Will you come up with me?" he asks once again.

"My father—"

"Your father knows you're an adult."

"True, but—"

"Please, Skye. Come up with me. Make love with me."

"You just said you weren't asking me to have sex."

"I'm not. I'm asking you to make love."

"Meaning...?"

"Meaning just you and me. No toys. No games. No bindings and no commands. Just the act itself. I want to experience something special with you."

"What's so special about vanilla sex?"

He pauses a moment, staring out the windshield, and finally, when I'm convinced he's never going to speak again—

"I've never done it before."

Chapter Fourteen

My mouth drops open. "Never?"

"How can that possibly surprise you?"

"I…" Words don't come. *Should* it surprise me? I already know that he and Addie got kinky, but I know nothing about any of his other conquests. He owns a BDSM club. Why is his revelation so surprising?

Because everyone begins at the vanilla level.

Right?

Everyone, apparently, except Braden Black.

"You've really never just made love? Without all the…"

"The word you're looking for is kink, Skye. Without all the kink."

I clear my throat. "Yeah. The kink. The dominance."

"No, I haven't."

"Why not?"

"Because"—he clears his throat—"I've never had the desire to. Not until now."

My flesh warms, and a tingle flashes through me. He wants to make love. Just make love. And he wants to do it with me.

"All right, Braden. I'll go up with you."

A few moments later we're in his hotel room. The bed is queen-sized, not what we're used to when we're together, and the décor is Early American, not the sleek sophistication that graces Braden's bedrooms.

Still, it seems perfect.

He stands and stares at me.

"Well...?" I say.

He smiles. Yes, a smile. Kind of a shy smile. Very un-Braden-like. "I'm not sure where to start."

"You've never had that problem before," I say.

"You're right, because I've always known where I'm going. Even when you challenged me at every corner, I knew where I was going and I ultimately got there. The fact that you made me work for it was part of the game."

"We were a *game*?"

"I don't mean it in a bad way, Skye, but you know as well as I do that we were playing a game of cat and mouse."

I sigh. He's right. I'm as guilty as he is of manipulation.

"Somewhere along the line I fell in love," he says. "And not because you succumbed to me eventually."

"Then why?"

He chuckles. "Do you have any idea how many times I've asked myself that question? And the only answer I've come up with is that love isn't always rational."

"So loving me is irrational? That's not really a compliment, Braden."

"That's not what I mean. You're smart, and you're beautiful. You're talented. And God, you're a challenge. I once told you that you're my Everest. You are. Even after you gave up all your control to me, you're still a challenge. I just didn't expect..."

"What?"

"To fall in love." He pauses a moment. "Usually, after I

conquer something, I go on to the next thing."

"And you feel you've conquered me?"

"No. That's not what I'm saying."

"What exactly are you saying, then?"

"Whether I conquer you is no longer the issue. The issue is that I'm in love with you, and I have no desire to go on to the next thing."

Again I feel warm and tingly.

"Never in my life have I had a desire for vanilla sex. But damn it, Skye, I want to make love to you. I want to touch you and I want you to touch me. I don't want to take away any of your senses. I don't want to deprive you of an orgasm or punish you. I don't want to tie you up this time. I just want to lie next to you, as your equal, and make love to you."

Again, he pauses. I open my mouth, but he gestures me not to talk yet.

"And Skye?"

"Yes?"

"I'm fucking…"

"What, Braden? What?"

"I'm scared, Skye. Fucking scared, and I've never been scared of anything in my adult life."

His eyes are tormented, and I melt into his arms. Braden Black just admitted vulnerability. To me. To Skye Manning.

Something he's probably never admitted to another human being, including himself.

"It's okay," I say against his chest.

"It's not," he says. "I don't like this feeling."

I pull back.

"I don't mean the love I feel for you. I just mean… I'm not sure I can put it into words."

I nod. "I think I can. Vulnerability means you're not in control. I went through this same thing a few weeks ago when we began. It's difficult, but it's not insurmountable."

"I feel like I'm not myself."

I can't help a soft laugh. "Boy, do I know where you're coming from."

He kisses the top of my head. "I don't want to talk anymore. I want to take you to bed and make love to you."

I smile. "Okay."

He leads me to the bed. He doesn't command me to undress or to undress him. We undress each other. Slowly. Methodically. Relishing each new inch of flesh we expose on the other, until we both stand naked. Naked and vulnerable.

Braden takes my hand and places it on his shoulder. "Touch me, Skye. Please."

So many times I've been bound and unable to touch him. How I've ached for a moment like this. I'm trembling—actually trembling.

I trail my fingers over the golden warmth of his muscled shoulder and down his upper arm all the way to his perfect hand, where I entwine my fingers with his.

He closes his eyes. "I ache for your touch, Skye. I fucking ache for it."

"Why do you bind me, then? Why do you make it so I can't touch you except on your terms?"

His eyes still closed, he sighs. "I ache for that, too. I've always wanted women that way. But it's different with you. I want the darkness, but I also want the light."

"And that frightens you," I say more to myself than to him.

He nods. "Please. Touch all of me."

I lean into him and kiss his muscled chest. I've kissed his lips before, sucked his dick, but I've never been allowed to touch him all over. Every beautiful and magnificent part of him.

His cock is hard and gorgeous, as usual, and though it beckons me, I choose to do as he asks. I touch him. Simply touch him, all ten of my fingers sliding over his majestic male flesh. He's warm, and he shudders at my caress.

I shake my head in amazement that my simple touch affects him like this, makes him tremble and softly moan.

His pecs are hard and muscled, and when I flick over one nipple, it hardens beneath my finger. I move downward, over his six-pack abs to the triangle of black hair. I entwine my fingers through it, avoiding his cock even though I want more than anything to fall to my knees and suck him deeply.

I move around his waist to his back, caress the cheeks of his perfectly formed ass, and then press into him as I glide around his back to his shoulders once more. I brush my lips over his chest, and another slight shudder racks through him.

I kiss his chest again, moving my lips slightly each time, until I press a kiss to a nipple.

He inhales. "Damn."

I flick my tongue over the nipple, relishing its erection, and then I close my lips over it and softly suck.

He trembles again, sucking in another breath.

"Tell me what you want," I whisper.

"You're doing it. I want your touch. Everywhere."

I lift my chin and kiss his lips softly. He opens and our tongues meet gently for a few seconds. Then I end the kiss and rain soft pecks along his stubbled jawline, giggling as his stubble tickles me. I move to his neck then, kissing down to his broad shoulder once more. Where before my fingers led, now my lips take over, as I sprinkle soft kisses over his chest and abs. When I reach his cock, I give the head a few flicks of my tongue, resulting in more sucked-in breaths and groans, and then I head downward to his hard-muscled thighs. I explore him with my hands and lips simultaneously, delighting in the pleasure of pleasing him.

Giving him something he's never asked for before. Something he's probably never experienced with any other woman before.

And I feel power.

Power in the fact that he wants my touch.

Power in his surrender to me.

So it's not technically a surrender, as we're going to make love to each other, but for Braden? It's a relinquishment of his control.

This must be huge for him. No wonder he's scared.

He's as scared as I was when I first gave up control to him.

And now it's my turn.

My turn to take control. Not just over his body for these few precious moments, but over my life. It's time to figure out Skye Manning.

I'll begin here. In this hotel room with the man I love.

Chapter Fifteen

I travel down his thighs, over his knees, down his calves to his bare feet, touching, kissing, pleasing him.

Then I stand, entwine both my hands with his, and lead him to the bed.

Yes, I lead *him*.

His magnificent body is mine tonight. All mine, just as mine is his. "You're so beautiful, Braden," I say breathlessly.

"No one's ever said that to me before."

I can't help a chuckle. "Probably because you don't let them speak."

He smiles. That smile I saw tonight at dinner. That smile I so seldom see. He's letting a part of himself out with me tonight, a part he keeps trapped inside. I don't yet know why he does this, but I'm honored that he's sharing it with me.

Which means I owe him the same. I need to find out why neck binding and breath control are so important to me so I can share it with him. Make him understand.

"Touché," he says. "But as far as beauty goes, I'm nothing compared to you. You're lovely, Skye, and not just on the outside."

"Yes, I know. I'm a challenge."

"That's part of it, but you go deeper than that, and you know it."

Warmth envelops me. "Thank you. I'm not sure anyone's ever given me a more profound compliment."

"I mean it. Yeah, you drive me wild, sometimes to anger. But it's because you're so provocative."

"I provoke you, huh?"

"God, yes."

"Is that good or bad?"

"It's both." He sits up and flips me onto my back. "My turn to touch you all over."

I moan softly. "Please, Braden. Please touch me."

He begins at the top, gently kissing my forehead. It's an almost nurturing feeling, as if he's checking if I have a fever. Yet it's not nurturing at the same time. It's sensual because it's Braden—the man I love and who loves me back.

I let my eyes flutter closed, and then his lips touch my eyelids in the softest of caresses.

He kisses my eyes. Such a minor thing, but it sends me reeling. Goosebumps erupt all over me, and my core pulses with aching need.

How will I survive this? Braden kissing and touching me all over when I need him inside me, fucking me?

I sigh as he moves his lips down my jawline while cupping my breasts at the same time. Fingers tease my nipples, and then he pinches them. I lift my hips with a moan. He's kissing my neck now—that sensitive neck—and I shiver.

"God, you're beautiful," he says against my skin.

My hips rise again. Searching for him. His touch. His tongue. His fingers. His cock.

But I won't give this up. As much as I need him inside me, I want to experience his touch. His ultimate caress.

He brushes his hands down my sides to my hips, which puts his mouth on target with my nipples.

"Please, Braden."

"Tell me what you want."

"My nipples. Suck my nipples."

He flicks his tongue over one, making me gasp, and then he sucks on it lightly.

And it occurs to me. He asked what *I* want! Such a strange sensation, coming from Braden.

I just want to lie next to you, as your equal, and make love to you.

Such lovely words.

Am I missing the kink?

Yeah, sort of. He probably is, too. But this is something we both want, and it has its merits. A lot of merits, actually.

"I love you so much, Skye," he says, after releasing the nipple.

"God, I love you too."

"Your tits are so gorgeous."

Nothing he hasn't said before, but in his deep voice that sounds a little breathless right now, it's completely different from the way he's said it before in that dark and commanding voice.

Dark Braden isn't gone. I know that instinctively. He's only on hiatus. He'll be back. He'll be back when I can answer his question.

And I *will* answer his question.

I will find my truth, and I'll share it with the man I love.

He slides from my breasts to my belly, dipping his tongue into my navel as he grips my hips. Then he flips me over like a pancake and slides his tongue between the cheeks of my ass.

"Mmm," he groans. "Mine. This ass is mine."

Dark Braden. I recognize him. Dark Braden has returned, and he wants my ass.

Then, almost as if he realizes what he's doing, he slides

downward, kissing the backs of my thighs and making me shiver. He kisses and caresses all the way down my legs to my feet, and then he kisses each of my toes and slides his tongue between them.

I never knew my feet were so sensitive.

He turns me over once more, this time a little more gently, and then he spreads my legs.

"So beautiful. Your pussy is wet for me."

"God, yes."

"I wanted to go slowly. To make real love, but I need you, Skye." He climbs forward and thrusts his cock into me. "I need you now."

So full. So complete. I close my eyes, expecting him to order them open. He doesn't, but I open them anyway and meet his fiery gaze.

His eyes are full of need and passion. Full of love.

And I hope, as I gaze into them, he sees the same in my own.

For I feel all of that. Lust. Need. Passion. Love. So damned much love.

He descends slowly toward me until our lips touch. Then our tongues, and then the soft moans from each of our throats—his an octave lower than mine. It's music, a discordant melody borne of our passion.

I realize, in this moment, that I've never made love with any man except Braden Black. And though this time is different, the other times with him were no less making love.

Making love isn't about the act or how you do it. It's about the love you feel in your heart and in your soul for your partner.

Braden increases the tempo of his thrusts, and I know he's going to come. I'm close myself, not from the friction I usually crave, but from our bodies vibrating together in perfect synchrony.

"Skye," he says, "I'm going to come. Come with me. Please."

As always, at his urging, my body responds, and I burst into a shattering climax.

Never do I take my gaze from his. I wrap my arms around him, bring his head down to mine, and kiss him as we orgasm together. I thread my fingers through his silky hair, slide my hands down over his shoulders and then down his back to his ass, grabbing it and pushing him farther into me.

For a moment, as my climax sends me soaring, I don't know where he ends and I begin. He is me and I am him and the whole world is us.

And I know I'm truly home.

When our orgasms finally subside, he withdraws and rolls onto his back, one arm over his forehead.

Elation fills me. Elation mixed with love mixed with peace.

I haven't figured everything out yet, but I will. I must. For Braden and for me.

For us.

Chapter Sixteen

"Stay," he says softly, his eyes closed.

"I can't."

"Please."

Braden hardly ever says please, but he's said it several times tonight. I want to stay. I want to sleep in his arms and wake up together. Make passionate morning love—the kind where morning breath and bedhead don't matter.

But even though I'm at home with Braden, I'm also in my hometown, and I need to be respectful of my parents.

I kiss his lips lightly. "I want to stay more than anything, but I can't. I hope you understand."

He nods. "I'll walk you down."

I laugh out loud. "Braden, Liberty, Kansas is the safest place in the world."

"Doesn't matter. I'll walk you down anyway." He gets up, pulls his slacks back on, and slides his bare feet into his dress shoes. He grabs his shirt and buttons a few buttons.

Man, he looks sexy. Just fucked and sexy.

I hastily dress as well, and we leave the hotel room.

"You want to come over for breakfast in the morning?" I ask. "You'll get better coffee from my mom than at the Sunrise."

He kisses my cheek lightly. "What time?"

"Around eight, I guess. My mom and dad get up with the birds, but I won't be ready for public viewing until eight."

"Okay. I'll be there."

"I can pick you up."

"That's okay. I'll get there."

I smile. "Okay, Braden. Thanks."

"For what?"

"For…tonight. For telling me a little about your childhood. For…"

He lifts his eyebrows.

"…everything," I finish.

"I love you, Skye," he says. "I'm trying."

"So am I. Goodnight."

Even though I long to be in Braden's arms, I sleep better than I have in a long time. I wake up refreshed and feeling alive.

Braden and I will work things out. I feel certain. But he's not my only issue. I still need to work out my friendship with Tessa. It's an hour later in Boston, so I can catch her on her way to work. I grab my phone and make the call.

"Hi there! This is Tessa. I'm either on another call or out clubbing! Leave a message and I'll call you back right away. Or whenever I feel like it!" Then a giggle.

I sigh. I don't really want to leave a message, but she'll see my number and know I called. I have to leave something.

"Hey, Tess, it's me. I'm at my parents' for a week. Just needed to get away. I miss you. Call me, okay? Let's work this out."

Not my most eloquent message, but I think I got my point across. I head to the shower. It's seven, and Braden will be here in an hour.

After my shower, I amble to the kitchen, where Mom's working on some pie crust.

"Morning, sweetie."

"Hey, Mom. I invited Braden for breakfast at eight. I hope that's okay."

"Of course. I'll whip up some apple turnovers with some of this crust. Will he like that?"

"He's kind of a bacon and eggs guy, but I think he'll love it."

She laughs. "He can have bacon and eggs, too. We have plenty."

"I'll make it."

"Don't be silly. I'm happy to do it. Your dad and I really like him, Skye."

How can they not? He was amazing last night. More friendly than I've ever seen him. "I do, too. But…we're not actually together right now. I hope we can fix it."

"I'm sure you can. He's lucky to have you."

My lips curl into a smile. "You think so?"

"Of course I do."

"Mom…?"

"Hmm?"

I sigh. My talk with Braden last night brought back memories I've never quite gotten over. "What happened between you and Dad those months when I was seven?"

"Skye…" She wipes the flour from her hands onto her apron and turns to look at me.

"Please. I'm an adult now. I can handle it."

She sighs. "Why do you need to rehash all that?"

"We used the good china last night," I say absently.

"Yes. So?"

"I remember breaking a plate once, and that day…" I open the refrigerator door and stare into it, not looking for anything in particular. "I'm trying to figure some things out."

"Close the refrigerator," Mom says. "You're wasting electricity."

I chuckle softly. So like my mother. I close the door and meet her gaze.

"I don't like to think about those days," Mom says.

"I know that, and I'm sorry. But it means a lot to me."

She turns back to her crust, picking up the rolling pin. "Why? Why should it mean anything to you? You were a child."

"Because it's important to me."

Mom cuts large triangles in the rolled out pie crust, seeming intent not to look at me again. "We put this to bed long ago. You haven't asked me about it in years."

"Since my freshman year of high school, right after you and Dad had a big fight. I remember."

She places filling on one of the triangles and seals it shut. "It has nothing to do with you."

Irritation boils through me. "How can you say that? You're my parents. When one of you leaves for three months, and the other spends a lot of that time crying, of course it has to do with me."

"I mean it wasn't your fault."

"I never thought it was. But it affected me, and like I said, I'm trying to figure some things out."

Mom slides her turnovers onto a cookie sheet and opens the oven door. "What kind of things?"

"Like, why I am the way I am."

"You're an intelligent and generous young woman, Skye. You know who you are."

She's not getting it, and I don't know how to explain it any better without mentioning my foray into BDSM, and that's *so* not happening.

Hey, Mom, I wanted my boyfriend to bind me around the neck and choke me, but he refused.

Yeah. *Really* not happening.

This is getting nowhere. "Never mind, Mom."

She closes the oven door and wipes her forehead, leaving a smudge of flour on her left eyebrow. "I thought you let this go years ago."

"I never let it go. I just stopped asking."

She turns back to her pie crust and cuts out several more triangles for the turnovers. "The past is the past. It doesn't do any good to revisit it."

"That's not true," I say. "In therapy—"

She turns abruptly and meet my gaze. "You're in therapy?"

"No. Not currently, but I haven't ruled it out."

Her pallor whitens. I stiffen in my chair. For a moment I wonder if she's about to faint.

"What's wrong with therapy, Mom?"

"Nothing, of course. Nothing at all. But you're a success, honey. You've always seemed happy to me."

My mom's apparent aversion to therapy disturbs me. What exactly is going on?

"I'm happy enough, but that's not what therapy's always about, Mom. There are some things I don't understand about myself. Things I *want* to understand."

"Oh, God." She quickly fills the dough with apples and throws them onto another greased cookie sheet. Then she sits next to me. "I hoped this wouldn't happen."

Apprehension edges into me. "What are you talking about? You don't want me in therapy?"

"No, that's not what I mean. If you need therapy, I definitely want you in therapy. I just always hoped…"

"Hoped what? What exactly are we talking about here?"

She bites her lower lip. "Where do you think your father went for those months?"

"Honestly? I assume he had an affair."

"Oh?" Mom cocks her head. Is she surprised?

"If you just tell me, I'll know."

She shakes her head. "I can't."

"For God's sake—"

I jump at the doorbell.

Braden. Braden is here, just when I'm making some headway with my mother. I rise to answer the door. "This isn't over," I tell her. "Not by a long shot. He's leaving tonight to go to New York, but I'm here for the rest of the week."

Braden doesn't smile when I open the door, but he does seem relaxed, which is a good thing.

"Good morning," he says as he walks in. He kisses me chastely on the cheek.

"Good morning. My mom has a treat for you. Homemade apple turnovers."

He inhales. "Is that what I smell? Sounds delicious."

"Plus bacon and eggs. And strong coffee."

"Perfect." He follows me into the kitchen. "Good morning, Maggie."

My mother pastes a smile on her face, though she's not fooling me. Something's got her freaked.

"Good morning, Braden," she says. "Please, have a seat. I'll get you a cup of coffee. Cream and sugar?"

"Just black. Thank you."

Mom sets a cup in front of him. "Turnovers will be out in five minutes. How do you like your eggs?"

"Scrambled," Braden and I reply in unison.

"Scrambled it is." She turns back to the stove and takes four eggs from the carton.

I feel like I'm sitting on a block of ice. What have my parents been keeping from me all these years? But next to me sits Braden, the man I adore, looking scrumptious in jeans and a blue button-down the exact color of his eyes. I'm fraught with ambivalence. My body doesn't know how to react. Braden's nearness warms me, makes me feel all mushy inside. But my discussion with Mom has me frigid, ready to either fight or take flight.

Perhaps my father didn't have an affair. That should please me. But all I really know is that my mother has to confer with my father before telling me anything.

Which makes me think it can only be bad.

Chapter Seventeen

"When do you fly out?" I ask Braden when we've both cleaned our breakfast plates.

"Not until five p.m. I've got a car meeting me at the hotel at two thirty."

"Okay. What would you like to do until then?"

His gaze burns into me.

Yeah, I know the answer.

"Not here," I say under my breath, though I don't need to be so cautious. My mother escaped the kitchen as soon as she served breakfast. She's freaked out in a major way. I'm not sure I've ever seen her like this before.

Except maybe…

Fragmented images float through my head. My mother. My father. Me. But they're like puzzles missing that one essential piece that remains elusive no matter how hard I look for it.

"Show me around," Braden says.

"Why? You've seen the house. And the cornfields are huge, but if you see one acre, you've seen them all."

He reaches toward me, trails a finger over my forearm.

"Show me a certain part of it."

"What part?"

"The part where you got lost."

Again I'm sitting on that damned block of ice. I never ventured so far into the fields after that time. I haven't given it any thought in ages—at least not until I told Braden the story a few weeks ago.

But maybe this is important. Maybe I need to face that part of me to understand the other parts. I swallow. "All right. I'll take you there."

I'm an adult now. I'm not seven years old. I'm taller than the corn, and even if I'm not, Braden certainly is. We won't get lost.

He touches my hand. "You're frightened."

"Not frightened exactly. A little apprehensive."

"Why?"

"Why do you think?"

"You've never gone back there, have you?"

My eyes widen. "How did you know that?"

"You got rigid. Tense at the mere thought."

"You can tell that by looking at me?"

"Of course. I know you, Skye. Sometimes I think I know you better than you know yourself." He looks toward the entry and then lowers his voice. "I have to know my partner. I have to be able to read her body when she can't speak to me. It's part of the lifestyle. Part of how I keep you safe."

His words give me hope. "Will we ever get back there, Braden?"

"I hope so," he says, "because I don't think I can exist without that part of my life."

"You mean last night didn't mean anything for you?"

"Last night meant *everything* to me. It was completely new to me, and I wanted it with you. But I can't deny I still crave the darker side of sex. I always will. And if you and I can't go there,

I'm afraid there's no future for us."

Sadness sweeps through me. "We *can* go there, Braden. You're the one who stopped it, not me."

"True. But as long as you have that need—for the neck binding—I can't be with you. That's why I need you to figure out why you want it. That's the only way we can deal with it, but until you know the reason behind that need, you'll always want something I can't give you. And that's no way to begin a relationship. To begin a future together."

"How can there be no future? We love each other."

He cups my cheek, trailing his thumb over my lower lip. "Love isn't always enough, Skye."

"Love conquers all."

"You're better than a cliché," he says. "You're smarter than that."

I nod. I can't fight the truth of his words. Love doesn't always conquer all, no matter how strong it is. For whatever reason, he won't bind me at the neck. And for whatever reason, I need him to.

"I will answer your question, Braden," I say. "That's why I came here. To figure this stuff out. But when I answer yours, I expect you to answer mine. I want to know why it's your hard limit."

He nods. "I always intended to."

"Then I'll hold you to it."

Our backyard is large, and one of our fields juts up against it, separated by chain-link fencing. It is, of course, the field where I got lost. I was never allowed to go anywhere near the other fields, as there's no access from the house.

I breathe in deeply, willing my heart to remain steady. It wants to race, but I won't let it. If I can't control my body, what can I control? Not much.

I lead Braden to the chain-link gate at the far side of the yard.

"Is this where you went into the cornfield?" he asks.

"Yes. The gate was open."

"Did you know how to open the gate?"

"Yeah. But I never did."

"Were you allowed in the field?"

I nod. "As long as my mom was nearby and as long as I didn't go in too far."

"But that day, you went in."

"Yeah. I was chasing a praying mantis, remember?"

"Right. You liked bugs."

I smile at the memory. "I was never a girly girl. I played in the mud. I never wore dresses except on special occasions. I didn't even wear makeup until my senior year of high school."

"Did you help with the farming?"

"Not the actual farming, no. But I helped Mom dry and can corn in the fall. I helped her with her craft fairs and baking. That kind of stuff."

"Did you ever want to help in the fields?"

I shake my head vehemently. "Not after that day."

"Okay. Where did you go from here?"

I point. "See that post in the distance?"

"Yeah."

"That's where the scarecrow used to be. It's where I hit my head and knocked myself out."

"That's pretty far for a little kid."

"Believe me, it seemed like miles, especially when you can't see over the corn stalks."

He looks around. "Praying mantises are green, right?"

"Yeah."

He wrinkles his forehead. "How the hell could you chase it in here? Didn't it blend in with the stalks?"

"Not really. It's a different shade of green."

"Ah," he says. "Your photographer's eye."

"I suppose so. My mom actually asked me the same thing once I came to and told her what I was doing. To me, the greens are totally different." I let out a breath. I'm feeling better. Talking helps.

"Totally different?" Braden says, one eyebrow quirking.

"Okay. Subtly different. But I can see the difference."

Braden grabs my hand. "You're cold as ice."

"Am I? I thought I was feeling better."

"It's okay. Nothing is going to hurt you."

"Because you'll protect me, right?"

"Always," he says, "but you don't need me to protect you here."

"I know." I choke out a laugh. "I was kidding."

"I know you were. Do you realize that you use humor when you're nervous?"

"Do I?"

"You do."

We walk through the plowed pathway, moving farther and farther out, toward the old scarecrow pole. We don't seem to be getting any closer, though, until it juts out from the ground and stops me in my tracks. I resist the urge to cry out in surprise.

"Here we are," Braden says.

"Yes."

"Take this place back, Skye."

"What do you mean?"

"Here it is. It's an old pole. Nothing can harm you here. So take it back. Take back the power it stole from you all those years ago."

"Have you ever done anything like that?" I can't help asking.

"This isn't about me. It's about you."

"But have you—"

"You have no idea what I've had to take back in my life."

"Will you tell—"

"Damn it, Skye. Must you always be so obstinate?"

I let out a nervous laugh. "Isn't that why you love me?"

He shakes his head. "God help me. You're partially right."

I smile. Sort of. "I understand what you're trying to do, but I don't need to take this back, Braden. It doesn't scare me."

"Doesn't it?"

"No. I admit to being reluctant to come here, but I'm fine now. Really."

I'm not lying. My heart is beating normally, and my skin is no longer chilled. I'm okay.

"Then perhaps you're wrong."

"About what?" I ask.

"Maybe this isn't what gave birth to your need for control."

"No, this is it," I say. "I didn't realize until I got here, though, that this place isn't anything to hamper my life. Besides, I gave up control. To you. Remember?"

"You did. Or rather you may think you did."

"What do you mean?"

"Feeling out of control is related to anxiety. That's how you feel when you lose control in a situation. That's probably how you felt when you got lost here all those years ago."

I nod.

I remember so vividly when he puts the situation in those words. My heart thumping, fear flowing through me. My little legs trying to run but tripping, and then the pole springing up just as it did today, breaking my path.

Hitting my head.

Then waking up in bed.

"But," Braden continues, "is that how you feel when you're

not in control now?"

Is it? "No," I reply. "Not really."

"So you see, Skye, your need for control isn't really who you are at all, is it?"

Is he right? Is that how I was able to succumb to his mastery so easily?

"I... I don't know."

"What you define as being a control freak is really just a preference. You prefer to be able to think clearly. That's why you don't get drunk."

"You think?"

"It's possible. In fact, your willingness to give up control to me in the bedroom may be because it's nice *not* to have to think sometimes. It's nice to let someone else be in charge."

My mouth drops open.

He's right.

He's exactly right.

"Tessa says I don't let my hair down enough."

"You seem to let it down with me."

"Yeah, I do... In fact..."

"What?"

Say it. Just say it. "I want to let it down farther than you're willing to let me."

"That's true."

"So...what do we do now?"

"You have to figure that out for yourself, Skye. I can't help you."

"But you just—"

"I just got lucky on a hunch. Most self-professed control freaks aren't actually control freaks. For example, you don't micromanage."

"How do you know?"

"Addison wouldn't have let you."

He's not wrong. "Since you brought her up—"

"Nice try." His lips tremble, as if he's trying not to laugh. "We're not talking about me yet."

I huff. "Fine."

"You also didn't change yourself or your situation for me."

"I would never do that."

"That's exactly my point. You are who you are. You don't change yourself to control the situation." He pauses. Then, "Let me ask you something."

"Okay."

"Were you attracted to me from the beginning?"

"Of course."

"A true control freak would have attempted to manage my impression of her. You didn't do that."

I cock my head. Is he onto something? I want to hear more.

"Did you want to sleep with me that first night?"

"Of course!"

"But you didn't."

"No, I—"

"See what I mean?"

"But I *was* controlling the situation."

"No, you weren't. You gave up something you wanted that you could have had. How is that being in control?"

"It was… It was too soon."

"According to whom?"

Good question. "I don't know. According to the rules I set in my own head?" I laugh nervously.

"Bingo. That's your illusion of control—those rules in your head. But that's not what makes a true control freak. You control only yourself. A control freak takes charge of *others*."

I drop my jaw. His words make an eerie kind of sense.

"What did you gain by controlling yourself?" he asks.

"Nothing. I mean, I made you wait, I guess."

"You did. You made us both wait for something we both wanted. But you know what?"

"What?"

"I never doubted you'd come to my bed. And I never doubted you'd eventually yield to me."

I cock my head. "You said I was a challenge."

"Yes, and you were. You *are*. But I never back down from a challenge, and there's not one thing I've gone after that I haven't gotten."

"So you're saying…"

"I'm saying there's only one true master of control standing here, Skye, and it's not *you*."

Chapter Eighteen

Braden's voice has gone dark once more, and my knees weaken.

As wonderful as last night was, I will always crave the darker side in the bedroom…and thankfully so will he.

"What if I said I wanted to fuck you right now, Skye? Right here, against this pole that frightened you so long ago. I'd like to blindfold you, tie you to it, and take you from behind hard and fast while forcing you to stay quiet the whole time."

I don't even have to think about my response. "I'd say do it."

He groans. "You have no idea how much I want to."

"No one's stopping you that I can see."

"Only you."

I widen my eyes. "Did I not just tell you to do it?"

"You did, and I'm tempted." He grabs my hand and leads it to the firm bulge below his waist. "You feel what you do to me? What you always do to me?"

I nod, shaking.

"But if we go back there—back to that place we both desire—you will still want things I can't give you. Until you can tell me why you want those things, I can't go there."

"I can live without it." I gulp.

"Can you?"

"For God's sake, Braden, I've lived without all of this for the first twenty-four years of my life. I've had sexual relationships before. Satisfying sexual relationships."

He wraps his arms around me, pinning me to the scarecrow post. "As satisfying as ours?"

My body is jelly. Total jelly. I'll yield to him any way he wants right now. "Well…no. But that's because I love you. I didn't love any of them."

"Is that the only reason?"

I don't reply right away. Instead, I reach forward, squeeze and rub his erection.

He whisks my hand away. "Stop it, Skye."

"We both want it."

"That doesn't matter."

"Why? I can live without the choking, okay?" I gasp back a sob. "I don't know why it spoke to me so much. Maybe if I knew why you won't—"

He places his fingers over my lips. "Knowing my story won't change yours."

"But—"

"It won't, and it shouldn't."

I don't reply.

"This place doesn't scare you anymore."

"No." I give him a mischievous smile. "It would scare me less if you fucked me here."

He touches my cheek. "Nice try. Let's go back now. I'll buy you lunch in town, and then I need to get on my way to New York."

"I'll miss you."

"I'll miss you, too. Take some time for yourself. I'd like you to be able to answer my question when you return to Boston."

I nod. "I will, Braden. I promise."

It's a promise I'm determined to keep.

After a delectable lunch of pasta at Luigi's, Braden's ride came for him and he drove off. I stood on Main Street in front of the red brick hotel and watched the car until it was no longer visible.

Hope fills my heart. We can work this out. I know we can now, because I know he wants it as much as I do. I just need to give him an answer to his question. I stroll along Main Street for a few minutes, taking in the sights. Two years have passed since I've been here, and though it still looks like a small town straight out of the 1950s, I notice one small change. What used to be the Tabor Brooke Law Office now has a different tenant. Rosa Brooke, Family Therapist. Tabor Brooke's daughter.

Hmm.

I know Rosa. She and I went to high school together. She was a townie. One of the beautiful people and a cheerleader, but she was always nice to me despite my being a rural kid. Maybe she'd be willing to chat about my…issue.

I gather my courage and walk through the entrance.

A small desk sits between two closed doors. "May I help you?" the receptionist asks.

I sigh. "No." I turn.

Then, almost as quickly, I turn back to her. "I'm sorry. I don't have an appointment."

"Mr. Brooke isn't in today. He's in court."

"I was actually hoping I could see Rosa."

"Oh. She's with someone at the moment, but they're almost

done. What's your name?"

"Skye Manning."

A teenaged girl walks out through one of the doors. She waves at the receptionist. "See you next week, Mary."

"Have a great day," Mary replies. Then she picks up her phone. "Rosa, there's a young woman here to see you. Skye Manning."

A few seconds, and then out walks Rosa, still as blond and beautiful as she was in high school. "Skye, how nice to see you!"

"Hi, Rosa. I was walking by and saw your sign."

"When did you get into town?"

"Just yesterday. I'll be here all week."

"I don't think I've seen you since graduation. You look amazing, but then, you always did."

I smile. Yeah, she was always nice to me. "Thank you. You look amazing as well."

"We should do lunch while you're home."

"That'd be great. I'd love to talk."

"Of course. We'll catch up. I hear you're a big photographer in Boston."

I nod. "I wouldn't say big, but I'm at least taking pictures."

"Wonderful. I can't wait to chat. What's your schedule like?"

"Well." I clear my throat. "I'm free now."

"I have a half hour. Sure. Let's go get a soda."

I twist my lips. "Rosa, when I said I wanted to talk, I meant... professionally."

"Oh!" She widens her eyes. "Of course. Come on into my office."

I follow her, and she shuts the door.

"Have a seat."

I choose the couch, and she takes the wingback chair adjacent to me.

I clear my throat again. "I have insurance. I can pay you."

"I'm not worried about that. What can I help you with?"

God, where to start? "I'm in a relationship. Sort of. With…
With Braden Black."

Her eyes nearly pop out of her head. "You are?"

"We're kind of off again at the moment."

"Seriously? Braden Black?"

"Just for the past few weeks. I guess the tabloids didn't get
here yet."

"Liberty's the last to get any kind of news. So tell me all
about him."

I fold my hands in front of me to keep from fidgeting. "That's
kind of why I'm here, actually. We have an issue that I need to
resolve."

"I'll try my best to help, but if you're only going to be here
for a week, there's a limit to what I can do."

"I understand. If you tell me I need further guidance, I'll find
a therapist when I get home."

"One session of therapy isn't usually enough."

"I'm here all week. I can come in more than once."

"If there's room in my schedule, I'll be happy to see you. But
we're getting ahead of ourselves. What brought you in today,
Skye?"

"It's Braden," I say. "He and I have a rather…unconventional
relationship."

"How so?"

"Our sex life is"—my cheeks warm—"kind of…" I swallow
down a wave of nausea. "This is all confidential, right?"

"Of course. I wouldn't be a very good counselor if I blabbed
my clients' stories all over town." She smiles.

I know she's telling the truth, but her words make me edgy.
Maybe this was a bad idea.

She seems to sense my apprehension. "Skye, something's
obviously bothering you. I assure you that you can trust me. I'm
a professional and I'm bound by the ethics of the profession."

I sigh. "Okay. Our sex life is… He's into BDSM."

She nods, not looking surprised at all. Has she heard this kind of stuff before? She's a counselor, yes, but she's a young counselor from Liberty, Kansas. How much could she have come across in her brief professional life?

"How do you feel about the BDSM in the bedroom?" she asks.

My cheeks are full-on blazing now. They must be fire engine red. "I resisted a little at first. But just a little. I actually"—damn, my cheeks are on fire!—"really like it."

"All right. That's good. He's not coercing you to do anything you don't want to do."

"No, he isn't. He's been very respectful. I was surprised how much I like it, though."

"Why is that?"

"Because I've always been pretty type A, and submitting in the bedroom takes all my control away."

"Not necessarily," she says.

I widen my eyes. "What?"

"Some say it's the submissive who has the control in that kind of relationship."

"How can that possibly be true?"

"Because the submissive—at least in a healthy Dominant/sub relationship—gets to choose how far they want to go. The sub is the one with the safe word. The sub can stop what's going on at any time. Therefore, the sub has more control than the Dom."

I raise an eyebrow. "Hmm. I never looked at it that way."

"Most people don't, but it has merit."

"It does. But here's the weird part. I wanted to do something, and Braden said no."

"What did you want that he wouldn't give you?"

I bite my lower lip. Here goes. Rosa is a professional, and she may have an answer. "I wanted him to choke me."

If she's shocked, her face doesn't show it. "Why did you want that?"

"That's what I need to find out. I don't know."

"When did the idea come to you?"

"We were in a BDSM club, and I saw another Dominant do it to his submissive. It... I want to say it turned me on, but that almost seems too tame. It lit a fire in my belly, if that makes sense. The idea of being completely at Braden's mercy, with my life literally in his hands... It sparked something inside me."

"Why do you think you wanted it so much?"

"I wish I knew. Braden refused to do it, said it was his only hard limit, but he won't tell me why. Yet he wants me to tell him why I want it."

"Maybe he doesn't want his reason to affect yours."

"Yeah. He said as much."

Rosa jots down a few notes. "He sounds like a smart man. Of course, he wouldn't be where he is today if he weren't smart."

"He's brilliant, yeah," I say. "But he's also really private, you know? He's opened up to me a little bit, but I don't have any idea why he enjoys the darker side of sex so much."

"There may not be a reason for that, Skye. Some people like kink, and they're perfectly normal people psychologically. I've seen a few studies that show them to be psychologically healthier than people who practice solely vanilla sex. Though another study could show the exact opposite. That's the problem with studies. You can find one to pretty much say whatever you want." She smiles.

I return her smile and nod. "Yeah. You're right about that. How do you know so much about all this?"

She laughs then, but not in a rude way. "I wouldn't be a very good therapist if I didn't know about various sexual lifestyles."

I laugh as well. "I suppose you're right. How long have you been practicing?"

"Just under a year. But I did a three-month internship with a sex therapist while I was getting my masters, so I've heard it all."

"Can you help me, then? Can you figure out why I wanted the choking so much?"

"Only you can figure that out, but I can help point you in the right direction." She checks her watch. " I'm sure I have some time tomorrow. Check with Mary, and she'll set you up."

"Perfect. Thanks, Rosa."

"My pleasure. See you tomorrow."

I leave Rosa's office, and after setting everything up with Mary, I walk back out onto Main Street.

And I feel pretty darned good.

Chapter Nineteen

M om is out in her flower garden when I get home. "Hi, honey," she says.

I crouch down next to her and smile. "Can I help?"

She shakes her head. "Dinner's in the Crock-Pot, and I'm about done here."

"Where's Dad?"

"Where do you think? Out working."

I nod. Of course I already knew that. I want to broach the uncomfortable subject that we talked about this morning, and I'm resorting to small talk.

She sighs and meets my gaze. Her eyes are brown like mine. I look a lot like her. I always have. My dad's eyes are blue—dark blue, though, not like Braden's bright, fiery blue. My mother is pretty and looks great for her age. Hardly a line on her face, but her gaze tells a different story this afternoon. It reeks of resignation. Of something she doesn't want to face but must.

"You're not going to let this go," she says. It's a statement, not a question. She already knows.

"I can't, Mom."

"Why?"

"I told you. I'm trying to figure some things out about myself. About my relationship with Braden. About my relationship with everyone, honestly. And it all seems to come back to those few months when Dad left."

"Would it surprise you to know that him leaving wasn't his idea?"

My mouth drops open.

She blows out a breath. "I guess the answer is yes. You're surprised." She stands and removes her gardening gloves. "We didn't have a lot of money in those days, but that year we had a bumper crop and we needed extra help. We hired a hand. His name was Mario."

I cock my head. "I don't remember anyone by that name."

"Think, Skye. That day you ran off, chasing a praying mantis. It was Mario who found you."

I wrinkle my forehead. "I don't remember anyone finding me. I just remember waking up later in my bed."

"Mario found you." She pauses a moment. "Mario is the reason you ran off."

I squint, as if I'm trying to see something more clearly. "No, that's not true. I was chasing a praying mantis, and I—"

I stop abruptly. An image appears in my mind. An unwanted image.

Oh. My. God.

"You hit your head really hard, Skye. You had a concussion."

"Mario. He was young," I say. "Dark hair. Really good-looking."

"Yes, he was."

The images become clearer, and Mario's isn't the only face. I also see…

My mother. My mother as a young and beautiful woman.

My mouth opens, but words don't come. For there are no

words. No words to describe the image that is now so perfectly clear in my mind I could have photographed it myself.

Mario.

My mother.

In bed.

In my parents' bed.

She nods, tears welling in her eyes. "You remember."

I nod slowly.

"You were so upset you ran off. You broke one of the china plates, and then you ran."

I shake my head. "No. I remember the plate, but...I was chasing a praying mantis."

"You probably did chase a praying mantis. You loved all animals, even bugs." She laughs. "You were a little tomboy for a while, at home in dirty jeans and a T-shirt. The few times I tried to put you in pink frilly things, you ran outside as soon as you could and got them all covered in mud."

"The power of pink," I murmur.

"What?"

"Nothing. Just that...I don't hate pink anymore. I mean, I don't think I ever did. I just..."

"You just fought. You fought me on everything. You're so much like your father."

"I am?"

She opens her mouth to reply, but I stop her with a gesture.

"Don't get off topic. What the hell were you and Mario doing in bed?"

She shakes her head. "Exactly what you think we were doing."

Anger rises from my gut—the kind of anger that takes over your whole body. "All this time, I thought Dad had an affair."

"No. I did."

I stand, my hands curling into fists. "How could you?"

My mother drops back down onto the soft grass. "Skye, sit down. Please."

Reluctantly, I sit back down on the ground, but only because I'm not leaving until she tells me every detail of why she thought it was okay to do this to my father.

"Dad is a good man," I say.

"He is."

I work hard not to yell at her. "So why? Why the fuck did you do it?"

She doesn't scold me for my language. Good. I'm twenty-fucking-four years old, and I can speak how I want.

"There are things you don't know. Relationships aren't always what they seem."

"Of course there are things I don't know. I was seven fucking years old, for God's sake!"

She winces at the profanity this time. "Your father and I… We didn't always see eye to eye on how to raise you."

"So what? Do you think you're the only two people who ever disagreed about a kid?"

"It was more than that. He wanted more children," she says. Then, after a pause, "I didn't."

"And that's a good reason to fuck another guy? I'm not buying it, Mom."

"That wasn't the reason. I'm just giving you examples of what we disagreed on."

I turn my head, unable to look at her for a moment. Her daisies are blooming. My mother's favorite flower. And right now all I want to do is pluck every petal off every flower and grind them into the soil. "Fast forward to the part where you end up in bed with Mario. And why the hell I didn't remember it until now."

"After you caught us, I asked Mario to leave. It wasn't worth losing the respect of my child."

"But it was worth losing the respect of your husband?"

She buries her head in her hands, then, and a sob escapes her throat.

Does she seriously think I'm going to offer her comfort? So it was seventeen years ago. So what? To me, it's brand-new information, as if it happened yesterday.

She finally looks up, one tear streaking down her cheek. "Why are you pushing this? Why couldn't you leave it in the past? Why do you bring this up and let it affect what we all have now?"

I stiffen.

Déjà fucking vu.

Braden said almost the identical words to me after Betsy told me about him and Addie and I went storming into his office.

What the hell?

No. I reject the thought. This isn't *my* problem. This is my mother's.

"What happened? When did Dad come back?"

"He came back that day. I called him."

"Because of me."

"Yes, but he didn't move back in then. After Mario left, Dad needed a little more time to deal with things. I understood, of course."

"The crying," I say. "You cried a lot."

She nods. "I screwed up, and I knew it. I felt sorry for myself, and I missed your father."

"Did you apologize to him?"

"More times than I can count," she says.

"And…is he…?"

"It took some time, but he forgave me. We became close again, and in a way, I think I love him more because of it."

I can't help a scoff. "What? In what world does that make sense?"

"I can't make you understand everything when I still don't understand myself. Suffice it to say I grew up."

"Wait, were you and Mario…? Before Dad left?"

She nods. "Yes. I'm not proud of it."

I shake my head. "How could you? He must have felt replaced."

"Not replaced. Rejected."

"Semantics."

She says nothing. How can she? I'm right.

So many more questions flood my mind. Why was she in bed with another man when her small daughter was home? How did it begin in the first place? *Why* did it begin in the first place? What did my father do to make her want another man?

Why? Why? Why?

And why did they keep this from me for all these years?

Most important of all—why did I repress the memory of my mother in bed with Mario?

That's got to be some kind of key.

Maybe Rosa will shed some light when I meet with her tomorrow. God, I hope she has the rest of the week available.

Except I no longer want to stay here all week. I want to go home to Boston.

Braden won't be there. He'll be in New York. Tessa's not speaking to me, and Betsy's trying hard to avoid me.

A violent urge to tear fistfuls of my hair out of my scalp rips through me. Better yet, I want to tear out my mother's hair. To hell with her daisy petals. I'll take her own petals, strand by strand.

My mother, who, in her way, has been the most influential person in my life so far.

And then something dawns on me. Another question that needs to be answered.

I look at my mother, her eyes still tear-filled. I look long and hard at her full lips, her high cheekbones, and her eyes so like my own.

"Mom, why didn't you want any more children?"

Chapter Twenty

Why didn't you want any more children?

My words seem to hover in the air around us, blurring the colors of the daisies and other blooms in my mother's garden.

Why didn't you want any more children?

Is she going to answer?

Or will this question be another that no one will answer? Just like Braden about his relationship with Addie. Just like my mother never responding about their separation…until now.

Now.

Everything comes to a head now.

I already know the answer.

Me. I'm the answer.

My mother didn't want any more children because of *me*.

"You were so smart, Skye," she's saying. "You still are, of course, and you were so stubborn and resistant."

"I fought you on everything," I murmur, echoing the words she said just minutes ago.

She nods. "On everything. The most mundane things, like Frosted Flakes instead of Cornflakes with sugar for breakfast.

They're the same thing, for God's sake, and regular Cornflakes were cheaper."

"They're not the same thing," I say. "Frosted Flakes have the sugar coating *on* them. They taste better."

My mother throws her hands in the air.

I get it. I'm still doing it. I'm fighting her on something that is truly meaningless. I don't even eat Cornflakes anymore, and I never eat sugary cereal anymore.

The image of Benji, the little boy from the food pantry, squeezing the loaf of bread whirls into my mind. My mother hated it when I squeezed the bread, but still, I did it. Fought her every time…

"I was a problem, so you didn't want to risk having another kid like me. Yeah, I get it."

She takes my hands in hers. "No, Skye. Don't ever think that. I loved you more than my own life. I still do. That will never, never change."

"But it's my fault I don't have a brother or sister."

"Of course not. It's not your fault. It's mine. I'm the one who couldn't handle you. Your father could. He found your rebellion charming."

"But he wasn't the one who had to take care of me twenty-four-seven," I say.

"No, he wasn't. He even offered to, but I wasn't cut out to take over what he did on the farm. Farming is hard work, and obviously I'm not as strong as he is, plus, I just don't have the interest."

I smile slightly. My father would have become a house husband for me? For more children? That's amazing, and as much as I adore him, he just earned several more daddy points. Mom is right. Farming *is* hard work. I know, because I worked right alongside my dad sometimes. As I got older, I took my camera along and took some amazing photos of him in the fields.

Some of my best work even to this day.

You are a challenge, Skye Manning, and I never back down from a challenge.

Braden's words.

Apparently he's not the only one who finds me a challenge. The first person I challenged in my life was my mother.

I am who I am. Braden says I'm not a true master of control. Perhaps he's right, given my eagerness to submit completely to him, to the point that I wanted to give him control over my access to oxygen.

Not a control freak, no. Just a challenge. Just someone who fights at every step.

Basically, a big pain in the ass.

That's what I am.

That's why I don't have siblings. But is that why…?

"Mom, please tell me you didn't start sleeping with Mario because of me."

"Of course not! That's between your father and me."

"But I was one of the things you disagreed on."

"Trust me, there were others."

"What was the catalyst, then? Why did you do it?"

She sighs. "I'm not sure I even remember anymore."

"That's bullshit, and you know it."

She shakes her head, chuckling softly. "You continue to fight me. Always."

I dig in my heels. Literally, as I sit in the garden, my heels sink into the soft dirt. "This is important to me. I've already told you I'm trying to figure some stuff out about myself, and this seems to be part of the key."

"It had nothing to do with you," she says, "and everything to do with me. Mario made me feel…beautiful, I guess."

"You were always beautiful, Mom."

"I didn't think so. Being a farm wife isn't easy. It's a lot of hard work. I never had any time for myself. You were... I loved you so much, Skye, but you were..."

"Rebellious. I know."

"Yes. It was tiring, always fighting for everything with you. Your father was in the fields twelve hours a day, and he came home exhausted. That's not his fault, of course, but he was too tired to talk to me, let alone... You know..."

Yeah, I know. Have sex, make love—whatever euphemism you want to call it. The idea of my parents doing that kind of nauseates me, but less so than the idea of my mother with some young stud named Mario.

"Did you always love him?" I ask. "Dad, I mean."

"Yes, I did."

"Then why...?"

"Because I'm human, honey. Simply human, and I needed some intimacy. Mario offered it, and I accepted. I shouldn't have, but I did."

I shake my head. "Why didn't you control yourself?"

She opens her mouth, but nothing comes out. She doesn't have an answer.

Just like I, the self-professed queen of control, have no answer as to why I want the neck binding with Braden.

I just want it.

But he doesn't.

Maybe if he told me why, I'd understand.

But he's right. Knowing his why won't bring me any closer to my own.

Finally, my mother speaks. "I should have resisted. I should have controlled myself. I have no reason except that I wanted it, and I gave in."

"So you admit you were weak."

"Yes, Skye. I'm not you. I'm not strong like you and your father are. I gave in."

"That's an excuse."

She sighs. "Perhaps it is. I had a chance to take something I wanted, and I took it."

"Did you give a thought to Dad? To me?"

"Of course I did."

"But we lost, and you won out."

She lowers her head and fixes her gaze on the soil in front of her. "There's no use arguing about it. You're right."

"I feel no satisfaction in being right, Mom."

"Honey, this is why I resisted telling you everything. Dad and I worked through it. We're good now. In fact, we're better than we were before Mario. And we both love you so much, Skye. We always have."

Yes, they have.

Despite the fact that my mother apparently found me difficult—*finds* me difficult—there was never a time when I felt she didn't love me.

I don't feel that now, either. I know she loves me.

Still, I need one more answer.

Chapter Twenty-One

"Mom," I begin, "why were you in bed with Mario while I was in the house?"

"That was unfortunate," she says with a sigh. "You were supposed to be at your friend Myrna's house, but her little brother developed a high fever, so Myrna's mom dropped you back home on her way to the doctor. She called, but I didn't hear the phone."

"Who let me in the house?"

"The door was unlocked. You were seven. You let yourself in."

Myrna. I haven't given her a thought in years. She and her family lived on a neighboring farm, but they sold out and moved when we were in fifth grade.

Right. I remember now. I opened the door and walked in the house. I yelled for Mom, but she didn't answer. Then I heard sounds coming from her bedroom.

So I opened the door, and—

Funny how clear it is now. How did I forget? The concussion may have had something to do with it, but I remembered the praying mantis. I remembered getting lost in the cornfield. The china plate...

I never saw Mario again after that, so it was most likely easy for my seven-year-old mind to block out such an unpleasant memory.

And of course Mom didn't hear the phone. She was... God. My instinct is to fight her on that as well. What was she thinking, not hearing the phone?

But it's seventeen years in the past.

Perhaps I need to let it go. Perhaps...

Perhaps I need to choose my battles.

I don't need to fight everything.

Perhaps I need to choose my battles with Braden as well.

"It's so strange," I tell Rosa the next day at our session. "It's clear as day now, but for the longest time I didn't remember catching my mom in bed with that guy."

"Childhood memory repression isn't unusual," Rosa says. "Especially something so unpleasant. Then you have the added issue of the concussion, which can cause retrograde amnesia."

"It didn't, though. I remember chasing the praying mantis, and I remember getting lost."

"But did you remember being at Myrna's that day?"

"No, not until my mother told me."

"See? You don't recall everything from childhood. No one does."

"But finding my mom in bed with a farm hand... That I should remember."

"You do. Now. Like I said, it was unpleasant for you at the time, and children often repress unpleasant memories as a defense mechanism. My guess is you didn't repress it at the time, but it faded away after your parents got back together and everything went on smoothly. The young mind is very resilient, Skye. I'll say it again. What you're describing doesn't sound unusual to me at all."

"It's not like me, though. I prefer to be in charge of everything, especially my own mind."

She smiles. "You were seven."

I sigh. I know. I was seven. Just a kid. But still…

"Let's see if we can't pull some of this together," Rosa says. "Do you feel responsible for your parents' breakup?"

"Of course not. Why would I?"

She nods. "What if I told you that I think, on some level, you do?"

"I'd say you're wrong."

"Let's go back to you and Braden for a moment. When you asked him to bind your neck—to choke you—and he refused, he said he was concerned that you were becoming dependent on his punishment. In effect, he thought it was no longer a part of the sexual experience for you, and that it was becoming too real."

"I disagreed then, and I still disagree."

Rosa makes a few notes and then meets my gaze. "What if I told you that I think he may have a point?"

"Then I still disagree with you. I enjoy kinky sex. So does he."

"But he's in charge, right?"

"You told me last time that I'm in charge."

"You are, in some respects. But so is he. He can refuse to do something you want. That's his right, but you're resisting him."

"That's not it. He won't tell me why he won't do it. Why it's his hard limit."

"Should that matter? You're resisting him. You're not letting him have the control in the bedroom, which you said you gave up."

"Well…technically we weren't in the bedroom. We were at the club."

Rosa shakes her head slightly. "Skye, you know very well

what I mean."

I draw in a deep breath. She's right. She knows it, and so do I. I can't help a soft laugh. "My mother told me I fought her on everything when I was a kid. Not just important stuff, but silly stuff, too, like wearing a pair of socks that was dirty, or arguing over breakfast cereal. What the hell is wrong with me?"

She smiles. "Nothing's wrong with you. You're strong willed. There's nothing wrong with that. If you were vindictive and irritable, if you blamed others for your stubborn behavior, you might have a touch of obstinate defiance disorder, but I don't see that in you."

"I guess I just didn't realize I've been this way my entire life."

"Our personalities are formed by the time we're five years old," Rosa says. "You're a fighter. That's not a bad thing. It's why you're successful."

I pause for a moment, thinking. *Is* that why I'm successful? I'm a good photographer, and I studied the discipline in college and became even better. I took the job with Addison so I could take pictures, and that job, plus my relationship with Braden, inadvertently resulted in my own budding influencing career.

Does that equal success?

Is it because of me after all?

Not because of Addie and Braden?

"You look like you're thinking," Rosa says. "Your forehead is all wrinkly."

I nod. "Yeah. I am. I'm wondering…"

"Wondering what?"

"I guess I'm wondering if I truly am the reason for my success. I guess I'm not even sure I *am* successful."

"Of course you are. You're a talented photographer and an up-and-coming influencer. Sounds like success to me."

"I always figured no one would care what I thought if I weren't Braden's girlfriend."

"I won't lie to you. That probably helped. But if you were Braden's girlfriend but couldn't write good copy or take a good photo, would you still be where you are?"

"I... I honestly don't know."

"You *do* know. You just don't want to admit it, Skye." She pauses. "Let's attack this from a different angle. Braden is concerned about you getting too much pleasure from punishment. What if he doesn't actually mean pleasure?"

"Braden always says what he means."

"He may think that's what he means, but what if it's not the pleasure from the punishment you're after? What if it's the punishment itself?"

"Why would I want to punish myself?"

"For one, because you think you're not worthy of your success."

I raise an eyebrow. What Rosa says isn't completely out of left field. How many times has the thought crossed my mind that I'm a fraud? More than a few.

"Let's go one step further," she says. "What if I told you it's not just that you feel unworthy of your success? What if you blame yourself for what happened between your parents all those years ago?"

I shake my head. "Why would I do that? It wasn't my fault. I was a kid."

"Yes, and you're right. It *wasn't* your fault. But somewhere inside you is that seven-year-old girl, and she might think it *was* her fault."

Did I?

Do I?

"I'm not sure I gave it any conscious thought at the time."

"This isn't your conscious mind at work, Skye. It's your subconscious. You didn't think about the fact that you fought your mother on everything, or that you were part of the reason she didn't want more children. But inside your psyche, you knew.

And perhaps your subconscious has always wondered if you drove your father away and drove your mother into another man's bed."

"I didn't even remember Mario until yesterday."

"But your subconscious mind did. Otherwise it wouldn't have come blaring back to you when your mother told you."

She's not wrong. The image is now so clear in my mind that I could have photographed it myself. In color. Freaking Kodachrome.

"How does this relate to my need for punishment?"

"How does it *not* relate? You're punishing yourself not only for your success, which you think you don't deserve and won't take any credit for despite having earned it, but also for your parents' split all those years ago."

"But…"

"What?"

"I…*enjoy* the punishment."

"Do you?"

"Well, yeah… But…"

"But what?"

"The punishment isn't really punishment. When Braden truly wants to punish me, he doesn't tie me up or flog me. He denies me a climax. The other stuff isn't meant to be punishment."

"There you go. *He* doesn't mean for it to be punishment, but on some level, you *do*. And that's what is disturbing to him."

I can't deny that her reasoning makes an eerie kind of sense. "Are you saying I'm addicted to punishment?"

"I wouldn't put it in those terms, but it's possible that what Braden sees as kink and part of what he enjoys in the bedroom, you see as actual punishment. As you say, when he wants to truly punish you, he takes your orgasm. The other stuff is for pleasure, both his and yours. Or so he thought."

"But I enjoy it. It *does* please me."

"I know it does. The question is why?"

Chapter Twenty-Two

Why indeed?

My phone buzzes, and I pull it out of my pocket. It's Braden.

"Do you need to take that?" Rosa asks.

"It's him. It's Braden."

"Tell you what." She checks her watch. "We only have five minutes left, and I've given you a lot to think about. So go and think about it, and I'll give you an extra five tomorrow."

I sigh. "I'm leaving tonight."

"I thought you said you were staying the week."

"I was. But after my conversation with my mother yesterday, I just want to go home."

She smiles. "Don't run, Skye. Work it out."

"With my mother?"

"With your mother. Your father. Braden. All of them. It's time to forgive your mother. And it's time to forgive yourself."

"Myself? For what?"

"For being a difficult kid. For fighting your mother so much. You weren't abnormal. Lots of kids have a stubborn streak. I had one myself."

"Did you drive your mother into another man's bed?"

"No, but neither did you."

I nod. I get what she's saying. "It wasn't my fault."

"No, it absolutely wasn't. Both of your parents would probably tell you the same thing."

"My mom already did."

"See?"

My phone stops buzzing. "I missed the call."

"Go. Call him back. Then call me tomorrow at two p.m. and we'll talk some more. If you need more help after that, I'll find a referral for you in Boston. But, Skye?"

"Yeah?"

"You're going to be okay. I promise."

Back on Main Street, I reach for my phone to return Braden's call, when it buzzes again.

I put it to my ear, smiling. "Hey! Sorry I couldn't answer. I was just getting ready to call you back."

"You were?" A female voice that sounds vaguely familiar. Not Addie, but Addie-like.

Shit. I didn't look at the number. I just assumed it was Braden trying again.

"Sorry, I was expecting another call."

"Are you Skye Manning?"

"That depends. Who are you?"

"I'm Apple Ames. Addison's sister."

Apple. Addie's hippie twin sister. I met her once, a year ago. She prattled on and on about Zen and motorcycles and the Dalai Lama. Despite their duplicate DNA, she and Addie are like night and day. Though which is which, I couldn't say.

"Hi, Apple. Why are you calling me?"

"I need to talk to you," she says, "about Braden Black."

My heart thunders. "Why?"

"There are things you need to know. Things Addie will never tell you. Things no one knows except Addie and me."

"Not Betsy?"

"Betsy?"

"Betsy Davis. Your friend from your childhood."

"Right. Wow. I haven't given her a thought in ages."

"You haven't? Addison posts for her all the time."

She scoffs. "You seem to be under the delusion that I pay a lick of attention to Addie's Instagram. I couldn't care less."

Yup, night and day, all right.

"I'm out of town, currently, but I'm returning tonight."

"Great. I'll meet you at the airport. Give me your flight information."

"Wait, wait, wait… How about sometime tomorrow?"

"This can't wait, Skye. I'm serious."

My heart begins beating like a snare drum during a Sousa march. "You can't leave me hanging like this. Seriously. What's going on?"

"All I can tell you is that Addie's watching you both. I'm concerned for you."

"I already know she's up to something. I've been watching her. I'm sure Braden has as well."

"Yeah, probably. But he can take care of himself."

"All right. Why, though? Why are you telling me all this?"

"Well, as someone wise once said, the enemy of my enemy is my friend, grasshopper."

I've heard that phrase before. From *The Art of War*? Maybe. Not the grasshopper part. I'm not sure where Apple got that. "Okay. But you can't tell me anything now?"

"Not over the phone. Sorry. I don't trust my sister as far as I can throw her. She could be monitoring calls."

True. When she ends the call, I toss my phone into my purse. Braden is in New York, and I have no idea when he'll be back in Boston. Probably not tonight. What does Apple want to tell me? More importantly, what is so important that she can't say it over the phone because she thinks Addie might be listening in?

What have I gotten myself into?

I head home. My mother and father are sitting together on the deck in back. I regard them before they're aware of my presence. They're not touching each other—Dad is paging through a magazine and Mom's reading a book—but the comfort between them is palpable. They belong together. They love each other. They've long overcome the events of seventeen years ago.

The least I can do is the same.

"Hi, Mom. Hi, Dad."

They both look up.

"Hi, sweetie," Dad says. "I didn't hear you come outside."

"You both seemed buried in whatever you're reading."

Mom hold up a tattered copy of *Jane Eyre*, one of my favorites. "Bet you forgot you left this here."

I nod. "I have another copy from the lit course I took in college."

"I just started it. Since you love it so much, I figured it was time I gave it a read."

"What do you think so far?"

"It's a little slow."

"At first, yeah. But don't give up on it. It's a fantastic story. What are you reading, Dad?"

He holds up his magazine. "*Agriculture Weekly*."

I smile. Dad really loves what he does. He always has. Those several months away from the farm must have been hell for him, and not just because he knew his wife was sleeping with someone else.

Anger rears its ugly head.

I take in a breath. Then another. *Seventeen years ago, Skye. Seventeen fucking years. Just because it seems like yesterday to you doesn't mean it was.*

"Guess what?" Dad says.

"What?"

"Mom and I just opened up Instagram accounts. It's time for us to get on board with your new career. You look gorgeous in all those posts, sweetie."

I smile. "Thanks, Dad."

"Have you eaten lunch yet?" Mom asks.

"Not yet."

She puts her book down. "I'll make you something."

"No, it's okay. I'll get something for myself."

Dad stands then. "I should be getting back to work. See you at dinner, sweetie."

"Actually…" I begin.

"Yeah?"

"I've decided to fly back to Boston tonight."

"But you just got here," Dad says.

"I know. And I promise I'll be back as soon as I can, but I'm under contract, and I need to get back to work."

"Then why did you plan to stay the week?" Mom asks.

Good question. I let out a breath as I decide to be honest. "I came back to figure some things out about myself."

"And have you?"

I nod. "Not all of it, but I've got a good start. I appreciate our talk, Mom. And between Rosa Brooke and Braden, I think I'm on the right track."

"What are you talking about, sweetie?" Dad asks.

"Didn't you tell him?" I ask Mom.

"Tell me what?"

"Oh, Skye…"

"Sorry, Mom, but he has a right to know." I turn to Dad. "I asked Mom about why the two of you separated all those years ago, and she finally told me the truth."

Dad clears his throat. "Maggie…"

"I made you look good," Mom says. "It was my fault."

"It was both our faults," he says. "Your mother wasn't getting what she needed from me."

"Dad, I—"

"That's all I'll say on the matter, Skye. Some things are between a husband and wife and aren't anyone else's business, especially their daughter's."

"But I had to know," I say. "It explains so much about me."

"She's right, Steve." Mom nods. "I should have talked to you first, but she's right."

Dad heaves a sigh. "What's done is done. Your mother and I got past it, and you need to as well."

"I will. Try to understand, though. This happened a long time ago, but because I didn't remember, it seems like yesterday to me."

"Is this why you're leaving early?" Mom asks.

"No. Okay, maybe partially. I just need to let it sink in and give myself time to get over it. Also to get over my part in it. But I also have to get back to work. Susanne Cosmetics is naming a new nail color for me."

"Pink Skye?" My mom smiles.

"Not after *me*. After some copy I wrote," I explain. "It's going to be called The Power of Pink."

"That's wonderful, sweetie," Dad says, "but I'm concerned about your feeling that you had a part in what happened between Mom and me. It had nothing to do with you."

"Thank you for saying that," I say.

"It's true."

Yes, it's true. For him. Not so much for me, but I don't want to argue with my father. He and I have always been close, and with all those memories rushing back, I also remember how much I missed him during those months. He came for me every weekend, and we spent the whole day together, but it wasn't enough.

But if my parents could get over it, so can I.

I head to the kitchen and fix a light lunch for myself.

Then it dawns on me.

I haven't returned Braden's call.

Chapter Twenty-Three

"Sorry I missed your call," I say to him. "I was…"

"You were what?"

I inhale deeply. No need to be nervous. "In a session. A therapy session."

"Why didn't you want to tell me that?"

"I don't know. It's personal, I guess."

"You mean you were ashamed."

"No, not really. I know I have no reason to be ashamed."

"But it's kind of a stigma, right? The great Skye Manning should be able to fix everything herself."

I can't help a chuckle. "It's scary sometimes, how well you know me."

"I see a lot of myself in you."

"Except, as you told me the other day, I'm not actually a master of control. Not like you are, anyway."

"No, you're not," he says. "But that doesn't make your need to be in charge any less valid."

"I know."

"Would it surprise you to know I've been to therapy?"

My eyebrows shoot up. "Uh…yeah, actually. It would."

"I have. In fact, I have a standing monthly appointment with my therapist, just to check in."

"You do?"

"I do."

"Why?"

"Because I can't run a billion-dollar company if I'm not mentally healthy."

I let out a short laugh. "When you put it that way, it makes all sorts of sense."

"When I put it that way? What other way is there to put it?"

"No other way," I say. "Absolutely no other way. You're right."

"As usual." He smirks.

Yeah, I can't see him, but I know he's smirking.

"Did your session help you figure things out?" he continues.

"It helped a lot, actually. I can't say I have all the answers, but at least now I'm asking the right questions."

"Good. That's good, Skye. I'm proud of you."

"I'm flying back to Boston tonight," I tell him.

"Why?"

Why indeed? The lie I told my parents won't fly with Braden. "I need a little distance from my parents. I found something out that has me disturbed."

"Do you want to tell me about it?"

"Not over the phone, but I can tell you that I think it has something to do with why I am the way I am."

"Something related to the cornfield?"

"Yeah."

"I'll be home in a few days. We can talk then. Or whenever you're ready."

"Okay."

"Goodbye, Skye."

"Bye, Braden."

Only after I end the call do I realize something profound.

Braden didn't pester me to tell him. Not the way I pester him about his childhood, his mother, and mostly about his relationship with Addison.

Whenever you're ready.

I could attribute his words to any number of things. Maybe he's busy right now, needs to get back to a meeting. Or maybe he's at a late lunch and his food arrived. Maybe another call came in that he had to take right away.

But in my heart, I know it's none of those things.

It's Braden giving me time to work stuff out, to be ready to talk about certain stuff.

A luxury I never afforded him.

I will now. I'll see Apple, but only to find out why Addie's stalking me. I won't ask her about Addie and Braden, and I won't ask Braden about his mother or about Addie no matter how much I want to know.

He deserves the same respect he's granting me.

I recognize Apple at once. Of course, because she's Addie's identical twin. At the same time, she also looks nothing like her.

Their facial features are identical, but that's where the resemblance ends. Apple's hair is jet black now, obviously a dye job, as she and Addie are naturally blond. Her dark tresses are wound into a French braid that drapes over her left shoulder a la Katniss Everdeen. Apple has two nose rings and a lip ring, and black stars are tattooed around her left eye. She dresses similarly to Betsy except for the colors. Her peasant blouse and boho skirt are dark gray and black, respectively. Her fingernails and toenails are painted black as well, but her Birkenstocks are dark brown.

She's the anti-Addie, and it makes me want to chuckle.

She approaches as I stand at the carousel waiting for my suitcase. "Skye?"

"That's me." I hold out my hand. "How are you, Apple?"

"Hanging." She takes my hand and gives it a hard shake.

I spy my black bag and grab it.

"Come on," Apple says. "I'm parked in the economy lot. You want me to take the bag?"

"No valet?" I can't help asking.

She scoffs. "That's Addie, not me. I don't believe in spending money just because I can."

I smile. Definitely the anti-Addie. "I can handle the bag, but thanks." I follow her to the parking lot where we take a long walk to her—I kid you not—VW Beetle. Lime green VW Beetle, at that. Not black.

I'm beginning to really like Apple Ames.

She unlocks the trunk and opens it, and I place my suitcase inside.

"I thought we'd hit a bar and have a quick drink," she says. "Somewhere public."

Man, she really *is* worried about Addie's ears. "Okay. It's early yet."

Somehow we end up at a small pub on the edge of Swampscott, the suburb where Bobby Black lives. I don't mention that. Apple probably knows anyway.

The bar is kind of a dive, but it's quiet. We snag a small table in the back, and after a server takes our order, Apple starts talking.

"I know Addie's been warning you away from Braden Black," she says.

"Oh?"

"Are you kidding? I know her MO. She's been obsessed with him for over ten years."

"Is it true she stalked him?"

Apple laughs. "Stalked? That's a pretty tame word for what she did."

"What word would you use then?"

"Ambush is more like it."

My heart nearly stops. "What do you mean?"

"After he dumped her—"

"Wait, wait, wait," I say. Curiosity is killing me, but I can't hear anymore. "I get that she was shaken and all, but I really don't want to—"

"Shaken?" Apple fiddles with one of the many rings she's wearing on her fingers. "Addie wasn't shaken. Unless you mean shaken to the core by his rebuff."

"O…kay. That's not how I heard it."

The server brings our drinks, and Apple takes a sip of her club soda. "Not surprising. There are only three people in the world who know what really happened. Addie, Braden, and me."

"How do *you* know?"

"Because I was *there*, Skye. I was there."

Chapter Twenty-Four

I take a sip of my bourbon. It stings more than usual.
Or is the sting from Apple's words?

If she's telling me the truth—if she *was* actually there—then she knows what went on between Addie and Braden.

She knows what I've been trying to get out of Braden for weeks now.

She fucking knows.

And then my own thoughts haunt me.

Didn't I just promise myself, after talking to Braden this afternoon, that I'd give him the space he seems to need to tell me everything?

On *his* terms?

In his own time?

If I get the story from Apple, I'm breaking my silent promise to Braden.

Damn, though. She's here. Now. Ready to tell me what I'm dying to know.

Ready to tell me…

I almost lost Braden after Betsy told me what she knew. Then

I *did* lose him because I couldn't tell him why the neck binding was so important to me. But he loves me. He made love to me. And I love him more than anything.

I still haven't quite figured myself out, but I'm on my way. It has to do with punishment. Dire punishment that I feel I deserve. Rosa is right.

Braden is right.

Braden means everything to me, and if he finds out I got his story from someone else, he may never forgive me.

Right now, he and I have a chance. I'm well on the way to being able to answer his question, and he's not pushing me for information.

That's why I promised not to push him, either.

If I let Apple give me her scoop, I'm betraying him.

"You were there," I echo her words.

"I was." She takes another sip and winces. "Soda water tastes like shit, but it's color and preservative free."

"You don't drink?"

She shakes her head. "Not since I was a kid. I'm sure you've heard all about the parties Addie and I used to throw."

"Not really." Just the one where Braden and Ben showed up, and Addie became obsessed with Braden.

"Yeah, they were legendary. Once I got into Zen Buddhism, I stopped all the alcohol and drugs and began treating my body like the temple it is."

"I see." Except treating the body like a temple apparently doesn't negate ink and piercings. But hey, all God's children…

"Anyway," she says, "the whole thing with Addie and Braden started at one of our parties. The folks were out of town, and Add and I had just finished high school."

He deserves the same respect he's granting you, says the little angel on my shoulder.

She's willing to spill everything, chants the devil on the other side. *You want to know. You know you want to know. It's been killing you.*

"Anyway, that's how it started. I'm not sure how, but Braden and Ben Black ended up at one of our parties."

I hold up my hand. I can't do this to Braden. "Stop. Please."

"Why? You want to know, right? Of course you already know how incredible looking they both are, so they were a big hit."

"A couple guys from South Boston?"

"Yeah, weird, right? But somehow they found out about our shindig, and they showed up. Addie and I were barely eighteen, and we were intent on slumming it a little that summer. Braden and Ben Black were the perfect candidates."

"How did she and—"

He deserves the same respect he's granting you, says the little angel on my shoulder.

She's willing to spill everything, chants the devil. *Everything.*

I take another sip of bourbon. "I can't listen to any more."

"You're kidding, right?"

"I wish I were, but I made a promise to myself that I'd let Braden tell me this stuff when he was ready."

"He won't be ready," Apple says. "Ever."

"How do you know that?"

She doesn't reply. Just takes another sip of the soda water she hates. Then, "I'm trying to help you."

"I know, and I appreciate it. I really do."

"Tell you what." She finishes her soda water. "I'll take you home. You have my number. If you change your mind, I'm here."

"Why do you care about telling me this stuff?"

"I already told you. The enemy of my enemy, sweetheart."

"Addie and I aren't enemies."

"You may not think so. *She* does."

"Why? I'll never have her following."

"Doesn't matter. You have something else she wants.

Something she's always wanted and could never have."

"Braden?"

"Partially, yes."

"Braden and I aren't even together right now, so I no longer have him."

"He's really into you, though," Apple says. "And Addie knows it."

Chapter Twenty-Five

The next morning I awake from thrashing dreams all night. *The cornfield. Running. The praying mantis. But I'm also running from the image of my mother and Mario in bed together. Naked.*

The scarecrow. The pole.

The fear and pain when I hit it...

How could I have buried that memory?

How?

But the how doesn't matter so much. I'm aware of it now, and though it hurts, it has a purpose to serve. I rise and start a pot of coffee. I have a phone call with Rosa at three—two her time. Before then, I need to do a Susie post...and I need to call Tessa. She hasn't returned my call, and it's time to work this out. I need her.

I scoff at myself. *I need her.*

I'm not wrong. I do need her, but maybe I should be focusing on *her* needs and not my own. This controlling part of my nature... Is it rooted in selfishness? In self-absorption? Man, something else to ask Rosa this afternoon.

I made a promise to myself yesterday that I'd let Braden have the space he requires concerning his past. That I'll no longer ask.

Oh, yeah, it will be difficult, but I'm determined. He deserves the same respect he's giving me.

And so does Tessa.

Yes, I need her, but this isn't about me. It's about her. And I know what to do.

I grab my phone and call her.

It goes to her voicemail, of course.

I exhale. "Hi, Tess, it's me. Skye. I'm back home now, and I want you to know I'm here for you if you need me. I really want to work things out, but if you need space right now, I hear you. Feel free to call me. Or not. It's up to you. But I'm here and I love you."

I end the call, hoping the message comes across the way I mean it. I do need her, and I do want to work things out.

I also want to give her whatever time and distance she needs.

A few minutes later, though, my phone buzzes. A wide smile splits my face. "Tess?"

"Hi, Skye." Her voice is…different. Tessa is usually so upbeat.

"I didn't expect to hear from you quite so soon, but I'm so glad you called."

A few seconds pass. Then, "I'm sorry."

"No, Tessa. I'm sorry. I should have called you when Braden and I went to New York. Our shopping trip."

"Yeah, you should have. But I should have told you it bugged me instead of brushing it off. That wasn't fair."

"I should have been there for you. With the whole Garrett situation. I'm sorry. More sorry."

"We can both be sorry, Skye."

"I suppose we can, but this is all my fault. I didn't mean to forget about you, but I can see that I did. I promise it won't happen again."

"I don't need any promises," she says. "I just want my best friend back."

"Deal," I say. "You want to grab some breakfast? Then yoga?"

She chuckles. "I have this little thing called work."

"Fuck. Of course. I'm not getting off to a great start."

She pauses. Is she rethinking her position? I can't blame her. Asking her to go to breakfast and yoga when she has to be at work in an hour was a foolish move. A self-absorbed move.

"It's okay," she says. "How about drinks tonight after work?"

"Absolutely. I have so much to tell you."

"About Braden? Work?"

"All of the above, but mostly about some things I'm figuring out about myself. I've been talking to…a therapist."

"You have? That's terrific!"

I chuckle. "I didn't know you'd be so excited about that news."

"I'm not. I mean… I just think therapy is good. For everyone."

For me. She means for me. I could argue with her, but what's the point? She's right. "How are things with you?"

"I'm okay. Garrett Ramirez is a jackass, but whatever."

"What happened with you two?"

"You wouldn't believe it if I told you."

"Sure I would."

A few seconds pass before she speaks. "I caught him with someone else."

"Tess, I'm so sorry."

"It's not like we were exclusive or anything, but I went over to his place one night to surprise him, and a woman in a towel answered the door."

"Wow."

"Yeah. What could I do? I'm sure I looked like a complete ass. So I told him it was her or me, and he chose her."

Ouch. "You gave him an ultimatum."

thru. By the time I'm home, it's time for my call with Rosa.
h in her number.

i, Skye," she says. "I trust you got home safely."

did. In fact, I have some good news. My best friend and I
ck on speaking terms."

at's great! How about you and Braden?"

e's still in New York, but I spoke to him after I left your
yesterday, and I think I had kind of a breakthrough."

nd of a breakthrough?"

augh a little. "Yeah. I told him I'd talked to a therapist
at I had some stuff to tell him when he got back. He said
t matter when. Whenever I was ready."

?"

ah, and that was the breakthrough. I've been pushing him
his past. About his relationship with Addison Ames, and
his mother. He's close-lipped about both, though he has
a little about his mom and his childhood. Anyway, when
he'd give me the time I need, I realized I have to do the
or him. I have to stop thinking about my own needs and
inking about his."

ur needs are important, too," Rosa says.

gh. "I get that. I do. And in my heart I know I'm not a
person. But this desire I have to take charge of everything
me want to know everything. Knowledge is power, right?"
e."

t he's not ready to tell me about some parts of his past,
ve to accept that."

pauses for a second. "Are you willing to accept that he
ver be ready?"

aw in a breath. "I think I have to be, whether I want to

od for you," she says. "I know it's hard."

a have no idea how hard. Last night, I met Addison's

"I sure did. I'm not overly proud of it, but…"

"You have every right to want to be the only person in a
guy's bed, Tessa. You're worth so much."

"Thank you for saying that. You want to know the best part?"

"What?"

"Three days later, he calls me and says he made a terrible
mistake. That he hooked up with Lolita—can you believe that's
actually her name?—on Tinder, and he was just angry at me for
making him choose, so he chose her."

"Seriously?"

"Yeah. So he starts to tell me he's falling in love with me,
and… God, Skye, you have no idea how much I missed you
while this was going on. I talked to Betsy and to Eva and even
to a couple other girlfriends from work and yoga, but it wasn't
the same."

"I know. Trust me. I know."

"Anyway, I told him to fuck off."

"Good for you."

"Good for me. Right. Except Betsy and Peter are kind of an
item now, and Pete and Garrett are best friends, so it's been a
little awkward."

"No reason to be."

"It is. I still have feelings for him."

I'm not sure what to say. This isn't like Tessa. She never
worries about losing a guy because there's always another
waiting in line. "Can you forgive him?"

"In a way, I have nothing to forgive him for. We never talked
about exclusivity. But he hooked up with someone he didn't
know, Skye. That bugs me."

"You've done it before."

"Not while I was seeing someone else."

"True."

"He's called me a couple times since then. I've let them all go to voicemail."

"Sounds like he's serious about wanting you back. That's a good thing, right?"

She sighs. "I guess."

"Maybe he's willing to be exclusive now."

"Maybe. It's tempting, but I can't forget how I felt when I found him with another woman. It was humiliating."

"I understand." Well, not exactly, but sort of. I caught my mother with another man once.

"So. How are things with you?"

"Good." Except Braden and I sort of broke up. As much as I want to spill everything—about Braden, about Susanne Cosmetics, about Addie and Apple—I don't. I want Tessa to know I'm here for her. That I'll no longer forget about her. Especially after my breakfast and yoga blunder in the middle of the week.

"I'm glad," she says. "I've got to get dressed and get to work. See you tonight. I'll text you with a place."

"Sounds good."

"Thanks, Skye. For calling again."

"Absolutely. Best friends forever, right?"

"Right."

I smile and end the call, and then I plug my phone into the charger, grab a cup of coffee, and head to the shower. Time to get my creative juices flowing for today's Susie post.

Chapter Twenty-

*L*ove my Susie Girl tinted moisture! G *#sponsored #susiegirl #susieglow*

The photo is a selfie—right out of the sh in a pink tank top, my hair still wet. My lips I'm blowing a kiss to my audience. And yeah, glowing. I'm not wearing any other makeup. tinted moisturizer before, but I will from no face feeling hydrated and healthy, and the sl my skin tone. These cosmetics may be inexpe truly top notch.

It's a great feeling to like the product I'm

I flash back to Addie's posts for Bean The woman despises the smell and taste of co oodles of dough from the company to adverti she has no qualms about doing so.

If I get successful at this influencing thing post about products or places I truly love. I' with integrity.

I catch a quick yoga class and then gra

sister, and she was ready to tell me everything about Addie and Braden. I stopped her."

"Really? That took some willpower."

"You're not kidding. I had all the answers right in my back pocket, and I told her not to tell me."

"I'm proud of you, and I'd like you to look at your decision in a different way."

"How?"

"It took a lot of control *not* to listen to what she had to say."

Rosa isn't wrong. "You're telling me."

"So there you are. Control. The only difference is you put someone else's needs ahead of your own. By letting the information go, you were exercising the control you crave, just in a different way. And you did it because you care for another person more than you need the information."

"I never thought about it that way."

"You're young, Skye. We both are." She laughs. "I may understand psychology, but I still have a lot of growing up to do. The more I know, the more I realize what I don't know."

I laugh along with her. "If that isn't the truth."

"So tell me. Yesterday we left with the question of why submitting to Braden's punishment pleases you. Or rather, what we're calling punishment for lack of a better word, since to him, you don't feel it's punishment."

"Right. His idea of punishment is to deny me an orgasm."

"Yes. So the spanking, the flogging, the tying up… All those things. You gain a lot of pleasure from that."

I swallow. "Yes. Especially the bondage."

"Perhaps you're just a natural submissive."

"Maybe, though it goes against everything I know about myself."

"Sometimes that's the key," Rosa says. "We think we know ourselves, but we don't always. Sometimes our subconscious comes into play, as I think it may have with your repressed memory of your mother in bed with another man."

"Braden says he doesn't think I'm a true master of control."

"Why does he think that?"

"He says I only control myself, and that a true master of control will desire to control others."

"Do you feel you control others?"

"No. He's right about that. I only control myself, and apparently I'm not even good at that anymore."

"Why do you say that?"

"Because I gave him my control in the bedroom."

"And what was the result?"

I sigh. "The most amazing and passionate experiences of my life."

"So you have no regrets."

"Not a one."

"Then we come back to the question. Why do you gain so much pleasure from what you see as punishment?"

I take a moment to think. "It probably stems from my insecurity. I feel like I'm only getting into influencing because of Braden."

"Exactly. On a conscious level. How about on a subconscious level?"

I sigh again. "My parents' separation. They fought about me a lot. Wow. They did. I haven't thought about that in ages."

"The repressed memory will start to bring back other memories. Memories that weren't repressed but seemed insignificant until now. What did they fight over that was about you?"

I chuckle. "My stubbornness. I'm a lot like my father, and it was too much for Mom to handle, having two of us. I fought her on everything. The example she gave me is Frosted Flakes versus Cornflakes with sugar sprinkled on top. Regular Cornflakes were cheaper, and we didn't have a lot of money back then, so that's what she bought. But there were other things. I fought her on everything, from getting my homework done to cleaning my room to gathering eggs from the hens we used to keep. Which is really weird, because I loved those hens and I loved gathering eggs, so why did I fight her? Even now, it seems so inconsequential to me, but apparently to her it was a huge deal. Enough so that she didn't want any more children. Or chickens, for that matter. We kept the hens until they died, but we never replaced them."

"You may have been stubborn and obstinate, but what you're describing is still in the range of normal for a child. It's not like you did anything super horrible."

"No, I didn't."

"Have you considered that being a mother was difficult for her?"

"No." I shake my head against the phone.

"I can't speak from experience yet, but from everything I've studied, parenting is quite difficult for some people. That doesn't mean they don't love their children."

"I'm starting to understand that. It seemed easier for my father."

She pauses. "Your father worked all day."

"Yes, he did."

"He wasn't home all day with his stubborn daughter. If, as you say, he's as stubborn as you are, the two of you would have butted heads, but he would have won, because he's the parent."

Interesting, but I feel Rosa isn't being fair to my mom. "My mother's a strong woman."

"I'm not saying she isn't. I'm only remarking that parenting you was difficult for her. That's not a slight to her or to you, and that's what you need to understand."

"My father said it was both of their faults. My mother wasn't honest with him, and he wasn't making sure her needs were met."

"That's usually the case. Relationships are almost never a one-way street."

"They both say none of it was my fault, though."

"It wasn't. You were a child. You need to believe them."

"I never thought it was my fault."

"Not consciously. But your subconscious may have. And that may play a big part in why you crave what you perceive as punishment."

I pause a few seconds.

"You there, Skye?"

"Yeah," I say. "Still here. Just thinking."

"About what?"

"That I need to stop thinking about the kink in the bedroom as punishment. But what if that's the only reason I want it?"

"Does it matter?"

"Of course it does. If I stop thinking of it as punishment, maybe I won't want it anymore. And if Braden *does* want it, where does that leave us?"

"All Braden needs to know is why you wanted the neck binding so much. Can you answer that question now?"

I sigh. "Yes. I believe I can. When I witnessed the scene— the woman bound around her neck and the man pulling on the makeshift collar and choking her slightly—I got turned on. But it was different than a usual turn on. It felt almost…"

"Almost what?"

"Almost…*necessary*. Necessary to who I am."

"Except, knowing who you are—a smart and talented young woman who's on her way to becoming a big success—that doesn't make a lot of sense."

"Right," I agree. "It doesn't."

"So how was it necessary?"

"I wish I knew."

"Let's attack this from another angle," she says. "Do you know why most people practice breath control in BDSM?"

"Not really."

"Have you heard of erotic asphyxiation?"

"Yeah. It's dangerous."

"It is, which maybe is why it's a hard limit for Braden. But the restriction of oxygen also intensifies the orgasmic experience."

My eyebrows nearly fly off my head. "Yeah, I've heard that, but…"

"But that isn't why it felt necessary to you."

"No, not at all. I wanted it because… Because it seemed like what I deserved."

"Skye," Rosa says, "I think we're on the right track."

Chapter Twenty-Seven

Atonement.

That's the word Rosa used at the end of our conversation, and suddenly I'm able to see things from another angle.

Although I know what atonement means, I look it up anyway.

Reparation for a wrong or injury.

If my desire to be punished was based on the fact that my success was due to my relationship with Braden and my previous tie to Addie, it's not atonement at all.

But if it's related to the fact that I feel responsible for my parents' breakup all those years ago...

Then it's definitely the right word.

And it clicks so much into place.

Rosa and I made arrangements to continue to see each other via Facetime once per week and tapering off as needed. She was ready to recommend a therapist in Boston, but I'm comfortable with her and prefer to continue as we are for now.

I feel so much better, and already, I'm willing to respect Braden's hard limit. He doesn't want to engage in breath control because it's dangerous, and he doesn't want to harm me.

That's a good thing. A noble thing.

What's more? I don't need to atone for anything. Yes, it will take time to totally banish the idea that I was responsible for my parents' separation, but I'm on the right track now, as Rosa said. And I deserve all the success I'm having with my influencing career. I take damned good photos and come up with clever ideas and copy. Hell, it's the reason Addie hired me in the first place.

I can't wait to tell Braden.

I want to tell him that I respect his hard limit. That I respect his wishes and desires. That I respect *him* so much.

And I do.

Even more? I love him so much.

"Amazing," Tessa says over our drinks this evening after I relay the whole story. "So much was happening to you, and I didn't know about it. I'm sorry I wasn't there for you."

"I'm sorry I wasn't there for you, too, with the whole Garrett thing."

She takes a sip of her blue margarita. "I guess we both fucked up."

I nod. "I guess we did, though I think I fucked up more."

She bursts into laughter. "Skye, you slay me. You even want control over this."

I join in her giggles because she's right. "I give. We're both guilty."

"And degree of guilt doesn't matter. Say it with me, Skye."

"Degree of guilt doesn't matter," I echo.

"Say it like you mean it," she throws back at me.

"We're both guilty. Degree of guilt doesn't matter. We'll both do better."

"There you go. Best friends forever." She finishes her drink. "You want to order some food?"

"Sure." I signal to our server.

We place a quick order for some street tacos and another

margarita for Tessa. I'm still working on my bourbon.

"Selfie time!" I rise and move to the other side of the table with my phone.

"Do I look okay?" Tessa asks.

"Are you kidding? You always look gorgeous." I snap a few photos and let Tessa choose which one to post. I do some quick edits and then post.

Nothing better than drinks with the BFF! @tessa_logan_350 #bffsforever #margaritaville #menwhoneedsthem? #tessaandskye

And I realize, even with Braden and me not right yet, I haven't been this happy in a long time.

I've been using the Susie skincare line for a little over a week now, so it's time to compare my before post to how I look now.

Hmm. Not bad at all. I don't have acne or anything, but my complexion is noticeably more even-toned.

Before and after one week of Susie skincare. My skin is more even-toned and it feels great! #sponsored. #susiegirl #anyonecanbeasusiegirl #susieglow

My last post about the tinted moisture earned me a thumbs up text from Eugenie. The copy for this one isn't as inspired, but I want my audience to focus on the photos. I'll post again in another week.

Today is Saturday. The day I was supposed to return from Kansas.

The day Braden is due to return from New York.

We've spoken on the phone every day, just checking in. Yesterday, though, I let him know I need to talk to him about something important.

I'm going to answer his question.

Where will it lead?

I don't know. What I do know is that Braden is in love with me and I'm in love with him.

What I also know is that Braden himself has something he's hiding, something he keeps buried inside him. I've made the decision not to force it out of him. Not like I'd be successful anyway.

Tonight, I'll share a part of myself with him that I've only just discovered.

I hope it inspires him to share something more with me.

If it doesn't?

That's okay. I still love him, and I'll give him all the time he needs. If he needs to be without me, I'll accept that.

I hope he decides to come back to me, though.

I miss him so desperately.

He's due at my place by seven. I'm going to cook him dinner. My shrimp étouffée that was ruined, spurring our second trip to New York.

The beginning of the end.

Tonight, though? Tonight will be the beginning of the beginning.

I'll will it to be.

I make a quick trip to the liquor store to pick up a Beaujolais-Villages, posting a selfie along the way.

Posting is beginning to become second nature to me. To be a success, I must be a friend to my audience, not just an advertiser. I need to show them that I'm human. I'm the same as they are. Skye Manning has drinks with her BFF. Skye Manning goes to yoga class. Skye Manning shops for étouffée ingredients and the perfect wine accompaniment.

It's actually pretty fun.

Plus, I'm using my talents, arranging my ingredients just so. Finding the perfect spot in the grocery store where the lighting will set off the colors so they're the most vibrant.

I whip up the étouffée and let it simmer. I've already made my chocolate mousse for Braden, so I decide on another French favorite to complement the meal—crème brûlée. The custard part is tricky. It needs to be thick and creamy but not too much so, or it becomes more like flan.

After everything's done except the burnt sugar coating on the crème brûlée—which has to be done with a small blow torch right before we eat it—I check my watch. Six thirty. Time enough to shower before Braden arrives.

I turn and—

Someone knocks on the door. I wipe my hands on the apron I'm wearing. It can't be Braden. He's never early.

I look in the peephole.

Shit! It is Braden. A half hour early. I open the door slowly, knowing I'm a fright.

"Skye," he says.

"You're early."

"I know."

"Well, come on in. I was just going to hop in the shower."

"That's a great idea," he says. "I'll join you."

I wrinkle my forehead. "That wasn't an invitation."

"I've been in meetings nearly twenty-four-seven since I left Kansas," he says. "I need a shower, too."

"Be my guest, then." I gesture him toward the bathroom.

"Oh, no. You can't dangle the idea of a shower with you in front of me and then take it away."

"I didn't dangle anything, Braden. You know that as well as I do. We're not together right now, despite—"

"Fuck it all, Skye. I don't care." He grabs me and slams his mouth onto mine.

The kiss is more than pent-up passion. It's primal, like a mark. Like when he bit the top of my breast that time.

He's missed me. He's missed me every bit as much as I've missed him.

He can't stay away from me any more than I can stay away from him. Still, tonight was supposed to be special. I was going to share something with him. I was going to answer his question.

Granted, I want to answer it after a shower so I look good. But now will have to do.

I break the kiss and push him away.

He cocks his head. Is he going to say something? He looks inquisitive.

But he remains silent.

"You're the one who ended things," I tell him. "Then you go to my parents' home without telling me. Then you tell me you want to have vanilla sex."

"All true statements," he says.

"But you can't be with me, you say. Not until I can answer the question you asked me after the club."

"That's true."

"So why are you kissing me? Why are you trying to get into the shower with me? Because we both know what will happen in the shower." I'm getting wet just thinking about it.

He stalks toward me and pushes me against the wall, pinning me, his hands gripping my shoulders. "Why am I kissing you? Don't you know by now?"

"N-No. I mean, yeah. You love me. You desire me."

He shakes his head. "It goes so far beyond that, Skye. You know that, because you feel it, too."

I nod, shivering. Yes, I know it. And yes, I feel it.

"You've become a drug to me, and damn it, I can't leave you alone, no matter how much I know I should."

"Y-You don't have to leave me alone, Braden."

"Don't I?"

"No. Because I have an answer. Tonight I'll answer your question."

He crushes his lips to mine once more. My apron is a grimy mess, and I know I'm getting God knows what all over his expensive suit. But if he doesn't care, why should I?

Our tongues tangle and duel. The kiss stays primal, as if we're two animals getting ready to mate.

For that's what our desire is — animalistic. It has been from the beginning. We're drawn to each other as if the universe has forced us together for some divine purpose.

And perhaps it has.

Perhaps I needed to figure some things out about myself to live a happier life.

Perhaps Braden needs to do the same thing.

Our love came after the primal instinct to come together, as if our hearts followed our souls.

The best kind of love.

We kiss and we kiss and we kiss, until the savory scent of the shrimp étouffée wafts to me. I break my mouth away from his and inhale a deep breath.

"I have to check dinner. I can't let it get ruined again."

He trails one finger down my cheek. "Okay. We'll have the shower after dinner."

"After we talk," I say.

He nods. "After we talk."

Chapter Twenty-Eight

Unlike my first attempt, this meal for Braden turns out perfectly. The shrimp étouffée is spicy and delicious, and the Beaujolais-Villages I picked complements it very well. We don't talk a lot at dinner. Just a little about his trip and about the posts I've done this week. He seems pleased with my progress as an influencer.

"I've been using the skincare line for a week now," I tell him. "What do you think?"

"I think you're as beautiful as you always were."

"Seriously. My skin tone is a little more even, don't you think?"

"I honestly have no idea."

"Are you kidding me? I look better, and you don't even notice?"

He chuckles. "Contrary to popular belief, beauty routines aren't for men, Skye. They're for women."

"I just mean—"

"You mean you want me to tell you that you look better. What if I did? The first thing you'd say then is, 'You mean you didn't like how I looked before?'"

I scoff. "Maybe some women. I wouldn't."

He shakes his head. "You aren't like any other woman I've ever met, so maybe you wouldn't. But I'm telling you the truth when I say I don't see a difference. You were beautiful a week ago, and you're beautiful now."

My cheeks warm. I'm not beautiful like Tessa, but in Braden's eyes, I am. That's all that matters.

Already I see I've come a long way in a short time.

"Ready for dessert?" I ask.

"Let's talk first," he says.

My heart beats hard. Here it is. The time of reckoning. I'm going to open up to Braden, and I have to accept that he may not be ready to do the same thing.

That's okay.

It has to be.

Plus, maybe he'll surprise me.

"All right," I say. "You want any coffee?"

"I think just a little more wine." He fills his goblet halfway and then lifts his eyebrows at me.

"No thanks." I smile. "You want to sit on the couch? It's more comfortable."

"Sure." He picks up his wineglass and walks to the living room.

I follow him, sit down, and pat the seat next to me.

He sits.

"You asked me a question the last time we were in New York together. A question I couldn't answer then."

"I did."

"You didn't think I was brave enough to find the answer."

"That's not exactly what I said. I said I was going to have my say, and then you could have yours, *if* you were brave enough."

"All right. The exact words don't really matter, because I've realized it's not the answer that's important in the long run."

"Oh?"

"No, it's the question. You see, Braden, I asked myself the

question. I asked why the choking was so important to me, and I have an answer, but it's not even the answer that's important."

"What do you mean?"

"Figuring these things out isn't black-and-white. I know you like to think of things that way. You're a lot like Tessa in that way."

He chuckles. "Am I?"

"Don't laugh at me." I give him a friendly swat on the upper arm. "I'm serious. She's an accountant. A mathematician. There's always a right and wrong with her. You're the same way."

"I'll admit to being analytical, yes."

"I'm an artist. Black and white only exist to me as opposite ends of a spectrum. There's so many colors in between. And then in between the in-between."

"Am I in for a philosophy lesson?"

"I'm just trying to explain that yes, I have an answer to your question, but I'm not going to stop asking the question. It's a journey. And while the answers themselves are important, they are only points along the way of the journey. To me, the answer isn't as important as the question. And the question you asked me was why the neck binding was so important to me. I have an answer to that question, but before I got there, I had to ask another question."

"You're talking in circles, Skye."

"I'm not, actually. You're just refusing to see the shades and layers between black and white."

"That's not true. I wouldn't be much of a businessman if I didn't recognize that there aren't any absolutes."

"There you go, then. There is no one absolute answer to your question. I have an answer today—and that answer makes sense today—but I feel there's more to learn about myself, and that might change the answer later."

"Fair enough. What's your answer today?"

"I was punishing myself."

He raises an eyebrow. "Why?"

"Once I figured out that I saw the bondage as punishment, I knew right away why I wanted it. It's because I feel like a fraud. The only reason anyone cares what I think is because I'm your girlfriend. Things went down and down after that. I lost my friendship with Tessa. I did a half-assed post for Susanne because I didn't think I was any better than that. And then, that night in New York, you left me, too."

"But that was after—"

"I know. I know. I'm getting to that."

"Okay," he says. "Go on."

"So I talked to my mother, and I talked to a therapist, and with their help, I figured something out." I hold back tears as I pour out the story of the cornfield with the added memory of catching my mother in bed with Mario. About how my mother didn't want any more children.

"I guess she agreed with you," I tell him. "I was a challenge."

"I hope you're not blaming yourself for any of this."

"I'm not anymore. But I was for a long time."

"But you didn't remember."

"I didn't, but somewhere inside me, my subconscious did. You see, I felt like a fraud, but that was only the top layer. The icing on the cake. The cake and filling were much more significant, and they were hiding in my subconscious. When Rosa asked me what I like about our lifestyle, I told her how much pleasure it gives me. But when she asked me why I desired the neck binding so much, even after you told me it was a hard limit, I had to really think how I felt at the time."

"And how did you feel?"

"I wasn't thinking of it as a turn-on. I was thinking of it as a necessity. Then I had to figure out why it was a necessity."

"And now?"

"It's no longer a necessity. I can't deny that I was enthralled by the concept. Part of me still is, but I can accept that it's a hard limit for you. And I can accept that without knowing why."

He pierces my gaze. "Can you? Really?"

I nod. "I understand your reticence. You know me well, but once a few things click into place, everything changes. I'm not telling you that my stubborn nature will be gone overnight."

"You wouldn't be you, otherwise."

"Exactly. And you like a challenge."

"I do."

"Knowing myself better doesn't change the essence of who I am," I say. "It only changes my reaction. I was a difficult kid who was a lot for my mom to handle. I'm still that way, and she loves me despite all of it."

"I love you, too, Skye."

I smile. "I know. And I love you."

"Are you sure you can give up the breath control?"

"Absolutely. I can do it because it's no longer necessary. Admittedly, I'm intrigued by it, but I love you more than I need it."

He fingers my hair. "I'm very glad to hear that."

Can you tell me why it's a hard limit for you?

The words are lodged in the back of my throat. My curiosity, my need to know…all of it is trapped there with the words I want to say.

But I keep them there.

I will not nag him for information. Not anymore. I respect him too much to do that.

But there is something else I need to get off my chest.

"Braden…"

"Hmm?" He kisses my forehead and sniffs my hair. "Love that raspberry shampoo."

My skin tingles, and the tickle between my legs intensifies.

No. Have to talk first.

"There's something else I need to tell you."

"What?" He stiffens slightly.

"Relax. It's nothing bad, but I want complete honesty." At

least on my end, though I keep that last part to myself.

"All right."

"Addie's sister called me."

"Apple? Why?"

"She offered to tell me what went on between you and Addie ten years ago."

He stiffens further. In fact he's rigid. He could be a statue carved in marble. "I see."

"I was tempted," I say. "I went for a drink with her and was ready to hear the whole story, but then I remembered something you said to me."

"Oh?"

"Yeah. You said I could take my time. That we could talk when I was ready. You didn't push me, Braden, and I love you for it. I owe you that same respect and courtesy."

His lips curve upward into a half-smile. "That must have been difficult for you."

"Oh, you have no idea."

He cups my cheek and kisses the tip of my nose. "You deserve a reward."

"I think so."

He kisses my nose again. "You're an amazing woman, Skye. I've never met anyone like you."

I can't help myself. "Is that a compliment or an insult?"

"Woman!" He rakes his fingers through his hair. "Don't you know by now what you do to me?"

"Yes, I know. You do the same thing to me. You have since I first laid eyes on you. No one can deny your obvious physical appeal, but it was your demeanor that got to me. Your presence. You fill every room you're in, Braden. Nothing scares you. Nothing."

"Only one thing," he says, cupping my cheek once more.

"What's that?"

"The thought of my life without you."

Chapter Twenty-Nine

I open my mouth, but only a soft sigh emerges.
I've brought him to his knees.

I've brought Braden Black to his knees.

He places two fingers over my lips. "Don't say anything. I know I ended our relationship, and I did so for good reason. But being without you…" He shakes his head. "It's not something I want to experience again."

"You don't have to," I say.

"I didn't think this would happen to me." He shakes his head. "We started out the same way I always start out. I saw something I wanted, and I went after it. But you got inside me somehow. And then, right before that last trip to New York, you broke me. Your tears, your sadness. I would have committed murder to keep that sadness away from you forever."

I smile. "You don't have to become a criminal for me. I took care of it myself. Or I at least began the journey."

"I've said it before. You're an amazing woman, Skye."

"And you're an amazing man. What you've accomplished is beyond the scope of what most people can even imagine. You pulled yourself up by your bootstraps, without any help, and you made it to the top. You're incredible."

His facial muscles tense. Just a little, but I notice. Have I upset him?

He softens again within a few seconds, thumbing my lower lip. "God, this mouth."

Then his lips are on mine, his tongue delving between them. The kiss is firm and drugging, and I ache for more, more, more…

As if reading my mind, he reaches down and pushes my shirt up over my breasts. He squeezes one, finding the nipple over the fabric of my bra and tantalizing it with his fingertips.

Images flow into my mind. Our lovemaking in Kansas. Our initial scene at the Black Rose Underground. Our first time together at his place. Mere weeks ago, yet it seems like a lifetime has passed since then.

He releases my breast and trails his hand downward, unbuttoning my jeans. Then his fingers are inside my underpants, toying with my folds.

He breaks the kiss and gasps in a breath. "Fuck, you're so wet. So wet for me."

"Always," I breathe.

"Need to taste you." He pulls my jeans off my legs and then discards my panties as well. He spreads my legs and then stares between them. "Your pussy lips are swollen and pink. So beautiful. I'm going to eat you, Skye. I'm going to eat you until you beg me to stop."

I close my eyes as he swipes his tongue over my opening. He moves away for a moment and nibbles and sucks on my inner thigh.

I moan softly, my eyes still closed.

"Open your eyes," Braden says. "Watch me eat you."

I open them and meet his burning blue gaze. He's on fire—on fire as I am. I want his mouth on me. On my pussy. On all of me.

"Keep those gorgeous eyes open," Braden commands. "Don't take them off mine."

He buries his face between my legs, his lips and mouth touching all of me at once. My own fingers trail to my breasts, first cupping them and then probing the nipples covered by my bra. They're hard. Hard and taut and they want their freedom. I hastily lift my bra up, exposing them.

Braden lets go of my clit. "I fucking love your tits. Play with them, baby. Play with them while I eat your pussy."

I twirl my fingers around my nipples, giving them only a slight touch. Teasing myself, because I want my focus on Braden's lips between my legs, but when I give one nipple a pinch, an arrow of current surges through me.

I close my eyes on a moan.

He stops licking me. "Open those eyes, damn it."

His rich, commanding voice sears into me. My eyes pop open nearly of their own accord. This is the power he possesses. All the power. And I'm good with it. So good with it.

"Don't close them again, Skye. You won't like the result."

No orgasm. That will be the result. Damn him! Except I love him so much. I love the power he has over me. I love his commands, his darkness, his control.

I love it all.

I must be on fire. Invisible flames encircle me, make me hot. Chain me to this couch, to Braden. I never want to be free from his control and his lips and those blazing blue eyes burning into me.

He sucks at my clit, and already I'm running toward the peak, the precipice, that paradise that exists only in my climactic haze. A finger fills me. Then another, and I jump. I fucking jump into the abyss where nothing exists except Braden and me and our love. The orgasm radiates through me, up into my abdomen and then my chest. Soon my body is trembling all over, and I squeeze my nipples harder. Harder, until the pain bursts through me like a skyrocket and adds to my pleasure.

"Braden, I'm coming! I'm coming!"

"That's it. Come. Come for me."

His fingers continue to tantalize me, moving in and around and finding every crevice that sends me splintering even further.

And all this time, my gaze never wavers from his. Even as I'm whirling through a spiral of physical and emotional sensations, even as the azure of his eyes gives way to torrid blue flames, I keep my eyes locked on his.

Then he's over me, his cock released, and he's inside me, pumping.

He fills me, completes me, makes me whole, and as he fucks me, my orgasm continues to flourish.

"Fuck, Skye," he says through clenched teeth. "I feel you coming. All over my cock. Your pussy squeezing it. Fuck!"

Still I'm gazing into his beautiful blue eyes, even when he squeezes them shut and pulses into me and releases. I don't close mine. They stay open, locking with his eyelids.

He told me not to close my eyes, and I do not.

He stays embedded in me, his cock pulsating, his shirt abrading my sensitive nipples. And when he finally opens his eyes, they're smoldering like the ash of a dying fire.

Only his fire isn't dying.

It's only beginning. I see it come to life once more in his gaze.

His lips meet mine, then, in a hard and bruising kiss. No ordinary kiss, not even the feral kiss we shared earlier.

No. This is a kiss of two souls lost and now found.

And I know, in that instant, that Braden has shared a part of himself with me that he's never shared with anyone.

It no longer matters whether he tells me about him and Addie. Or even about his mother.

I know him in a way no one else ever will.

Chapter Thirty

Once I come down from my dreamy high, I can't help a chuckle.

"What?" Braden asks.

"You're still fully dressed, as usual."

"As usual?"

"You mean you don't know that you usually stay dressed when we make love?"

"I guess I never thought about it. Though I admit it's on brand for me."

"Yeah, it is. Always in control." I gaze at him. His lips are swollen and red from that last punishing kiss. Except it wasn't punishing. It was violent, yes, but not punishing. It was a meeting of souls.

"I won't deny it," he says.

"Ha! You better not. I'll know you're lying."

"I don't lie, Skye."

No, he doesn't. He may keep things from me, but he doesn't lie. "I know. You want some dessert now?"

"Sure."

"Coffee?"

"Yeah, that'd be great."

I rise and hastily pull my bra and shirt back over my breasts. "Where are my jeans?"

"I don't know. I threw them somewhere."

"Ah." I spy them underneath a chair.

"You can leave them off," he says. "In fact, take off the rest. I want you to serve me dessert naked."

"Will you be naked, too?"

"Are you forgetting who makes the rules here?" he asks.

I smile. "Braden, does this mean our relationship is back on?"

He cocks his head. "Do you want it to be?"

"Do *you*?"

He shakes his head. "You're still the same Skye, arguing about every little thing. Yes, I want it to be, but I'm giving you an out."

"Why?"

"Because I'm not ready to give you what you gave me. I'm not ready to tell you the things you want to know, and to be honest, I may never be."

I can always get it out of Apple.

But I know I won't. I won't betray Braden. I love him and respect him too much.

I strip off my shirt and bra and walk naked into his arms. I kiss his lips softly. "It's okay. I want to be with you. Sure, I wish you'd be honest with me about those things in your past, but if I have to choose between you and knowing about you and Addie, I choose you."

"You're a stronger person than I am," he says.

"I doubt that."

"You are. I gave you a challenge, and you ran with it. You figured yourself out even though it was difficult and it caused you pain."

"I'm far from having myself all figured out," I say. "Like I said, it's a journey, and the journey is what's important."

"I agree. And I want to give you something."

"The truth about you and Addie?" I raise my eyebrows, hoping.

"No. That I can't do. But I want to tell you a little more about my mother."

I look down at my bare breasts. "Now?"

He pulls something out of his pocket. "Maybe after dessert."

A flash of red. Then a flash of black. "What are those?" I ask.

He holds up two pieces of fabric, each red on one side and black on the other. "Restraints," he says. "Silk restraints."

"And you just happen to have those lying around in your pocket."

"Have you ever known me not to come prepared?" His voice holds a touch of amusement, but his expression remains stoic. This is dark Braden. The Braden I first fell in love with.

My nipples harden in an instant, as if a chilly wind is blowing over them.

"Silk isn't the best material for restraining someone," he continues. "It can get knotted tightly and is sometimes difficult to release. Fortunately, I'm experienced enough that it doesn't pose a problem."

I shudder. For the first time, his talk of experience doesn't arouse jealousy in me. No, no jealousy. Only desire. I want that silk touching my body, binding me.

I look around. Where will he bind me? I have a headboard, but unlike his, it's not built for bondage.

"To answer your question—"

"What question?" I interrupt.

"I see you glancing around. Wondering what I'm going to do to you with these restraints. You've underestimated me, Skye. Remember that evening when you turned off your phone so you wouldn't get my email?"

I nod. Not my finest moment.

"I had some time here alone, and I looked around this place." He glances to the hanging planter in my kitchen. "That hook is secured by a molly bolt. It can support at least fifty pounds."

"I appreciate the compliment, but I weigh a lot more than that." I give him what I hope is a teasing smile.

"That doesn't matter, because your feet will be on the ground. The hook will simply hold your bound wrists above your head. All I need is to slide your table to the right slightly."

The table still holds some of our dinner dishes, but with a flourish he slides it over without so much as jarring them.

"Your ceilings are low as well." He steps on a chair and grabs the hanging plant, setting it gently on the table. "Where's that crème brûlée?"

"In the fridge, but I have to do the topping."

"Not tonight. Tonight I want only the cream." He raises an eyebrow. "Though I know it won't be as delicious as *your* cream."

I squirm, squeezing my thighs together. My nipples are so hard they may pop off.

"Hold out your wrists."

I obey. He wraps the bindings around them in an intricate pattern, securing me tightly but not so tight as to be uncomfortable. Two strips of silk—a little over two feet long, by my estimation—hang from my wrists, presumably to secure me to the hook in the ceiling.

"Don't you need to measure?" I ask.

He shakes his head and then meets my gaze. "I never miss."

My body throbs with anticipation as Braden steps on the chair once more and secures the other ends of the restraints to the hook.

"Good?" he asks.

I have a little slack, and my feet are flat on the floor, about fifteen inches apart, so I guess that's good. "Yeah. Good."

He moves the chair out of the way. "You're going to stand there, Skye. You're going to stand there quietly. No talking. And you're going to take what I dish out."

Chapter Thirty-One

He walks around me until he's out of my vision.

"Oh!" I squeal as his palm comes down on my ass.

"No talking!" He slaps me harder this time.

I press my lips together to keep from squealing again.

"You have the most beautiful ass, Skye. I still haven't had the pleasure of fucking it."

Right. That night. We were supposed to…

"Not tonight," he says.

Disappointment flows through me.

"Soon," he continues, "but not tonight."

He picks up the dish of crème brûlée that he set on the table previously. He sticks his finger into the cream, swirls it around, and then holds it to my lips. "Taste."

I lick his finger clean, letting the lushness of the dessert sit on my tongue before I swallow.

He twirls his finger in the cream again, and this time he tastes it. A low growl rises from his chest.

I'm on fire. The image of Braden sucking crème brûlée off his thick finger has me ready to burst. My nipples strain, and I instinctively pull against my bindings.

"Don't," he says. "Don't resist. You're mine, bound and ready for my pleasure."

I nod.

Into the cream goes his finger once more, but this time he smears it over one of my nipples. The heat of my skin melts the thick cream, and it dribbles down over my large breast.

Braden's eyes smolder. "You look so enticing."

Please lick it off. Please.

Instead, he smears the other nipple with cream as well, and soon it's melting down my abdomen, heading toward my throbbing pussy.

What he does next makes me gasp. Braden, who's always so meticulous, scoops all of the crème brûlée out of the dish and covers my body with it. He fingerpaints me, cream sliding down his forearms onto his cotton shirt.

"You're delectable," he says. "Covered in thick and gooey sweetness. And now I'm going to lick every bit off of you."

God, yes. Please.

He lowers his head and licks one nipple, slurping and sucking. I ache to thread my fingers through his thick hair, ache to tell him how good his lips feel on my flesh. But I'm bound by silk and by his command.

And I want it no other way.

He sucks and eats custard from both nipples, tormenting me with pleasure. His lips and tongue travel downward, but damn him, he avoids my clit. He sucks the cream from my inner thighs, my calves, even the tops of my feet.

"Delicious." He swipes his tongue over his lips.

And I think I may faint from desire.

"Did I miss something?" he asks innocently.

He knows he did. He knows exactly what he did. I won't say it, even though I want to scream it.

Eat me! Eat my pussy! I'm dying here! Please.

Finally he slides his tongue between my legs.

And I nearly implode on the spot. I can't move my arms. I can't speak. I can only feel—and I feel enraptured. Tantalized.

This man of mine eats pussy like no other, and even though we fucked only moments earlier, I'm wet and ripe and ready to go again. I resist tugging on the silk. I don't want to pull the hook out of the drywall. So I stand, not suspended but nearly, as Braden licks me, tantalizes me, eats me like I'm a feast.

I slide into a climax, my core throbbing, and then another. My whole world shatters around me and implodes between my legs. He licks, and he licks, and he licks, and when I think I can't take one more tug on my clit, he sucks it between his lips and jams two fingers inside me.

And I come once more, this time not in my clit but inside. My G-spot. The climax surges through my body, lighting every cell on fire.

"Braden!" I cry out. "Braden, I love you! I love you so much!"

Braden and I share a shower so I can wash the sticky crème brûlée off my body. He didn't take me after my ultimate orgasm, so he lifts me in his arms and fucks me hard against the shower wall, and another orgasm shoots out of me.

He thrusts harder, my back slapping against the wet tile in the shower. "Fuck, Skye. Fuck, you feel so good."

I'm still in the clouds of my climax when he erupts, his words buzzing in my head.

I love you. I fucking love you, Skye.

And I'm not sure those words have ever sounded so sweet.

Chapter Thirty-Two

Since Braden came straight from New York, he has his luggage with him. He puts a pair of lounge pants on while I cover myself in a satin robe. He holds my hand as we walk to the couch where we fucked only a little over an hour earlier.

I don't say anything. I promised I wouldn't push him, and I'll stick to my guns if it kills me. He has to make the first move.

He takes my hand and rubs circles in my palm with his thumb. "This isn't easy for me."

"I know. It's okay. Take your time. Or don't say anything. It doesn't matter." And it doesn't. Oh, I'm still curious. Nosy as all get-out. But this isn't about me. It's about Braden. About what he's comfortable with.

"I loved my mother," he says. "So did Ben."

"I'm sure she loved both of you, too."

"She did. We were all that kept her going sometimes. I'm not sure she'd have had the strength to go to the food pantry if she didn't have our two mouths to feed."

"It couldn't have been easy for her."

He pauses. Inhales. For a moment I fear he may clam up,

but then he continues.

"After the fire, she spent several weeks in the hospital. She was in constant pain. Ben and I weren't allowed to see her because she had to be kept in a sterile environment until her skin grafts took."

"I'm so sorry."

"I'm not looking for sympathy, Skye. I never am."

"I understand. Can't I still be sorry that your poor mother had to go through all that?"

"I suppose." He sighs. "Anyway, before the fire, we always had enough to eat. It wasn't gourmet food, by any means, but we didn't go to a food pantry, and we weren't on government assistance."

"Beef stew," I say quietly.

"Beef stew?"

"That evening when you showed up here unannounced and I served you leftover beef stew. You said your mother used to make it."

"She did. Tough stew meat was a staple at our house. She'd cook it forever, and it was delicious. That was before the fire, though. After the fire, we couldn't afford even the toughest beef."

"I'm sorry."

"Still not looking for sympathy. Anyway, like I told you before, insurance wouldn't pay even though the fire was an accident. My mother eventually came home, and I think she would have been okay if…"

"If what?"

Braden buries his head in his hands.

I wait. And I wait.

He needs time, and I aim to give it to him.

Finally, he looks up and meets my gaze. "Ben and I weren't able to visit her at the hospital. So when she finally came home…"

I gulp. Instinctively, I already know what's coming.

"I cried when I saw her. Screamed even. The scarring was so...so... The word that comes to my mind is ugly. Scary. I was seeing it through the eyes of a six-year-old. I expected to see my beautiful mother, but..."

"Didn't your father prepare you?"

"He tried to. But have you ever seen a burn victim, Skye?"

I nod. "Yes. Not in person, but I once went to a photo exhibit where the artist's subjects were all burn victims. It was beautiful work. Their humanity shone through."

"You were an adult, then."

"Yes."

"And you didn't know any of the victims personally." He threads his fingers through his hair still wet from the shower. "You can't prepare a young brain for that. This was my mother."

Braden's face contorts as he squeezes his eyes shut. In a way, he's that little boy again, tortured by the visual of his mother.

I give him a few minutes. Then, "How did Ben react?"

He opens his eyes, seeming calmer. "He didn't scream. That's all on me."

"But he was younger."

"Younger, yes. But he didn't react the way I did. I can't explain it."

"Have you talked to him about it?"

"Are you kidding? I don't talk to *anyone* about it. Except my therapist on occasion. And now you."

I'm honored that he's sharing this part of himself with me. I put my hand over his. "Braden, you aren't responsible for what your mother went through."

"I know that. But she was never the same person after that, and if I hadn't screamed when I saw her—"

"Stop," I say. "Just stop. You were a child, first of all. Second, she'd already been traumatized by the fire and the burns and the pain. Her time in the hospital. The small part you played had little bearing."

"I know. I've been through enough therapy to know that."

"Good."

"The problem is, I'll never forget. I'll never forget how seeing her made me feel."

"How did it make you feel?"

"It made me feel... God I can't even say this."

"You can." I squeeze his hand.

"I was repulsed, Skye. The sight of my mother repulsed me."

Chapter Thirty-Three

He squeezes his eyes closed once more.

You have no idea what I've had to take back in my life.

Braden is a six-year-old boy again, seeing his beautiful mother with ugly burn scars.

And I understand him more than he knows.

"It's okay," I say.

"It's not okay. It'll never be okay. What kind of child thinks his mother is repulsive?"

"A six-year-old who's expecting to see his beautiful mother after being without her for weeks."

"I've heard it all, Skye. I've heard all the reasons why this feeling was valid at the time."

"Did you still love your mother?"

His eyes glow with blue fire. "Of course I did!"

"And did you grow used to her scarring?"

"Yes, within days. She was still Mom."

"Then what are you blaming yourself for?"

He rubs his chin. "She was never the same."

"Wasn't she? You were six, Braden. Are you sure you're

remembering right?"

He shakes his head. "No, I'm not sure. I've been around and around on this with my therapist."

"Have you considered that you weren't the problem? Maybe your father was. The fire was his fault, after all."

He nods slightly.

He knows. He and his therapist have been through this. He knows. But it still haunts him, how he feels he rejected his mother when she came home.

"She and my dad were never the same after that, either," he continues. "She had to stay with him. She had nowhere else to go, plus she had Ben and me."

"Did she love your dad?"

"In her way, yeah, I think she did. But…things were never the same."

"How so?"

He chuckles. "In some ways, things were better. Dad stopped drinking, but he had trouble finding work for a while. We lived in a mobile home rental, and we could barely afford that. So we went on government assistance, which my mom and dad both hated."

I listen intently. No surprise where Braden got his need for control over his own life and others.

He had it worse than I ever did. So much worse. Yet look where he ended up.

"What eventually happened to your mom?" I ask hesitantly.
"She died."

"I know that much."

"I don't like to think about it," he says. "I still feel somewhat responsible."

"You're not."

"There are things you don't know. Things no one knows. You can say the words. I can even believe them. But none of it changes anything."

I snuggle against his chest and give him a hug. *I'm here. I'm here for you.*

I want to take away this pain, and the only way I can do that is by letting him off the hook.

"Stop, Braden. Don't go any further. I don't want you to hurt."

He kisses the top of my head. "You're sweet. So sweet and amazing. You're giving me an out that I never gave you."

"You did. You said you'd give me the time I needed. I just didn't need as much time."

"I don't know what I ever did to deserve you," he says. "But if I figure it out, I'll do it again a million different times."

"You don't have to." I kiss the top of his hand. "You already have me."

"And you have me," he says, "though sometimes I wonder why anyone would want me."

I pull back slightly. "You're kidding, right?"

"You know I never kid, Skye."

"You're the catch of the century!"

"Only on paper."

"Green paper," I add.

He wrinkles his brow. Again, I've succumbed to something that sounded funnier in my head.

"Wait," I say. "That didn't come out right."

"Sure it did. I'm loaded. You're not the only one attracted to my money."

"The money's a nice fringe benefit. I won't lie. But that's not what I meant, and you know it. It was a joke, Braden."

"I know. I never thought you were after my money. I pursued *you*, remember?"

I smile. "You did. And I resisted, even though you were the most attractive man I'd ever met."

"It's your nature to resist. It's what drew me to you."

"I was a challenge," I say.

"You still are."

"Am I? You're not going to dump me now that you have me?"

"Why would I do that?"

Betsy's story pops into my mind. How Braden allegedly dumped Addie because she wouldn't engage in BDSM play with him again.

It's not true. It can't be true.

Can it?

I'd know for sure if I'd listened to Apple. If Braden never levels with me about Addie, I'll never know the truth.

"What if you want something I can't give you?" I ask.

"Did you dump me when you wanted something I couldn't give you?"

"No. You dumped me."

"Only because you needed to figure things out before I could take you further into the lifestyle. I don't want you in the lifestyle for the wrong reason, Skye. You could get hurt."

I nod. "I know. I understand that now."

"This lifestyle isn't for the faint of heart. I know that, and so do you. It has to be something we both enjoy for the right reasons. In the beginning, I saw your controlling nature, but I sensed part of it was a façade. Part of you seemed submissive to me, and I wanted to wake up that dormant part of you. But then things went a little awry."

"Meaning?"

"I fell in love."

I warm all over. "So did I."

"If I didn't love you, maybe I'd be okay with taking you through all the steps of the lifestyle for the wrong reasons, but you mean more to me than that. I couldn't do it. If it's any consolation, ending things with you was the hardest thing I've ever had to do."

I can't help a soft scoff. "You didn't even do a very good job."

"You're right about that. I couldn't let you go, Skye. I went running to your parents, hoping I could find some clue as to why you wanted the breath control so much. Then, once you arrived, you know the results. I couldn't stay away."

"Neither could I, obviously."

"But I promised myself I wouldn't take you back to the lifestyle until you could answer the question I posed. You see, Skye, the lifestyle isn't about punishment, even though I will punish you from time to time. But it's my choice to punish you. Not yours."

"I understand all that, Braden."

"I believe you're beginning to."

"Beginning to?"

"That's not an insult. It's just an accurate statement. You said yourself that this is a journey."

"It is. I also think your lifestyle is a journey."

"I don't disagree. But it's a journey I must have control over. I choose what we do, and you can then choose whether to consent to me or say no."

"I understand. Truly. Perhaps I said those words before and didn't actually understand, but now I do."

He nods. "Then perhaps we're ready to go back to the club."

Chapter Thirty-Four

Shuddering chills rack my body. The club. Black Rose Underground. The thought still excites me.

My pussy tingles, and…

Damn.

My asshole is throbbing. Seriously throbbing. Is that even physiologically possible?

Braden hasn't taken me there yet.

He was going to, that fateful night that led to our breakup.

But he didn't. I'm still a virgin in that sense.

"What else is there at the club?" I ask, my voice coming out nearly breathless.

"Oh, Skye, there's so much more. You've only been to the bondage room."

I gulp. "What other rooms are there?"

"Some rooms are for light play only."

"Light play?"

"Yes. Basic spanking, light bondage. For example, how I bound your wrists with my necktie at my office."

"What's bondage, then? Is it light play?"

"Bondage, other than light bondage, is heavy play. What you saw at the club is considered heavy play."

"Especially the neck binding, right?"

"In my opinion, anything involving the neck is edge play."

"What's edge play?"

"Anything that involves a risk of physical or mental harm."

"Mental harm?"

"Yeah. I steer clear of edge play, for the most part. It doesn't interest me much. Most of it isn't allowed at Black Rose Underground."

"But I saw the breath control."

"Not everyone considers breath control edge play, so I allow it, but all practitioners have to sign a special consent form before they can do it at my club."

"I see. And I didn't sign that form."

"You didn't, but it doesn't matter. I wasn't going to do it anyway."

"Your hard limit."

"Yes," he says, but of course, he offers no further explanation.

"What else is considered edge play?"

"Anything that draws blood."

I gasp. "People actually do that?"

He nods. "Knife play, gun play, fire play. I don't allow any of that."

"*Gun* play? Fire play? People do that?"

He nods.

"Is that another hard limit for you?"

"I've already told you that I only have *one* hard limit, Skye."

I nod. I can't deny that breath play still intrigues me, but it no longer feels necessary.

So that's good.

"What other kind of heavy play is there at the club?"

"There's suspension play. Flogging and caning. Animal fetishes."

My stomach drops. "You mean sex with animals?"

He laughs then, and I feel ridiculous.

"Of course not. Some people like to be led around like they're animals. Horse play. Dog play. Things like that."

I widen my eyes. "People do that? To each his own, I guess."

"I take it you don't want to try that."

"Hard pass on that one."

"Not a problem. It's all up to you, Skye."

"Do you…like that kind of play?"

"It's not one of my favorites, but I'm not averse to it if it interests you."

"It doesn't."

"Fair enough. There's sensory deprivation. I've introduced you to that already on a minor scale. There's also larping."

"What's larping?"

"Live Action Role Playing. It's huge in the gaming community. The club takes it to a sexual level."

"Meaning…"

"Like Superman having sex with Wonder Woman. Stuff like that. Sci-fi is big. Sex with aliens. That kind of thing."

"So you have a room where…"

"Where you can watch people engaging in alien sex? Yeah. Except they're not real aliens, of course. Some of the costuming is pretty elaborate, though."

I'm pretty sure my jaw is on the floor somewhere. "Oh. My. God."

"I told you before that clothing is a fetish for some. So is costuming."

"But not for you."

"No. I prefer to be myself when I play. I'm Braden Black and no one else."

"Good, because Braden Black is who I want to have sex with."

"Anything sound intriguing to you?"

"What kind of things do you see in the larping room?"

He shakes his head. "I'm not sure you'd believe me if I told you."

"Can I see it?"

"Sure. The next time we go to the club. What else interests you?"

"Not larping. I'm just curious how that works, but I don't want to do it myself. I prefer to be with you. As me."

"Fine with me. Anything else?"

The bondage is what truly speaks to me. The trust required, and I do trust Braden with all my heart. Still, I'm willing to learn more. I'm willing to do what he wants me to do. So I know my answer.

"Whatever you want," I say. "I'll do whatever you want."

Chapter Thirty-Five

"We didn't finish what we began the last time," Braden says. "That ass is mine."

"It's yours." I smile.

"Good. I'm going to take it tomorrow evening. At my place."

I'm slightly let down. "Not at the club."

"No, Skye. I changed my mind about that. I'm going to take it here in Boston. Because this is my home, and this is your home. And that ass is going to be mine here and wherever else I want it."

I swallow. "All right."

How will he take me? Will he bind me? Blindfold me? Tell me not to feel anything?

I want to know.

Yet I don't want to know. I want to savor the anticipation. The surprise.

"I'm exhausted," he continues while typing something into his phone, "so I'm not going to stay here with you tonight. If I do, neither of us will get any sleep, and I need it after the week I've had."

I nod. "I'm disappointed, but I understand."

"Thank you. Christopher will pick you up here tomorrow evening at five. Be ready."

"I will be. What should I wear?"

"Whatever you like. You'll be changing at my place."

"Into what?"

"You'll find out soon enough." His phone dings. "Christopher's downstairs waiting for me."

I nod.

He stands up and pulls me alongside him. He touches my cheek. "It's never easy to say goodbye to you."

"Really?"

"Surely you know that."

"That night in New York, when you ended things. You seemed so…cold."

"I've learned to hide my emotions. I've had to, for business purposes. But as you know, I don't lie. That was the hardest thing I've ever done."

Pleasure rips through me along with sadness. It's an odd sensation. I'm pleased it was so difficult for him, but I don't like to think of him in any kind of pain.

In a way, before tonight, I almost thought of Braden as impervious to pain.

He presses his lips to mine without opening them. Just as well. If he opens them, we'll end up back in bed. Not that I'd complain, but if he needs his sleep, I want him to have it.

I want what's best for Braden. Always.

Tessa's downward dog is still flawless, and mine still sucks. "Ugh," I say. "Why do I even try?"

"Because it's good for you." Tessa pulls her body upward.

"I do love yoga, and yeah, it helps with stress and all that, but the fucking downward dog!"

"It's tough for some people."

"That's what you always say."

"And I'm still right."

I laugh. Being with Tessa back at yoga on a Saturday feels good. Damned good. We just completed a hot yoga class, and we're both panting and sweating. All is good.

Plus, I'm back on my game with my Instagram posts.

And Braden and I are back together. We still have a lot to learn about each other, but we're both willing. We're in love.

I emailed Eugenie this morning to let her know that Braden and I had reconciled. Even though she previously said it wasn't a problem, that she was willing to see how I did anyway, I know she was disappointed before. Yeah, Braden's the reason I have this contract. But you know what? It's an opportunity, and I'd be foolish not to take advantage of any opportunity that comes my way.

Braden taught me that.

I grab a towel and wrap it around my neck to catch the sweat. "I need a shower."

"See you in the steam room," Tessa says.

I nod, head to the locker room, and grab a quick shower. I wrap my wet hair in a towel and walk into the ladies' steam room. I inhale the peppermint and eucalyptus. That's why I really love the steam room. I don't need the heat. I just did hot yoga. I need the fresh spike of fragrance that opens my sinuses like nothing else.

"You in here, Tess?"

"Over here."

I follow her voice to the tiled bench and take a seat next to her. Tessa drinks from her bottle of water. "You're not going to believe this."

"What?" I ask.

"I just ran into Garrett."

"In the ladies' locker room?"

She chuckles. "No. After you left the yoga studio, he walked in."

"Garrett? At yoga?"

"He was wearing a muscle shirt and jock shorts. Fuck, Skye, he looked amazing."

"Uh-oh."

"Right? Anyway, he said he was waiting for our class to end so he could talk to me."

"Ugh. Stalker much?"

I regret the words. Garrett probably isn't a stalker. Not like Addie stalked Braden. Like she may still be stalking Braden.

"No, he just said he's sorry he's been bothering me, and if I tell him no this time, he'll leave me alone."

"So what did you tell him?"

"I told him...I'd have dinner with him tonight."

"Tessa..."

"Well, it's not like we said we were exclusive, right?"

"Right. You're right."

"I've missed him."

"Why don't we find you another guy?"

"I'm not getting on a website, Skye."

"That's not what I mean." A light flashes in my head. "You want to meet Braden's brother?"

"Ben Black?"

"That's the one."

"Is he available?"

"As far as I know."

She inhales a breath and lets it out slowly. "No, I don't think so. I mean, thanks for the offer, but I hate fix-ups."

I decide not to push it. "Okay. Let me know if you change

your mind."

"To be honest, I'm still hung up on Garrett."

"I know. Or you would have told him to fuck off."

"You got that right. So I need a favor."

"Of course. Anything."

"I need you to come to dinner with us tonight."

Fuck. Anything but that. Braden's tonight. Five o'clock. Something so special will occur between us.

I can't give that up.

I can't.

Not even for Tessa.

"I'm so sorry, Tess. I made plans with Braden."

She sighs.

"I'm sorry," I say again.

"I'm always going to play second fiddle to him, aren't I?"

She's a little out of line with that one, but I want to tread softly. I don't want to risk losing her again. "No, but I wouldn't break plans with you if he asked me to, either."

She takes gulps from her water bottle. "You're right. You have better things to do than be my babysitter."

"Maybe…"

"Maybe what?"

"I could check with Braden. Maybe we could join you guys for dinner and then—"

She holds up her hand, waving steam in my face. "No. Don't worry about it. I just…"

"What?"

"If I don't have a chaperone I'll end up in his bed."

"Be your own chaperone."

"That's such a Skye thing to say."

"And needing a chaperone is a Tessa thing. Black and white. If you don't have someone else there, you'll sleep with him. There's no middle ground. You're so much like Braden sometimes."

"I am?"

"Yeah. He says he doesn't accept anything as absolute, but in his way, he does."

"What do you mean?"

I haven't told Tessa about his hard limit, and I won't. Our intimate life is personal. "He just has his own ideas, and nothing will sway him."

"He sounds more like you than like me," Tessa says.

"He's a lot like me in other ways. I'll grant you that. But that's not even my point. My point is you don't need a chaperone. You *can* control yourself."

"Yeah. You're right. It would just make things easier."

"Life isn't always easy."

"Fuck," she says. "You sure got that right."

Tessa, you have no idea.

Chapter Thirty-Six

I'm tempted to ask Braden about dinner with Tessa and Garrett anyway. I really want to be there for my best friend, and it's just dinner, right? Whatever Braden has planned will take place after dinner, I assume. I'm ready to text him, but then I stop.

No.

I just got Tessa back, but I just got Braden back, too. I don't want to put either of those relationships in jeopardy. Tessa's okay, so why rock the boat?

Besides, I want this evening to be just about Braden and me and the intimate act we're going to share. That's not selfish. It's just sticking to plans I already made.

In the back of my mind there's an image of Ben Black. I really think he and Tessa would hit it off. Of course, I've met him for all of a couple hours, so what do I know?

Maybe I'll ask Braden tonight. He was the one who brought up the idea of Ben and Tessa in the first place, after all.

I'm ready early, in an army-green mini-dress that lingers between casual and dressy. I style my brown hair and wear it down, its waves flouncing over my shoulders. A little Susie

Girl tinted moisturizer, mascara, and lip tint, and I'm ready for whatever awaits me.

Topping it off! Susie Girl mascara gives me just the touch I need. #sponsored #susieglow #susiegirl #sexyeyes #simplyskye

I'm tempted to name drop, to tell my readers that I'm getting ready for my date with @BradenBlackInc, but I don't.

Tonight is special.

I don't want anyone there except the two of us. No followers wanting to know all about our evening.

Like I'd tell them anyway.

My phone buzzes.

Eugenie Blake.

Why is Eugenie calling me on a Saturday afternoon?

I pick up the call. "This is Skye."

"Skye, it's Eugenie. I'm sorry to bother you on the weekend, but I just read your email and I'm thrilled that you and Braden worked things out!"

"Oh." Of course she is. "Thank you. I'm happy about it, too."

"I'm sure you're both ecstatic. And since you're back together, we'd like to talk to you again about some additions to the campaign. Your hashtags #susieglow and #simplyskye are proving to be very popular with our customers, so we're going to create another campaign around them."

"That's...really generous of you, but we just did the pink campaign."

"That's not a campaign so much as a brand-new product. We'd like to cash in on the fact that you're the girl next door. Simplyskye is perfect for that. I've got Brian looking into the paperwork to file for a trademark. Same for susieglow."

"You mean you'd hold the trademark for susieglow and simplyskye, even though I made them up?"

"Well...yes. We're willing to put up some serious money, so of course we want to hold the trademarks."

I'm not sure what to say. I wish Braden were here. "I'll need to think about all of this."

"Of course! I just wanted to let you know how excited we are about this new step. And also how happy we are that you and Braden are back together."

Right. That's why the Saturday call. This is something they were thinking about, but they didn't want to push it while I wasn't with Braden. Just in case that hindered my influencing career.

Again, Braden is the reason I'm getting anywhere.

Oddly, it doesn't bother me as much as it used to. As I told Tessa, opportunity is opportunity. But Susanne holding trademarks for hashtags I came up with disturbs me a little.

Okay…a lot. It disturbs me a lot.

I'm no creative genius. These are two-word hashtags, after all. But still, they're *my* two-word hashtags. Shouldn't I get some kind of credit for that?

Braden will know what to do. I'll ask him first.

"Thank you for calling, Eugenie," I finally say. "As always, I appreciate your confidence in me, and I'll give all of this some serious thought."

"Wonderful! When will you and Braden be in New York again?"

"I'm…not sure." *But soon, I hope.*

"We'll have to do dinner again. We're getting the sample nail colors in late next week, and we'd love for you to be here for the unveiling."

"I'd like that, too. I'll talk to Braden about making the trip."

"We'll be happy to send you both tickets."

"I'm sure that's not necessary." She also knows this.

"Well, you let me know. Have a wonderful evening, Skye. And we're so happy about the good news!"

A knock sounds on the door as I end the call. Christopher

is prompt, as usual. I shove my phone in my purse. "Coming, Christopher."

"How are you this evening, Ms. Manning?" he asks.

I swat him on the arm. "It's Skye. How many times will we have this discussion?"

He smiles.

I never realized how handsome Christopher actually is. He's tall, nearly as tall as Braden, with sandy blond hair and hazel eyes. Nice full lips, and a muscular build.

Another perfect candidate for Tessa.

Although, I'm sure she'd go for the billionaire over the chauffeur.

But maybe not. Tessa surprises me more often than not.

I follow Christopher down to the street, where he helps me into the Mercedes.

And that's my last thought of Tessa.

Only Braden is on my mind now.

Braden...and what awaits.

Chapter Thirty-Seven

"You look beautiful," Braden says, once Christopher and the rest of his staff have made themselves scarce.

"Thank you. So do you."

God, he does. He's wearing faded jeans—I didn't even know Braden owned a pair of faded jeans—and a light blue button-down. No shoes, his feet are bare. Easier to get his pants off. I smile to myself.

His hair is still slightly damp, as if he just got out of the shower. I smile again.

"As beautiful as you are, though"—his eyes smolder—"you're going to have to take your clothes off."

I look around. We're standing in the middle of the foyer, and with Braden's open floorplan, pretty much anyone in the living room, kitchen, or dining room can see us.

"No one will see you but me," he says. "Now, do as I tell you."

I nod, trembling, and slip out of my sandals. I slide the straps of the green dress over my shoulders and shimmy out of the sundress. I stand now only in a strapless bra and thong.

Braden's jaw tightens, and a low growl emerges from his throat. "All of it."

I inhale. Tomatoes. Basil. Garlic. Italian. We're having Italian. "Do you want me to eat naked?"

"Absolutely," he says.

I part my lips.

He sucks in a breath. "That mouth."

I tingle all over, my nipples pushing against the satin of my bra. I reach around, unhook it, and let it drop to the floor.

He sucks in another breath. "Fuck. Those tits, Skye."

I slide my finger under the tiny waistband of my thong and push it over my hips and ass, letting it fall next to my bra.

No one's here. No one except Braden and me.

But anyone could walk in.

The thought excites me. Frightens me. Bedazzles me.

"I suppose you'll remain dressed?" I say.

His lips quiver, as if he wants to smile, but he's holding back. "We'll see. Follow me."

I hastily grab my clothes, assuming we're going to the bedroom, but instead he leads me to the kitchen.

I inhale again. Definitely Italian.

"Lean on the island," he says. "Put your hands flat on the counter."

I obey, sucking in a breath at the cold marble on my belly. I lay my hands flat as he instructed.

Braden trails his warm fingers over the cheeks of my ass. "I've waited a long time for this, Skye."

Oh. My. God. Is it going to happen now? In the kitchen? Against this cold marble countertop?

My legs quiver, nearly giving out, but I hold still, keeping my hands flat.

He moves his hands between the crease of my ass, their warmth welcome as I'm suddenly freezing.

"Are you as hungry as I am?" His breath is hot against my neck.

"Yes," I say softly.

"For food? Or for something else?"

"Both?" Damn that inflection. "Both," I say again, firmly this time.

"Then I'll feed you," he says, his voice low and hypnotic.

I nod, my body finally acclimating to the cold countertop. "But first…"

"Oh!" I jerk as he slides his tongue between my ass cheeks.

"Easy." He grips my hips. "I need to prepare you for what's coming."

He continues to lick me, his tongue warm and soft against my most intimate flesh. The feeling is sublime, and I close my eyes, leaning forward. I gasp as my breasts hit the chill of the marble.

"Easy," he says again against my ass. "Such a gorgeous ass, Skye. I can't wait to fuck you here."

"Wh-What's stopping you?"

I wince. Did I really just say those words?

If he dropped his pants right now and jammed into me, I'd have it coming.

"*You* are," he says. "You're not ready. But you will be. Hold still now."

A few seconds pass, and—

"Oh!"

He probes me with slick fingers. Lube. Like he used the last time with the butt plug. It feels nice and silky.

"I'm going to put the plug in you," he says. "You'll wear it during dinner. It will help for later."

I nod.

The stainless steel is warm this time. He must have warmed it in his hands. That was sweet of him. It probes my tight rim.

"Relax," Braden says. "Breathe in, and then out."

I comply, and as my breath flows out of my nose and mouth, he inserts the plug.

Nicely done. I hardly even felt it this time. Clearly, I'm ready for tonight.

He pulls me up and away from the counter and toward him. "Do you know what it's going to do to me, knowing you're wearing that plug while we eat dinner?"

"The same thing it did to you during your meeting while I was with Eugenie in New York?"

"Oh, you have no idea." His voice has a rasp to it. It's fucking hot. "That day, all I could think of was you sitting at Susanne Corporate with your sweet little ass filled. Filled with the plug I put there. You didn't know yet, but I did, where we were going that evening. I was hard all day. All fucking day, Skye."

"So was I." I let out an embarrassed giggle. "I mean, I was turned on all day, during my meeting and all."

"I know. That was my plan. I want you turned on while we eat our dinner." He takes my hand and leads it to his erection, huge and magnificent beneath his jeans. "I'm hard as a rock already. So ready to stuff my cock inside that tight little asshole of yours."

A soft moan echoes from my throat.

"But first, we eat. Don't eat too much. I want you to have energy, but not to feel full. I don't want you uncomfortable in any way tonight."

"All right. It smells divine. What are we having?"

"Something simple. Lasagna. We'll each eat a small portion, and there will be plenty of leftovers if we're hungry afterward." He lowers his eyelids slightly. "You'll be hungry, Skye. You're going to use a lot of energy tonight."

I nod hesitantly. "Whatever you want, Braden. I'll do whatever you say."

"Marilyn makes excellent lasagna."

"I'm sure Marilyn makes excellent everything."

He leads me to the dining room, where the table has already been set. Two glasses of red wine sit beside the plates, and the lasagna is covered. An Italian loaf with olive oil for dipping, and a small green salad.

That's it.

And it's perfect.

Braden pulls out my chair, and I sit, very aware of my nudity and even more aware of the pressure of the plug in my ass. My nipples are hard and turgid, and they don't escape his gaze. *Are you going to get undressed?*

The words don't make it past my lips, though.

This isn't about what I want.

Except that it kind of is.

Both Braden and Rosa taught me that. I have power in this relationship as well. Right now, I'm exercising my power to not speak. To not ask Braden whether he's planning to shed his clothes. Because ultimately it doesn't matter. Ultimately, we're going to end up in the bedroom where he'll take my anal virginity.

How we get there isn't up for debate, and I'm okay with that.

Braden sits across from me and serves me a small square of the lasagna. The salad has already been plated, and a slice of bread sits on my bread dish. Then he serves himself.

This is a casual meal. Normally we'd eat our salad first, but tonight it's all served together. I smile. He's doing this for me. To make me comfortable. Even though I'm naked, he's making this casual for me.

"Dig in," he says from across the table.

I begin with a forkful of salad. It's dressed with a honey-vinaigrette that sparks my tastebuds. *Nicely done, Marilyn.* I pull off a piece of my bread and dip it in the olive oil. More deliciousness and again my tastebuds react to a tang. The olive oil has been infused with something spicy, most likely cayenne or jalapeño with a touch of garlic.

And then the lasagna. The sauce is acidic with a hot spiciness due again to hot pepper. Something I wasn't expecting. This evening's meal seems to have a theme. Spicy.

Just like what's coming in the bedroom.

Braden was right about only eating small portions. Too much spiciness could cause gastric distress, which would put a major damper on the evening. Yet the tang of the food will also enhance what's to come.

He thinks of everything.

Braden raises his glass of wine. "To discovery."

I pick my glass up and clink it against his. "To discovery." Then I take a sip. The wine perfectly complements the meal, as usual. Its acidity and lusty spiciness is perfect.

"What wine is this?" I ask.

"It's a Brunello di Montepulciano from Italy, made from the Sangiovese grape."

"It's wonderful. So juicy and spicy. Perfect with this meal."

He nods and takes another sip. "Eat slowly. We'll only have one glass of wine, as well."

"Okay."

I'm so ready. So compliant. I think he could tell me to do anything right now and I'd do it.

Submission is a wonderful feeling. To give myself over to another person I trust… Never in a million years would I have thought I'd find it so rewarding.

I take dainty bites of my food. I finish all of my salad, most of my bread, and half of my lasagna.

I pat my lips with my napkin and then rest it on the side of my plate.

Braden meets my gaze, his eyes heavy-lidded. "Are you ready, Skye?"

"Yes, Braden. I'm ready."

Chapter Thirty-Eight

My eyes pop into circles when I enter Braden's bedroom. Candlelight emits a soft glow, and something occurs to me. I've never before seen a candle anywhere in Braden's place. Never. In fact, at our first dinner in New York, he asked the waiter to take the candle away from the table.

I never gave it a thought, but it makes perfect sense to me now, knowing how fire devastated his family.

This is for me. He's given me candlelight, to make the mood romantic.

And if it's possible, I fall in love with him even more.

He cups my cheek. "I was ready to take your ass that night at the club, but in retrospect, I'm glad it didn't happen there."

"Oh?"

"Yes." He thumbs my lower lip.

"Why?"

"Isn't it obvious? This is where we should engage in that intimate act for the first time. That's not to say we won't do it at the club, too, but for the first time, we should be here, in an environment where you're the most comfortable. Where you feel safe."

"I always feel safe with you, Braden."

"I know. I guess I'm not explaining what I mean very well. Let me be blunt. I changed my mind. I want to do it here. In my bedroom. I want to be here because this is something intensely personal to me. Personal and private, and I want us to be alone."

"But Christopher and the rest of the staff—"

"Aren't here. I sent them all away for the weekend. They'll be back tomorrow evening."

"Who will drive me home, then?"

"No one. You're not going home this weekend, Skye. You're staying here. With me."

I smile. "That sounds good."

"I'm going to take care of you. I'm going to make this good for you in a way I couldn't at the club. You'll be pampered."

I warm all over, and in the candlelight, my breasts glow. Braden takes notice, dropping his gaze and groaning from his chest. The low growl seems to flow from him and into me, lodging between my legs. I'm quivering. Naked and quivering, my ass ready to open up, drop the plug, and take all Braden can give me.

I'm so ready. I don't want to wait any longer.

But this is Braden's dance. We're both moving, but he's in the lead.

And I'm good with that.

"I've waited a long time for this," he says, "and we're going to do it right."

Being here means something to him. Here, in his bedroom in Boston, where he doesn't do things he may participate in at the club.

I simply nod. "Whatever you want is what I want."

The low growl hums from his chest into me once more.

"I'm going to bind you to the headboard as we've done before, face up."

"Face up?"

"Oh, yes. Face up. I want to look into your warm brown eyes when I take that ass."

"But…I just assumed…"

"That I'd take you from behind? That was my plan at the club, but this will be much more intimate. Plus, you'll get to watch. I want you fully engrossed in the experience."

"Using all my senses tonight?"

"Yes, every last one. This is something I don't ever want you to forget, Skye."

I smile. "I'll never forget anything we do together."

His lips quirk upward. "You definitely won't forget this. Lie down on the bed."

I obey, nudging the plug in my ass. I can't stop a soft giggle.

Braden walks to his wardrobe and pulls out the leather cuffs that he used on me once before. He places them around each of my wrists and then secures them to the rungs of the headboard, giving me only a slight amount of slack. I clamp my fists around the leather rope securing the cuffs to the headboard.

"Okay?" he asks.

"Yes."

"Good. You're not going to be able to touch me, and that's how I want it. You need to focus all your other senses on what I'm doing to you. Can you do that for me?"

"Yes."

"Excellent." He slides his tongue over his lower lip, just enough to be really sensual. "You look delectable, Skye. Better than the most glorious feast. You're the only feast I want tonight. A feast for my eyes, my ears, my lips and tongue, my nose." He inhales. "You're wet. I can smell your musk already. It's the sweetest perfume."

I lift my hips instinctively, his words igniting me. I'm so ready for this. So ready for him.

"Easy," he says. "I'm as anxious as you are, but I'm going to enjoy every morsel of my feast first. Beginning with those luscious tits of yours."

My nipples strain forward, as if they heard his words. They're tight and puckered and ready for his lips, tongue, and teeth.

Braden removes his shirt, and I suck in a breath, intoxicated as always by his shoulders, chest, and abs. He's even more striking by candlelight.

Candlelight.

Hot wax.

The idea intrigues me. Would he do it if I asked? He doesn't like anything to do with fire, but it's not a hard limit.

Quickly I banish the thought. Tonight is about something else. Something Braden and I have both been looking forward to. He's gone to such trouble to make this good for me, and I intend to enjoy every second.

He peels off his jeans and boxer briefs, and out juts his cock, illuminated by the soft glow of the candles. He's ready, all right. As ready as I am. But I've seen that look in his eyes before. He won't be rushed.

He joins me on the bed and kisses my lips softly, like a butterfly's wings. I part my lips, hoping for more, but he trails them over my cheek and down the side of my neck, giving me goose bumps. I know where he's headed, and my nipples are more than ready. Finally, he gets to the tops of my breasts, licking and kissing the rosy flesh. I quake beneath him, my nipples poised and ready. He strokes my breasts with his warm tongue, and just when I'm about to yell at him to suck on my nipple, he finally closes his lips around one.

"Oh, God," I moan.

It's so good. So damned good. I'm ready to spread my legs and let him plunder me.

"Shh..." he says against my nipple. "No more talking."

I nod, though he can't see my head. No more talking. Braden doesn't like me to talk when we're making love. Except for that one time in the hotel in Liberty when he suspended his rules.

I loved that experience with him, and I hope we have it again. But the truth?

I'm thrilled when he makes demands of me. More than thrilled. Captivated. Something in me craves his dominance, craves to obey him. Making love isn't set in stone. It's unique to each couple, and Braden and I have our own tastes.

I find all of it thrilling.

He sucks on one nipple while pinching the other in a discordant rhythm that I can't pinpoint. Just when I think I might expire on the spot if he doesn't suck harder, he seems to read my mind. He sucks harder, pinches harder, and flaming darts shoot straight to my clit. The anal plug seems to enhance every spark that blasts into me, making everything more vibrant and more beautiful.

Still pinching one nipple, Braden lets the other drop from his lips as he kisses the underside of my breast and then the top of my abdomen. The sensation makes me sizzle. Though my nipple misses his mouth, my flesh quivers at his every touch. He's getting closer. Closer and closer to tonight's prize.

And I can't wait.

Chapter Thirty-Nine

Braden's lips and tongue are on a quest, but he's taking the scenic route. He meanders along, kissing and sucking at every centimeter of my flesh as I undulate beneath him, trying to guide him to his destination.

He's going slowly. Making me crave him even more. My ass is pulsating along with my clit. It's an odd sensation. A very pleasant sensation. Anal sex. The forbidden. The taboo.

Funny, how I still think of it in those terms. Pretty much everything Braden and I do together is considered taboo to most. To me? It's intimacy with the man I love, and it's completely normal. I'm exactly where I'm meant to be.

Our souls linked, and our hearts followed.

And right now his lips are following a path we both want.

Finally he kisses the top of my pubic bone, a groan emanating from his throat. "I'm going to miss this sweet cunt tonight, baby."

I sigh at his words. He's never used "cunt" before, and the dirtiness of it makes me hotter.

"I'll take good care of that in the morning, but for now…" He pushes my thighs forward and gently eases the anal plug out of me. "Gorgeous. Dilated and perfect."

I moan and instinctively pull against my bindings. God, if I could only touch him. His warm flesh, his silky hair, his hard cock.

But I can't. I'm bound for his pleasure.

And for my own.

He traces my hole with his finger, his breath catching. Then he squeezes a bit of lube into his palm before rubbing it over me.

The lube is warm. He warmed it in his hand.

For me.

"I'm going to take you now, Skye. This is mine. Only mine."

The head of his cock nudges against me.

"Relax," he says, his voice dark. "It may hurt at first, and you have permission to speak if it gets to be too much."

I nod, but I already know I won't stop him, even if the pain is unbearable. I want to do this for him.

For us.

I breathe. In. Out. In. Out. I stay very aware of my breathing as I wait for him to enter me .

Then I gasp as he breaches my tight rim. I bite my lip to keep from crying out. The sharp pain knifes through me.

I can tell him to stop. I can end this now.

But I don't.

I let out a breath, forcing my muscles to relax.

"That's it," he says. "I'm going to go all the way in now."

I nod, and he thrusts swiftly. He's completely embedded in me, and I'm so full. So, so full.

Yes, the pain is still there, but I don't mind it anymore. In fact, I welcome it. This is the ultimate show of trust between Braden and me. I love it.

"I'm going to pull out now," he says.

A whimper leaves my throat, but soon I find out he doesn't mean pull all the way out. He just pulls out to the tip and then slowly pushes back in.

And I'm full again. Complete in a new way—a way that links Braden and me even more profoundly than we were before.

A sheen of perspiration glistens on his forehead. He's working hard. Holding himself back. He wants to fuck me. He wants to fuck me hard.

I long to open my mouth and tell him to do it, but I'm forbidden to speak.

"Your pussy is glistening, Skye." He grips my hips but then slides one hand over my center and dips a finger inside. "So wet." Then he slides his fingers over my clit.

I gasp, my whole body quivering.

"I love how you respond to me. So wet, so pink and pretty. Your ass feels so good around my cock. I'm going to fuck you now. And I'm not going to be able to go slowly."

I nod once more, and he plunges inside me.

So invasive. He's touching a part of me that no one's ever touched before, and though I feel pain, I also feel pleasure. Intense pleasure coming from the pain, but also from the closeness. From the intimacy and trust.

Braden continues to work my clit as he fucks me, and a new sensation envelops me.

Forbidden. Taboo. Like the fruit that tempted Eve. It's the darkness of the act. The darkness along with the trust and intimacy. I welcome the pain. I welcome the pleasure.

I become the pain.

I become the pleasure.

Braden's stimulation of my clit rolls me toward the peak. A climax is on the horizon. A new kind of climax.

And my God, it's beginning not in my clit but in my ass.

Then I'm racing, crying out, speeding toward the precipice as he pumps, pumps, pumps…

And I shatter. I break. I fucking collapse. And all the while he continues pumping, invading my body, his cock completing me. I close my eyes and see only flashes of light and color—the pleasure and emotion morphing into psychedelic visions behind the veil of my mind's eye.

Whether I remain quiet is a mystery. *I love you, Braden! I love you, Braden!* Are they words or thoughts?

I don't know.

I don't care.

Braden sucks in a breath. "Fuck, Skye, you're so hot. Feels so good."

Thrust. Thrust. Thrust.

And then he plunges once more, so deep inside me, and I feel every contraction of his release.

Every. Single. One.

I open my eyes when my own climactic waves begin to subside. Braden's eyes are squeezed shut, and he's gripping my hips hard. I'll have marks. Beautiful red marks.

For a timeless moment, we remain locked together. One being. One heart. One soul.

Until he opens his eyes and pulls away from me. "Stay put," he says. "I'll be right back."

I close my eyes once more, and a minute later, warmth slides over my ass. I open my eyes. Braden is taking care of me with a warm washcloth.

My God, I love this man.

"You may speak now." His voice is husky, dark, sated.

I open my mouth, but all that comes out is a soft sigh.

"Tell me what you're thinking," he says.

"It was… It was…" Words float around in my head as I grasp for the right one. "Unbelievable."

"For me as well. I want to be the only man who ever goes inside that ass, Skye. The only man."

Fine with me. I don't say it aloud, though. Is he telling me we have a future? A real future, including marriage, children, and all that white-picket-fence stuff?

I don't dare let myself hope.

He rises again from the bed and releases my bindings. I rub my wrists absently.

"Okay? Any chafing?"

"No."

"How about your arms? Any pain from the stretch?"

"No," I say again.

"Good." A pause as he rakes his gaze over me. "I love you, Skye."

"I love you, too, Braden. So much."

"Thank you for sharing that part of yourself with me."

Thank you. He said thank you.

I'm humbled in a new way. He's thanking me.

"Thank you, too," I say. "Thank you for everything, Braden."

Chapter Forty

B raden rises once more and snuffs out all the candles. Now the only light visible is what shines in from the Boston Harbor through his massive windows.

The scent of candle wax drifts toward me. "Braden?"

"Yes?"

"Why isn't candle play a hard limit for you?"

"Because I'm very careful. It's not play that I engage in frequently."

"You don't allow it in the club, though."

"I don't allow fire play in the club. Because it can lead to significant damage if not done properly. No insurance policy would cover it."

"Is fire play different from candle play?"

"In my mind, yes. Taper candles made from soy wax—which doesn't burn nearly as hot as paraffin or beeswax—don't cause much risk if handled properly."

"Would you, then?"

"Would I what?"

"Do it for me?"

He lifts his eyebrows. "You're interested in candle play?"

"The idea of hot wax on my nipples excites me."

"All right, Skye. For you. I'll do it for you."

"But not here," I say. "At the club."

"I agree. My bedroom isn't set up for candle play."

I smile at him. "I've never seen a candle here before tonight."

"I got them especially for you. To give you the romantic atmosphere you deserve."

"And it was perfect, Braden. The whole thing was absolutely perfect."

"Yes, it was. You were a trouper, too. I know you experienced some pain, but you relaxed and worked through it."

"A little. I mean, yeah, it was painful. Quite sharp at first, but... I don't know. The pain was always there, but it turned into pleasure. Kind of like when you spanked me. It was perfect in its pain. If that makes any sense."

"You like pain," he says.

"No. Not really. I'm not a masochist. But I like pain when it brings me closer to you."

No truer words.

"When will we go back to New York?" I ask.

"I don't know. I want to give you some time to continue to work through things before we go back to the club."

"Oh, I wasn't even talking about the club. Eugenie wants to meet with me again about a new social media campaign built around some of my hashtags. I need to talk to you about—" A yawn splits my face.

"You're exhausted, and frankly, so am I. You can tell me all about Eugenie's new brainchild in the morning. After our soak in the tub."

"A bath?"

He nods. "A soak will help ease your soreness."

"I'm not sore down there. Really."

"Not now. You're still on a high from the orgasm. You will be sore in the morning. Trust me." He brushes his lips over mine. "Now go to sleep."

"Mmm. Deal." I close my eyes—

Only to shoot them open again when my phone buzzes.

"Ignore it," Braden says.

"Ha! You know I can't do that any more than you can."

He chuckles. "I know."

I rummage the phone out of my purse on the nightstand. Tessa. At this hour? "Hey, Tess," I say into the phone, stifling another yawn.

"Skye?" Her voice is unusually high and squeaky.

"Yeah? Are you okay?"

"Not even slightly." She chokes back a sob and then sneezes.

I jerk upward, eyes wide. "What's the matter? Why are you crying?"

"Damn these allergies," she says. "I need you. Please."

"Okay, okay. Calm down. What do you need?"

"It's Garrett. I… I slept with him."

"Okay."

"Why couldn't you come to dinner with us? You knew what was going to happen."

"Tess, I—"

"I needed you tonight."

"Okay, okay. Calm down." This is all very un-Tessalike. She must have it bad for Garrett. And I'm her BFF. I should know this.

"Where are you? I'll come to you."

"At my place. He left, Skye. He fucked me, and then he left."

"Did you ask him to stay?"

"I did. He said he had an early meeting in the morning. But tomorrow's Sunday. He lied to get out of spending the night with me. How could I have been so stupid as to let him in my bed again?"

Again, this isn't like Tessa at all. "Are you drinking?"

She sniffles. "A little."

Shit. Last time she did ecstasy. "Tell me you didn't take anything else. Please."

"No. Not yet. But I'm a mess. Can you come over?"

I'm bone tired, but… "Yeah. Sure."

I hate the thought of leaving Braden's bed, but I won't let my best friend down. I've done enough of that recently.

But this is strange. Tessa doesn't get this upset over men. What's up with Garrett? When he broke her heart the first time, she did drugs, for God's sake. I need to make sure she doesn't go down that path again. Either she has it super bad for this guy, or…something else is going on. Something I'd know about if we hadn't been arguing.

"I'll be there as soon as I can. Hang in there, okay?"

"Thanks, Skye."

"No need to thank me. Get a hold of yourself, and I'll be there soon." I shove the phone into my purse. "Braden, I need to leave. Tessa's in a bad way."

"I'll drive you."

"You don't have to. I'll call an Uber. Besides, you gave Christopher the night off."

"I *can* drive, you know."

I smile weakly. "Thank you. This means a lot to me. I'm so sorry. After our wonderful night."

Braden dresses, and I head up to my bedroom and find something more comfortable than the green sheath I arrived in. A comfy cotton T-shirt and fleece joggers are perfect. When I descend, Braden is waiting for me at the elevator.

Fifteen minutes later, we pull up in front of Tessa's building.

"You may as well go home," I say. "I should stay with her tonight."

He nods. "I'll walk you up. It's late."

I kiss his cheek. "I'll be okay."

"I'm walking you up, Skye. It's not up for debate." He slides out of the car and opens the passenger door for me.

A few minutes later, I knock on Tessa's door. She opens it, her face streaked with tears, and her eyes…strange, like one is looking the other way or something, but not quite.

Again, so not Tessa. She's fond of Garrett, but she doesn't fall apart over men.

"Hey," she says weakly. "Hi, Braden."

"Hello, Tessa." He walks straight into her apartment, taking command. "What can we do for you?"

Shit. Just what Tessa doesn't need right now. Braden Black trying to fix things. He finds solutions, but Tessa doesn't want a solution. She wants to cry on her best friend's shoulder.

"Braden…" I begin.

"Have you eaten?" he asks.

"I had dinner with Garrett."

He picks up a nearly empty bottle of vodka. "How much of this have you had?"

"Braden…" I try again.

"A few shots," Tessa replies.

I grab Braden's arm and steer him out the door. "She doesn't need to be interrogated," I whisper. "Please, just go."

He cups my cheek. "Call me if you need anything."

"I will." I close the door and turn to Tessa. "Sorry about that."

"It's okay. I'm sorry to ruin your evening."

"You didn't." I wish I were lying in bed with Braden, but we accomplished the task for tonight. I let out a laugh. The task for tonight.

And now I'm beginning to feel that soreness Braden warned me about.

Oh, well. Tessa needs me, so my sore ass can wait.

I sit down on her couch and pat the seat next to me. "Come

on. Spill it."

She sighs. "It's so stupid. I went and fell in love with the jerk."

"That's not stupid."

"Why couldn't I meet a man like Braden? He treats you with so much respect and love."

"Have you forgotten he dumped me a couple weeks ago?"

"No. But things seem fine now."

"They're good, but it took a lot of work on both our parts. I even started therapy to get to the bottom of everything."

"I know." She shakes her head. "I guess I just want more than Garrett wants to give right now."

"So you're not in the same place. That doesn't have to be a bad thing. He did come back to you, and he's willing to be exclusive."

"That's what he says, anyway."

"Do you think he's lying?" I ask.

"I don't know. He could be. After all, he lied about having an early meeting tomorrow."

"Are you sure?"

"It's Sunday, Skye."

"Braden has meetings during the middle of the night sometimes. We flew out to New York early on a Sunday morning that one time so he could deal with some kind of contract in China."

I wince a little. That trip had cost me Tessa. I was so absorbed in Braden and my interview with Susanne Cosmetics that I neglected to call her to break our shopping date.

She doesn't bring that up, though, thank goodness. Instead, she says, "Garrett Ramirez isn't Braden Black. He's an architect."

"So maybe he has a breakfast meeting with the boss. Or a racquetball date or something."

"Then that's what he should have said. But what he actually said was 'I have an early meeting tomorrow.'"

I check my watch. After midnight. "It's too late to order pizza. How about I run across the street to the convenience store and grab a few pints of Ben & Jerry's?"

She smiles. "Would you?"

"I absolutely would. As long as you promise no more drinking. Alcohol solves nothing."

"I know. I know."

"This isn't like you, Tessa."

She sighs again.

"Are you really in love?"

"I think so. I realize I haven't known him very long."

"You've known him as long as I've known Braden, and we're in love. Sometimes you just know." I can't help a smile.

"And sometimes one person feels something the other doesn't."

"Tessa, you're a catch. We both know it, and so does Garrett."

"I'm not sure he does."

"Then honestly? He's not worth it." I grab my purse. "I'll be back in a flash. Dump the rest of that." I nod to the vodka bottle.

"Yes, ma'am."

I smile and leave the building. I don't like going out alone at night, but the convenience store is right across the street from Tessa's building. She and I go there all the time. Boy, if Braden knew I was going out alone after midnight, he'd be pissed as hell.

I walk into the store and head to the freezer section. Only two selections. Chunky Monkey and Cherry Garcia. It's more of a Chocolate Therapy kind of night, but any port in a storm. I grab a pint of each and head to the checkout counter—

Addison Ames stands at the cashier.

I nearly drop both pints.

Do I say something? She hasn't seen me yet. I can put the ice cream back and sneak out.

Fuck that.

I hold my head high and strut right up behind her. "Good evening, Addie."

She turns, her eyes narrow. She looks oddly unsurprised to see me. "You mean good morning, don't you?"

Yeah, she's right. It's after midnight.

She eyes my purchase. "Trouble in paradise?"

"Why would you think that?"

"Looks like an ice cream binge to me."

"Maybe we're going to eat it off each other."

She scoffs. "Braden play with ice cream? Not a chance. Besides, we're not anywhere near your place or his. Nice try, though."

For your information, bitch, Braden has licked chocolate mousse and crème brûlée off every inch of my body.

But the words don't come. No matter how much I'd love to taunt Addie, I can't bring myself to do it.

Interestingly, she's buying a pack of cigarettes.

"Didn't know you'd taken on the nicotine habit," I say.

"They're not for me. They're for my sister. She's staying with me for a while."

"Apple?"

"Only sister I've got."

Apple, who doesn't drink and regards her body as a temple. Who also can't stand Addie. Not buying.

"Why is she staying with you?"

"She's having her place redecorated. Paying some ungodly amount to make it look like a dump from the seventies, apparently."

Ungodly amount? That doesn't sound like Apple, either. Of course, I spent only an hour with her.

Addie pays for the cigarettes and then waits while I pay for my ice cream.

"Don't you have somewhere to be?" I ask.

"Not really. Apple can wait a few minutes for her smokes."

"You know what's interesting?" I say. "We're not anywhere near your place, either. And the last time I saw Apple, she wasn't smoking."

"When the hell did you see Apple?"

"Yeah, not your business," I say.

"The hell it's not. What did Apple say to you?"

I raise an eyebrow. "Something bothering you, Addie?"

She lowers her eyelids slightly, almost batting them for a second. "Of course not."

"Really? Because I'm thinking those smokes aren't for Apple. When did you start smoking?"

She scoffs. "I do *not* smoke."

"And also, when did you start hanging around this part of town?" A light bulb flashes in my brain. "Which one of us are you following, Addie? Braden? Or me?"

"I don't have to stand here and take this." She flounces off, heading God knows where. I don't see her car anywhere. This is a decent area, but no single woman should be walking alone after midnight.

"Whatever," I murmur. I take my ice cream and head back to Tessa's.

Once there, I knock.

No answer.

"Tess?" I say, trying not to shout too loudly. It is after midnight.

She doesn't respond, so I turn the knob. It's open. She didn't lock up after I left, which is not like her at all.

So un-Tessalike. What the hell is going on?

I walk in. "Tess, I'm back."

She must be in the bathroom. I jiggle the door handle, and—

"Oh my God!"

Chapter Forty-One

Tessa's body is slumped over the toilet bowl, which is filled with vomit. Maybe that's what she needed.

"Tess, come on." I jiggle her shoulder.

She doesn't move.

"Tessa! Come on!"

"What's wrong?"

I jump out of my skin at the voice.

Addison Ames stands in the doorway to Tessa's bathroom.

"How the hell did you get in here?"

"Same way you did. I walked in."

"Why the fuck are you— Oh, hell. Never mind. Help me get her out of here."

To my surprise, Addie helps me drag Tessa out of the bathroom.

"She's out cold," Addie says.

"Thanks for stating the obvious." I pat Tessa's cheek. "Tessa, come on. It's Skye. Wake up."

My heart beats wildly as fear settles in. Why isn't she responding?

Did she take more drugs? Were there any drugs in the house? Fuck. "Call 911," I say to Addie.

"She's just drunk."

"For God's sake." I leave Tessa for a moment to get my purse and grab my phone. I quickly dial 911 and explain the situation. "Please hurry," I say before ending the call. Then I call Braden.

"Hey," I say when he answers. "Tessa has passed out, and I'm afraid she might have done some drugs or something."

"I'm on my way."

"I may not be here. We called 911."

"We? Who's we?"

Shit. "Addie. It's a long story. I'll tell you when you get here."

"Addie?" he nearly snarls. "I might have known."

"Known what?"

"I can't explain now. I'm heading to Tessa's. If the ambulance gets there before I do, text me where you're going."

I nod into the phone. He can't see me, but I can't even think about that right now. He knew Addie was here?

But who cares? Tessa is unconscious, and I have no idea what she took.

I turn to Addie. "What do I do? What if she OD'd?"

"You mean Braden didn't have all the answers?" she says with sarcasm.

"Stop it. Just stop it. This woman is unconscious. What do I do?"

"Why do you think I'd know?"

"You're rich. You've probably experimented with drugs."

"Apple did. I didn't."

"Then call Apple. Please. I don't know what to do."

She actually nods and grabs her phone. A few seconds later, "Apple said check to make sure she has a pulse."

Good advice. Why didn't I think of it? I place my fingers on Tessa's neck. It's faint, but it's there. "Yeah, she's got a pulse."

"She's alive," Addie says into the phone. "Now what?"

Pause.

"She said make sure she's lying on her side in case she pukes."

"She already puked."

"Doesn't matter. She could puke again."

"Got it." I roll Tessa onto her side. "Now what?"

"Clear out her mouth."

I take a quick look. "She's clear."

Addie listens intently with her phone to her ear. Then, "That's all Apple knows. We just wait for the paramedics."

I nod. "Tell her thanks."

I sit, Tessa's hand in mine, actually thankful that Addie is here. Having another conscious human helps me, even if it's Addison Ames. Why she's here, I still have no clue. Braden didn't seem surprised, but I don't even care about that right now.

Each second passes like an hour. Only ten minutes have elapsed since I called 911, but every moment is one less moment that Tessa has.

"Addie, look around," I say, my other hand lodged on Tessa's neck over her carotid. "See if you can find evidence of drugs. We need to be able to tell the paramedics what she took."

Addie nods, her pallor two shades lighter than normal.

Is she as frightened as I am? She doesn't even know Tessa.

"I don't see anything. No pill bottles. No syringe. Just this empty bottle of vodka."

"She already drank that before. Something happened while I was out getting ice cream. Damn!"

Then a harsh pounding on the door that nearly sends my heart up to my throat.

Addie opens the door and lets the paramedics in. They rush over to Tessa.

"What's the story?" one of them asks us.

"She was drinking, and now I can't wake her. She might have

done some kind of drug, but we can't find any evidence."

"Got it. Her pulse is slow, but it's there. Is she an athlete?"

"Professional? No. But she's in good shape. Yoga and running."

"How old is she?"

"Twenty-five."

The paramedics get Tessa onto a stretcher.

"Where are you taking her?" I ask. "Can I ride in the ambulance?"

"Mass General. You family?"

"Friend."

"I suppose so, if there's no one else."

"I'll drive her."

My heart melts.

Braden's voice. He's here. Everything will be fine now.

"That's fine. We'll do everything we can for your friend."

I nod and gulp out, "Thank you."

"What are *you* doing here?" Braden demands of Addie.

Addie doesn't reply.

"It's okay," I tell him. "She actually helped me."

"I'm here now," he says to Addie. "Stay here. I'll call a cab from my car to take you home."

She nods nervously. This seems to have shaken her. I'm not sure why, but right now I'm concentrating on Tessa.

I don't speak as Braden helps me into his car.

I don't speak as he calls a cab for Addie.

I don't speak the rest of the way to Mass General.

I don't speak as he hands his keys over to the valet and we go into the ER.

Tessa's parents. I have to call them. What do I tell them? What if she really *was* doing drugs?

Braden walks confidently to reception. "Tessa Logan was just brought in. How is she?"

"Are you a family member?"

"I'm Braden Black. My girlfriend is Tessa's best friend. She's the one who called 911."

"I'm sorry, Mr. Black, but I can't give out any patient information unless you're a family member."

I half expect Braden to pull out a couple hundred dollar bills, but that's not his style. He follows the rules, even though he knows I'd give my left arm to know what's going on with Tessa.

He returns to me and sits down.

"I have to call her parents," I say numbly.

He nods. "You mean you haven't?"

"No. I... I couldn't think. I have no idea what to say to them."

He takes my phone from me. "What's the number?"

"It's in my contacts under Dan and Carlotta Logan."

Braden is in control, as usual. He finds the contact and presses call. "Hello, Mr. Logan? I apologize for calling at this late hour. My name is Braden Black, and my girlfriend is Skye Manning. I'm sorry to tell you that your daughter Tessa has been taken to Mass General ER."

Pause.

"She was drinking, and Skye found her passed out and couldn't wake her. That's all I know because they won't give any information to non-family members."

Pause.

"No problem. I'm sorry to be the bearer of bad news. We'll see you soon." He turns to me. "They're on their way."

I nod. At least we'll get some answers soon.

I just hope they're the right ones.

Chapter Forty-Two

Dan and Carlotta arrive in twenty minutes. They go straight to reception and don't say anything to us. Not that I blame them. Their little girl is back there, and for all they know she may have OD'd.

Damn!

Garrett Ramirez is so not worth this.

What hold does he have over her?

Shit. I should call Betsy. But not until I have some news on Tessa.

A nurse comes out and talks to Dan and Carlotta. Eventually, they make their way over to Braden and me.

I can't bring myself to speak.

"Hello, Skye," Carlotta says. "I'm so glad you found her."

I still can't speak.

Braden stands. "I'm Braden Black. How is Tessa?"

"She's going to be okay," Carlotta says. "They're pumping her stomach."

Then it *was* drugs. Damn.

"So soon?" Braden asks.

"It's a preventive measure," Dan says. "They won't get her toxicology lab report back for an hour or so."

Braden nods. "I see."

"You two can go home," Dan says. "We'll call you when we know anything more, Skye."

"Skye?" Braden asks.

"I want to stay," I finally say.

"All right." Braden returns to his seat. "Is there anything I can do for any of you?"

"Some coffee would be nice," Carlotta says. "Thank you, Mr. Black."

Braden takes my hand and pulls me out of my chair. I guess I'm going with him. Nothing in the hospital is open, of course, so we walk to a nearby convenience store. Braden grabs two coffees. "You want anything?" he asks.

I shake my head. "I should be there."

"They needed some time to deal with what they just found out."

"Is that why you dragged me along?"

"That, and because you needed to get away."

I don't reply.

"This isn't your fault, Skye."

"She asked me to have dinner with her and Garrett tonight. I said no, because you and I had plans. I knew we were going to... And I was looking forward to it. I wanted it so badly."

"Why didn't you call me? I would have understood."

"I know. But I didn't want to break our date. I wanted... Damn! How selfish am I?"

"It's not selfish to refuse to break a previous commitment, Skye. You and I both know that. Tessa is a grown-up. She's responsible for her own actions."

He's right. Of course, I know he's right. But after Tessa and I just made up, I should have been there for her. I should have put her first.

Instead I put Braden first. I put myself first.

I'm not sure I'll ever forgive myself.

A few hours later, a young doctor comes to the waiting room and approaches the Logans. "I'm Dr. Mary Hedstrom. I have good news. Tessa is going to be fine."

The anvil slides from my shoulders. My guilt doesn't subside, but at least Tessa is okay. That's the main thing.

"Could I speak to you two in private?" Dr. Hedstrom says.

"It's okay," Dan replies. "Skye is Tessa's best friend, and Mr. Black is Skye's…gentleman friend. They've both been very helpful. You may speak freely."

"All right. Tessa had an allergic reaction based on an interaction of two different substances that she ingested."

Drugs. She did drugs again. What was she thinking?

"What substances?" Dan asks.

"Alcohol and ketamine."

Braden lifts his eyebrows. "Ketamine?"

"What's ketamine?" Carlotta asks.

Good. I want to know as well, but I don't have the energy to ask.

"Technically it's an anesthetic," Dr. Hedstrom says, "but it's also used sometimes to treat pain or depression."

Finally, I find my voice. "Tessa's not depressed."

"Skye's right," Carlotta says. "Tessa has never been prone to anxiety or depression."

Though she did take the breakup with Garrett hard, which is so unlike her. And tonight…she got so upset because he wouldn't spend the night. Again, unlike her.

Dr. Hedstrom clears her throat. "Ketamine in a smaller dose can make a person docile. It can also cause dizziness and diminished reflexes. Sometimes eye movements can seem uncoordinated."

"Her eyes were weird," I say. "Before she passed out, I mean."

"I'm not surprised. Mr. and Mrs. Logan, I checked Tessa's name in our database. I don't show her ever being prescribed ketamine. That doesn't mean she wasn't. If her provider isn't a part of our network, we wouldn't have the records. But most providers in Boston are part of this network."

"If no one prescribed it, then how did she get it?" Carlotta asks.

The doctor takes a deep breath before continuing. "Unfortunately, ketamine is a nightclub drug. Men sometimes use it to drug women. It's known as one of the date rape drugs."

Carlotta gasps, her hand flying to her mouth.

"Of all the…" Dan shakes his head.

"No," I say. "Tessa wasn't at a club tonight. She and Garrett went to dinner, and then they went to her place, and—"

"Do you know that for sure?" Dr. Hedstrom asks.

"I wasn't there, if that's what you mean. But that's what she told me. But…"

"What, Skye?" Braden nudges me.

"Tessa wasn't herself tonight. She was so upset over something that normally wouldn't upset her. Just like the last time."

"The last time?" Carlotta says.

Crap. I didn't mean to say that. I can't rat to Carlotta about Tessa taking ecstasy. I continue, "Either she's really in love with this guy, or…"

"Or he drugged her," Braden says matter-of-factly.

My blood runs cold. Garrett? No. He wouldn't drug her. He wouldn't. But if he would, then would Peter, his best friend, do the same?

"Mr. Black, if you know something, you need to tell us," Dan says.

"Call me Braden. If Tessa wasn't at a club tonight, how else would she have gotten ketamine?"

I have to say something. I don't want to, but I have to. For Tessa's own good.

"Tessa doesn't normally do drugs," I say, "but a couple weeks ago, when she and Garrett broke up, she took ecstasy."

Carlotta nearly loses her footing, but Dan and Braden both steady her.

"It's off brand for her," I say. "I was surprised as all of you are. But I felt I should say something. If she took ecstasy, it's possible she took ketamine."

The doctor talks to Dan and Carlotta, and soon their voices are only a buzzing between my ears.

Because none of this makes sense.

Images appear in my mind. That night I went clubbing with Tessa, Betsy, Garrett, and Peter. Tessa was on Garrett's lap within a minute, and by the end of the evening, Betsy was cuddled up with Peter…whom she'd just met.

They were lovey-dovey all the way, and I didn't think anything of it.

Except now?

Neither of them were acting like themselves.

Is Braden right?

Did Garrett give the ketamine to Tessa?

And did Peter give it to Betsy?

Oh. My. God.

Peter hit on me first, and Braden showed up and took me away from him.

Peter seemed almost afraid of Braden when we saw him at the Opera Guild Gala.

At the time, I figured it was because of the contract his

father's firm wanted with Black, Inc.

And Braden seemed adamant that I stay away from Peter.

Was it jealousy?

Partially, yes. But what if it was also something else?

I break through the buzzing voice. "Braden."

"Yeah?"

"You're serious, aren't you? You think Garrett gave Tessa the ketamine."

"I have no proof of that."

"Then why did you bring it up?"

"Let's just say I think he may have access to it."

The doctor's voice is still buzzing to the Logans.

Finally, I break through. "Can we see Tessa?"

"Just her parents for now," Dr. Hedstrom says.

I nod. So many questions. Tessa promised me she wouldn't do drugs. Yet somehow ketamine got into her system. Would Tessa lie to me?

No, I don't believe she would. She never has before.

Which means Garrett gave it to her or someone else did.

And whoever did, they did it without her knowledge.

She was drugged…and Garrett is the prime suspect.

"Doctor," I say, "could ketamine and alcohol have such a dire effect? Obviously it was a small dose of ketamine, right?"

"It's hard to say. We'll know more after we're able to speak with Tessa. If she doesn't have any retroactive amnesia, we'll know the dose was small."

"Retroactive amnesia?" Carlotta asks.

"Amnesia that causes you to lose time from before you took the drug. For example, if Tessa took the drug at—"

Dan clears his throat. "My daughter did not take that drug."

Did he hear me say she took ecstasy? Though I agree with him now. Tessa didn't take the ketamine.

Still, it got into her system somehow.

"I need to ask you both," Dr. Hedstrom says. "Does Tessa take anything else? Like I said, I couldn't find any prescriptions in our system, but does she take anything else?"

"You mean like over-the-counter stuff?" Dan asks.

"Yes, over-the-counter meds. Herbal supplements. Everything."

"I honestly don't know," Carlotta says. "She hasn't lived with us since she was eighteen."

"Her allergies were bothering her tonight," I offer. "She takes that stuff. I think it's echinacea."

Dr. Hedstrom raises her eyebrows. "Do you know how much echinacea she takes?"

"No, just that she takes it. She has terrible hay fever."

"That may be the issue. Echinacea can interact with ketamine and make the effects more profound. Then the alcohol on top of everything…" Dr. Hedstrom shakes her head. "But the good news is that Tessa is out of danger. She probably would've come to on her own, but I'm glad you brought her in, especially since she was vomiting."

"Mr. Black…" Dan begins.

"Braden, please."

Dan nods. "Braden, you seem to know this Garrett. I need to get in touch with him."

"Not a problem," Braden says. "If Garrett Ramirez gave Tessa ketamine, I will find out."

"Thank you," Carlotta says. "But what can we do now? The deed is done. I'm just thankful Tessa is all right."

"We're all thankful for that," Braden agrees, "but I will look into this. I've looked the other way far too long."

Chapter Forty-Three

"What did you mean back there," I finally get up the nerve to ask, when Braden and I are back at his place, "when you said you've looked the other way far too long?"

He sighs. "Remember when I showed up at the MADD gala, and Peter Reardon stayed away from you after that?"

"How could I forget?"

"I didn't want you with him because I wanted you, but that wasn't the only reason."

"Oh?"

"I'd already decided his father's firm wasn't going to get my contract, even though their bid came in the lowest."

"Are they not good architects?"

"They're excellent architects, actually. I just don't like the way they do business."

"I'm not sure what you mean."

"They're not the most ethical people, and it begins at the top with Peter's father, Beau Reardon."

"Braden, Betsy is dating Peter now. And they got cuddly awfully quickly. You don't think...?"

"It's possible. I hear things in my circles that don't become common knowledge. Beau Reardon sometimes uses unconventional methods to get what he wants." Braden's eyes are dark with anger. "I'll take care of it," he says succinctly.

"How?"

"Does it matter?"

"Well…yeah. I don't want you getting into trouble."

"I won't get into any trouble. Don't worry. But the Reardons and Garrett will wish they'd never crossed a friend of mine when I'm done with them. Now, let's get you that warm bath I promised you."

I lean back against Braden's hard chest and let the warm and fragrant water soothe every part of me. Yeah, my sore ass needs it, but the rest of my body needs it no less. This night has given stress a new meaning. I close my eyes.

At least Tessa's okay.

I have more questions. So many more. Like how did Addison end up at the convenience store across the street from Tessa's after midnight? For that matter, how does Addie always know everything about Braden and me?

Is she stalking me? Is she still stalking Braden? If she is, he must know. He has eyes and ears everywhere.

I can't ask, though. At least not now, when I'm breathing in the soothing lavender steam from this amazing bath. Braden turned the jets onto low, so they give the water just the gentlest of swirls, as if we're bathing in a lovely natural hot spring.

He moves his hand slowly up and down my arm, just the whisper of a touch, and it soothes me.

I'll figure everything out.

Later.

. . .

My eyes pop open. The sun streams through Braden's bedroom windows. I turn my head. No Braden. Then I sit up and grab my phone from the nightstand.

No way! One p.m.?

Makes sense, I guess. We were up almost until morning waiting for news on Tessa. Then we came back here and bathed together, which was amazingly sensual.

I rise, pad over to Braden's closet, and grab one of his shirts. I button it around me and breathe in his piney and masculine scent—my favorite perfume in the world. Then I grab my phone and call Carlotta. She lets me talk to Tessa.

"Hey, Skye." Tessa's voice is a little hoarse, but she sounds… okay.

"Tess, thank God. How are you?"

"Tired. But okay. Very thankful for you and Braden."

"Please. If I'd been with you in the first—"

"Stop," she interrupts. "Don't go there. Don't do that to yourself. I'm an adult. At least now I know why I was acting so strangely."

Fresh anger ignites in me. "I can't believe Garrett. Braden's going to take care of this."

"Good." Tessa lets out a hoarse scoff. "Tell him to let the pig have it."

"Don't worry. I will. When are they springing you?"

"Today," she says. "Mom's staying with me for a while. I couldn't talk her out of it." She coughs softly.

"I don't want to keep you. You need to rest. Do you want me to come by?"

"No. I think I'll take some time to hang with my mom. You don't mind, do you?"

"Of course not. Whatever you need. I'm here if you need me."

"I know. Thanks, Skye."

I end the call and walk out of the room. "Braden?"

"In the office."

I follow the sound of his voice to his home office. He sits behind his desk, staring at his laptop screen.

"Hey," I say.

"Good morning. Or should I say good afternoon." He finally looks up and sucks in a breath. "You look fucking sexy in my shirt."

I smile. I can't help it. The soft cotton against my body infused with his scent. I *feel* sexy in this shirt.

"What are you working on?"

"Nothing that can't wait. Come here." He moves his hand downward.

Once I'm behind his desk, I see that he's freed his cock from his lounge pants. I part my lips.

"Fuck, you're sexy," he says. "Climb on, Skye."

I'm wet already. No surprise there. Braden's mere presence makes me wet and ready, and right now, with his tousled bedhead and heavy eyelids, I'm ready to pounce.

I climb onto his lap and straddle him, slowly easing down onto his erection.

"God…" I groan.

His moan meets my own as we sit immobile for a few seconds, and I relish the feeling of him deeply embedded inside me.

"Fuck." He inhales. "I can't get enough of you. Never enough."

He takes charge then, and grips my hips, lifting me until his cock head is only teasing my pussy lips. He holds me there for a minute, my nipples abrading the cotton of his shirt. I struggle against his strength, trying to sink back down so I'm complete again, and just when I think I may seriously lose my cool, he finally pushes me back down onto his hardness.

It's quick. It's lusty. It's not romantic at all, but I don't care. It's us.

Simply us.

He grasps me harder and harder, and I feel like a piston on an engine. And I love it. I love it so much. The pressure builds inside me, and before I know it, an orgasm is imminent. "Braden! I'm going to come. God!"

"Do it, baby. Do it. Come."

With his words, I shatter, only to be forced together at the molecular level as I stare into his mesmerizing blue eyes.

Those eyes look at me with wonder.

With awe.

With lust.

With love.

"I love you," I say between breaths. "I love you so much."

He jams me down hard onto his cock, and as my climax continues, I feel every spurt of his.

Every last one.

I lay my head on his hard shoulder, still panting. He did all the work, but still my breath comes in sharp rasps. The climax. Braden. All of it. He literally takes my breath away.

I smile against his shoulder. This is so not us. Every lovemaking session is usually a huge deal. Either he's thought it out ahead of time, or he comes up with it spur of the moment. Either way, it lasts way longer than the few minutes of this one.

I wasn't bound. I wasn't told to focus on one sense. I wasn't told not to talk.

Even so, I didn't speak, except to tell him I was coming and that I loved him. I didn't move, so I may as well have been bound. And though I wasn't told to focus, I focused anyway, on each movement. On his scent.

On everything about this precious moment in time.

We've come to a new understanding, Braden and I.

And I'm all in.

"Skye," he says into my hair.

"Hmm?"

"Have you checked on Tessa?"

"Yeah. She's being released today. Her mom is moving in with her for a while to take care of her."

"Are you okay with that?"

"Sure. Carlotta's great."

"I mean"—he pushes a stray strand of hair out of my eyes— "do you need to be here for her?"

"No. I'll only get in Carlotta's way. Tess and I talked. She wants some time with her mom."

"All right, then."

I close my eyes, feeling dreamy. "All right what?"

"We're going back to New York. Tonight."

Chapter Forty-Four

Who loves to kiss? Susie Girl lip tint in Fab Fuchsia gives you the pink pucker you love! #sponsored #powerofpink #susiegirl #susieglow #simplyskye #lipsaremadeforkissing

The selfie is me puckering like a fish, and believe it or not, I don't look butt ugly. It's a fun pose for a fun post. Already the likes are heating up.

I don't have to look perfect in each shot. I'm not Addison Ames. I'm Skye. Imperfect Skye. And I'm beginning to see the merit in that—what Eugenie and the rest of the Susanne staff see.

It's okay to not be perfect, because you know what? Not one of us is.

Addie may think she is. Some of her followers may even believe it.

I know she's not.

And I wish I hadn't started thinking about Addie, because now I have more questions for Braden.

No.

No.

No.

I'll let him come to me in his own time.

We're heading to New York in a few hours. I've already contacted Eugenie and we're set to meet tomorrow with dinner in the evening.

And then…Black Rose Underground?

I don't know.

Braden seems distant. Not distant toward me. He's been very affectionate. But he hasn't mentioned the club. We've done the anal sex taboo, and I'm yearning for more. Candle play intrigues me. I still like the idea of neck binding, but it's a hard limit for Braden, and I understand. Just as I know he understands my hard limits. Blood sports, for example, which I didn't even know existed until he told me about them.

Not a hard limit for him. He made it emphatically clear he only has one hard limit. Has he done blood sports? Do I even want to know?

Plus, he was just in New York, and this new trip came up quite suddenly. Something's brewing in his head. I wish he'd confide in me, but I know better than to ask. He'll tell me when he's ready.

I can't push him. I won't. I'm learning to gauge his moods and his needs. At the same time, I'm learning how to control my own needs. Yes, I want to know all these things. I'm curious. But I can exist without knowing.

It's freeing, really, to let someone else take charge.

Tessa always tried to tell me. *Let your hair down, Skye.*

She was right.

Though her "let your hair down" attitude may have gotten her into some trouble. Thank goodness she's going to be all right. In fact…I want to see her. Sure, she said she's fine, but I don't feel right leaving Boston without seeing it for myself.

I finish packing my small suitcase for New York. Braden is still in his office. I knock softly and then enter. "Hey."

"I'm almost finished," he says.

"Great. I'm going to go see Tessa. She should be home by now. Her mom's going to stay at her place for a while, but I want to see her before we leave."

He nods. "Be back in two hours. That'll give us enough time to get to the airport."

"I will." I grab my phone. "Just going to catch an Uber."

"No need. A car's waiting downstairs for you."

"Is Christopher back?"

"No. I ordered a car today in case we needed one, and it turns out we do. I'd go with you, but I need to finish up this document."

"It's okay. I understand. I don't want to overwhelm her."

"You think I'd overwhelm her?"

"Braden"—I try not to laugh—"you overwhelm *everyone*."

The left side of his mouth twitches slightly. He's trying not to smile. I can't help myself. I laugh. I laugh like I've never laughed before. "You try so hard to be stoic all the time. Why? Let yourself go, Braden!"

"You sound like Tessa," he says.

"Yes, I do. And she has a point. Let it out! Let yourself laugh! For God's sake, I'm right and you know it. You *do* overwhelm everyone. It's who you are. Love yourself for who you are. Let it out!"

A smile forms on his lips. "Oh, Skye," he says. "You don't want me to let it out."

"Of course I do. Be happy!"

"I am happy. You know that. I'm happier than I've ever been with you."

His words warm me. Make me feel all cuddly like a teddy bear. "That's not what I mean, though I'm really glad about that. What I mean is that life sucks sometimes. We've had a few rough times. But we're back together. Tessa's going to be okay. Life is good, Braden. Enjoy it."

Braden's eyes smolder. "You really want me to let myself go?"

"Yes. I really do."

"Are you sure? Because I'm not sure you know what you're asking for."

My legs weaken, and I quiver all over. He's turning this into something sexual, and my body is all in already. Has he truly never let himself go sexually?

And if so, what does that mean for me?

"Maybe I *don't* know what I'm asking for," I tell him. "Most of what you've shown me has been new to me. But I love you, Braden, and I'm willing to go wherever you want."

His gaze burns into mine. "We'll see about that when we get to New York."

I'm so ripe from his words and gaze alone I'm ready to pounce on him again.

But I need to see Tessa.

"I'll be back," I say.

"Give Tessa and her folks my best."

"I will. Thanks for being there with me last night."

"Skye, where else on earth would I be other than with the woman I love?"

I nearly swoon. Nearly melt into a puddle right there on the floor. How is it possible that I got so lucky to have Braden Black fall in love with me?

I don't understand it half the time.

Right now, though, I need to see Tessa. I smile at Braden and turn to leave his office.

. . .

"I remember all of it," Tessa says to me, lying on her couch in bright red—so very Tessa—flannel pajamas. "And no, I didn't take any drugs last night. Certainly not ketamine."

"It's good that you remember. You didn't get enough to cause any amnesia."

"Do you really think Garrett drugged me?"

I shake my head. "I honestly don't know, but last night, while you were going through all this, I started thinking. That night when we went clubbing, and it was Betsy's first date with Peter, she seemed to get friendly with him really quickly. I mean, more quickly than I'd have thought she would."

"You and I have only known her for a little while."

"True," I say, "but I thought I had a pretty good feel for who she is."

"In other words, I might sleep with a guy I just met but Betsy wouldn't?"

"Well…yeah. You're Tessa, and she's Betsy. What made me think something might be going on with you was that you were so distraught over Garrett leaving last night. That's not you, Tess. You're usually a 'whatever' kind of girl, you know?"

She inhales. "I've been doing some thinking of my own."

"And…?"

"You're right. I haven't been myself the last couple times with Garrett. When he started calling me after I caught him with Lolita, I told him to fuck off. It wasn't until he showed up at yoga that I even considered giving him another chance. Then last night… I'm sorry, Skye."

"For what?"

"For blaming you. Laying a guilt trip on you for not going to dinner with us. I made my own choice to sleep with him."

"Are you sure it was your choice? It may have been the drugs."

"It felt like my choice," she says, "but at this point, I just don't know. I mean, I'm not going to cry rape. I don't have any regrets.

My only regret is getting all teary-eyed over him leaving. I must have been a complete flake."

"No, not at all. But I just kept thinking that it wasn't like you."

"You're right. It wasn't. Thinking about it now, I kind of want to hurl."

"You've hurled enough."

She shakes her head. "Ketamine. I can't even believe it."

"Tess…"

"Yeah?"

"What about the ecstasy you took? The last time?"

"Not my finest moment."

"Where'd you get it?"

"One guess."

"Garrett?"

"Peter, actually. He had it at the club that night. Betsy wouldn't touch it. I took it but just put it in my purse. Then, after the whole Garrett thing, I said what the hell?"

I'm not sure what to say, so I say nothing.

"I know," she says. "You're thinking that isn't like me."

"No, but you weren't on ketamine that night."

"I wasn't. Or I don't think I was. Who the fuck knows anymore? Ketamine isn't the only date rape drug. I'm more than a little freaked out by this."

"So am I."

"It'll be a long time before I accept a drink from anyone that I haven't had analyzed first," she says. "I'm thinking my days of clubbing are over."

I clamp my hand to my mouth in mock shock.

"I know, I know. I like the club scene. But seriously, Skye, this is fucked up."

"You don't have to tell me. I'm so sorry this happened to you."

"So am I. And if it's the last thing I do, I'm going to prove what Garrett did to me."

"Braden's looking into it," I say.

"He is?"

"Yeah. He thinks… Well, I don't have any information, really, but if anyone can figure it out, it's Braden."

"Tell him thanks."

"I will. You okay here?"

She nods. "My mom's out picking up some stuff at the drug store. She'll no doubt drive me back to the vodka bottle for the next couple of days while she stays here, but honestly? I'm glad to have her. It's nice to have parents sometimes."

I smile. "Yeah, it is."

And my heart swells a little.

I think I just forgave my mother.

Chapter Forty-Five

"I'm sorry," I tell Eugenie. "I can't let you trademark hashtags that I created. I'm not sure hashtags can even be trademarked."

"They can," Eugenie says. "Of course we checked with legal first. Hashtags can be trademarked if they serve as an identifier for the company's goods or services."

Crap. I really should have talked to Braden about this first, but with everything going on with Tessa, I didn't have the time.

"That might allow you to trademark susieglow, then, but not simplyskye."

"Of course we could. You're working for us."

I shake my head. "I don't work solely for you. I need to be able to use my own hashtag for other things."

"We're willing to purchase the rights to the hashtags from you," she says, "for ten thousand dollars each."

Twenty grand? Maybe I *can* be bought. I think she hit my price. But...

"I'm sorry. I might be willing to let susieglow go, since I wouldn't be using it for anything else, but not simplyskye."

"Simplyskye is a gold mine," Eugenie says. "We've already

drawn up the documents regarding both hashtags."

My stomach churns, and nausea begins to claw its way up my throat. Eugenie doesn't intimidate me. That's not what's going on here. But right now, Susanne is my sole source of income, other than my bakery at home that pays me in hundred-dollar bills and baguettes.

Braden, what would you do?

Maybe it's not too late. I check my watch. "It's about lunch time. Do you mind if I mull this over for an hour?"

She nods. "Of course. I already ordered lunch in, but if you need the time, I understand." She plasters on a smile that seems fake.

She's pissed off.

She really thought I'd just sign on the dotted line.

And then I know what to do. Not what Braden would tell me to do, but what I know is right for me.

"I changed my mind. I don't need the hour. I'll sign over susieglow but not simplyskye."

"What if we up our bid?"

I shake my head. "Eugenie, I appreciate everything you and everyone else at Susanne has done for my burgeoning career. You all mean the world to me. But I can't let simplyskye go. If my career continues, I'll need it."

In fact, I'll look into trademarking it myself as soon as I get out of this meeting.

"We'll have to draw up new documents." Eugenie frowns.

"I realize that will create extra work for you," I say, "but I didn't agree to this over the phone, as you know."

"Yes, I understand that." Her jawline stiffens. "Very well. Our lunch will be here soon. After we're finished eating, we'll go to the art department and take a look at your new nail color."

My steak-and-avocado salad tastes like dirt. My appetite flew the coop, but I smile and eat and make small talk with Eugenie and her team. By the time we're finished, I'm a little less on edge.

A little.

"All right," Eugenie says. "They're ready for us in the art department, so let's go see the new nail color."

I smile. "I'm excited to see it."

Her smile seems more genuine this time. Maybe she needed to fill her belly. The dirty martini she had her assistant mix for her probably helped as well.

The art department is at the other end of the floor. Eugenie opens the door and walks in. I follow, along with Louisa and Brian.

A woman approaches us. "Eugenie," she says. Then to me, "You must be Skye. I'd recognize you anywhere."

"Yes, hello."

"I'm Adrienne Ficke, the art director. We're thrilled to be working with you on the new shade. Come on. Let's take a look." She takes my arm and leads me to a conference room. Several bottles of nail polish sit on the table. A projector and screen are set up. "We have three prototypes, and we all love number one the best, but we need to get your input."

Amazingly, she's talking more to me than to Eugenie. Eugenie doesn't seem to mind though. She's definitely in a better mood. Adrienne begins going through her PowerPoint showing us how they came up with the shades.

"We took your color swatches and chose three shades to work with. Our main objective was to create a pink that could be worn with anything, so we couldn't go too neon. That's okay, though, because we already have the neon with the Make Things Happen that you used in your power of pink post. We needed a pink that was versatile, that could be worn day or evening, and we think we created three excellent prototypes. As I already told you, our team unanimously votes for number one, but we'd like your input."

My input. I can do this. Color is something I understand well. But I look to Eugenie. She's part of the company, and I'm just a contractor. She should speak first.

"Skye?"

I'm surprised when she defers to me.

"Hmm," I say. "Number two says millennial pink to me. It's a light blush color with just a hint of orange. Kind of like dogwood pink. It's quite pretty, but when I think of the power of pink, it's not really cutting it for me. Plus, even though Susie Girl is marketed to younger women, we don't want to target just millennials."

"My thoughts exactly," Adrienne says. "What do you think of one and three?"

"Three is what I'd call fuchsia or magenta. It's pretty close to the neon of the Make Things Happen that I wore in the original post. It's beautiful, but I'd be hard pressed to pair it with some other colors."

"Yes, yes," she agrees again.

"What do you think, Eugenie?" I ask.

"Color is the art department's baby," she says. "And yours, of course. You have an excellent photographer's eye, Skye."

Okay, maybe she's not upset with me after all. I can't be the first independent contractor to refuse to sign already prepared documents.

"Number one…" I let the color sink into my mind. "It's… It's gorgeous, like nothing I've ever seen before. It's a little watermelon, with…"

"Rosewood. Just a touch of brown."

"It's perfect. It's definitely pink, but that addition of brown gives it the neutrality you're looking for. This color exudes happiness yet will go with any color wardrobe. How did you do it?"

"It's my job." Adrienne smiles.

"I miss that part of being an artist," I say. "As a photographer, I have to work with the colors of my subject. Yes, I can edit, and I can manipulate the lighting, but to create a new color…"

"Nothing's stopping you from getting into art," she says.

"Well…I am. Photography is my first love, but color mixing has always fascinated me. Thank you so much for letting me be a part of this process."

"You came up with the slogan."

"I was simply having a bad day, and I put on some nail polish."

"And it made you feel better?" Adrienne asks.

Did it? I guess it did. It all led to this moment, anyway. The breakups with Braden and Tessa seem far in the past now.

"Yes," I reply. "It made me feel better. A lot better."

"And that's the power of pink," Eugenie chimes in. "I think we're all agreed that number one is the way to go. When will this be on the shelves?"

"That's up to manufacturing, purchasing, and distribution, of course," Adrienne says, "but we're hoping within a month, now that the color has been chosen. You and Skye should begin devising the social media campaign."

Eugenie closes the file folder in front of her. "We're on it. Thanks, Adrienne. This is a gorgeous color. I agree with Skye. I'm not sure I've seen anything like it."

"We're pretty proud of it. Thank you both for your input."

I glide out of the art department alone with Eugenie. This has been fun.

Of course, now we have to get back to the trademark of the susieglow hashtag.

"Tell you what," Eugenie says. "I can probably have the new hashtag paperwork drawn up by this evening. I'll bring it to our dinner date. I'm sure you'd like Braden to look it over."

I drop my mouth open. I haven't even told Braden about any of this. "There's no need. I can stop by and sign it in the morning."

"If it's all the same to you, I'd like to have this put to bed sometime today. I'll bring it to dinner."

"Of course, whatever's easier for you."

Odd. If anything, Braden will be more stringent than I am. But whatever. I love the pink that Adrienne and her team created, and I'm excited about The Power of Pink campaign.

Things are good.

B ack at Braden's Manhattan penthouse, I wait patiently. He's probably at his New York office, and I don't expect him before six at the earliest. Dinner reservations are at eight. No staff is here, so I help myself to a bottle of sparkling water from his fridge and think about what to wear for dinner.

I jerk when the elevator doors open.

It's only three p.m., but in walks Braden.

And he doesn't look happy.

"Skye," he says simply.

"Braden."

"I'm afraid I won't be able to join you and Eugenie for dinner this evening."

"Oh? Why not?"

He inhales. "Something has come up."

"What?"

"Nothing you need to concern yourself with."

"Braden, anything that concerns you concerns me." I draw in a breath. "Is Addison still stalking you?"

His eyebrows nearly fly off his forehead, but he doesn't answer.

"Come on. She has to be. Either that or she's stalking me. Or both of us. How else would she know all the things she knows?

How else would she have ended up at the convenience store across from Tessa's place the other night?"

"I have this handled," he says.

"So she is." I shake my head. "Why didn't you tell me?"

"This isn't as simple as you think."

"Of course it's as simple as I think. Make her stop, legally if you have to. I don't appreciate being spied on."

"Do you think for a minute that I don't have more tails on her than she has on me?"

My mouth drops open.

"I've told you before that I have her watched. Why does this surprise you?"

"What's up with the cat and mouse game, then? Why are you letting her do this?"

He draws in a deep breath. "There are things you don't know."

"Only because you won't tell me."

Have I gone too far? At the moment, I don't rightfully care. I just got through a stressful meeting with the business acumen of Braden Black. I love him, but I don't need him.

And I deserve an answer, damn it.

"Have you considered that I may *not* be able to tell you?"

I widen my eyes. "What?"

He paces away from me for a moment and stares out the window in the living area. Manhattan is gray, as usual. Why do people live here? Boston is so much more beautiful.

He *can't* tell me?

How is that even remotely possible?

Unless…

"Braden, does she have something on you?"

He turns toward me but doesn't meet my gaze. Very un-Braden-like.

Damn. I don't want to be right. I *really* don't want to be right.

If I'm right, that means…

Jesus. Why didn't I listen to Apple? If I had, I'd know right now. I'd know this big secret that Braden is keeping.

"Why are you protecting her?" I ask. "What am I supposed to think? You won't tell me. I can only deduce that she has something on you."

"She doesn't. At least not in the way you're thinking."

"How can you possibly know what I'm thinking?"

"I know *you*, Skye. You think what Betsy told you is true. You think I did something to Addison that I shouldn't have done. You're wrong."

"Prove it to me. Prove to me I'm wrong, then."

"I shouldn't have to prove anything to you. If you will never trust me, how can you still be in this relationship?"

I open my mouth, but find I have no words.

Because he's right.

If I don't trust him, I have no business being in a relationship with him.

I made a promise to myself. To him. That I'd give him time to tell me. And now I'm welching?

"I'm sorry," I finally say. "I promised I wouldn't push. I do trust you, Braden. I know you're a good man. I couldn't be with you if I didn't believe that."

He strides toward me and pulls me to his chest. "I know you trust me, Skye. You've proved that many times over. You have to trust me with this as well."

"I do." I nod into his shoulder.

He pushes me away slightly and meets my gaze. "I will tell you what you want to know, but I need your promise that it goes no further than you."

"I tell Tessa everything."

"Not this. I can make you sign an NDA like you did for the club."

"That's not necessary. I won't tell Tessa about the club, and

I won't tell her anything you don't want me to."

"Good. And it's not just Tessa. You can't tell *anyone* what I'm about to tell you. Especially not Addie or that friend of hers."

"Who?"

"The one who owns the dog supply store."

"Betsy? She and Addie aren't really friends."

"Maybe not, but she knows some of this. You can't tell her anything more. Got it?"

I look into those beautiful blue eyes. They're laced with a tad bit of sadness. Just a touch, but I can see it. He's sorry he has to do this, but he's willing to do this. For me.

"Of course, Braden. You can trust me. With anything."

Chapter Forty-Six

I listen.
Simply listen, letting Braden's words morph into pictures in my mind.

...

She was beautiful, if you like blondes. Braden had always favored darker hair.

"They're both on the prowl," Ben said to him. "And they've got their eyes on us. Might be a lucky night for the Black bros. We can get some high-class pussy."

"Shut the fuck up," Braden said.

"What's up your ass?"

"Nothing. I'm just not in the mood."

"Not in the mood for sex?" Ben laughed. "Fine. Have a drink. Have five drinks. I'm going to get me some of that." He walks toward the Ames sisters.

Identical twins, both blond and beautiful. Ben began working his magic on the one with longer hair. Soon they disappeared.

The other one, though.

She was... Braden couldn't put his finger on it. She was staring at him, trying to get his attention all night, but something was off with her.

Still...he hadn't had sex in a while. When you worked construction six days a week in the hot sun, you were dirty as a pig and fucking exhausted the rest of the time. What little free time he had he spent researching. He had an idea—an idea that could be big. He just had to figure out how to get it off the ground. With so little time and even less money, it didn't seem likely. Still, it was his dream, and he spent his off time working on it. No time to get dressed up and cruise for chicks. How could he find women who liked what he liked, anyway? Not all girls let a guy tie them up. At twenty-four, he was getting too old for casual sex. Ben was barely twenty-one and still liked flashing his ID at bars.

This was his scene, not Braden's.

Ben had heard about the party at the Ames' mansion through a friend of a friend. When he suggested they check it out, Braden finally agreed. They'd had the day off work, so he wasn't dead tired as he usually was. While the time might have been better spent working on his ground floor idea, Ben had finally persuaded him.

The other Ames twin approached him.

Braden looked around. Shit. No escape. The house was getting crowded.

She smiled at him. "Hi there. Welcome. I'm Addison Ames."

"Braden Black."

"Who's your friend? The one who went off with my sister?"

"He's not my friend. He's my brother, Ben."

"Oh. So what do you do, Braden Black?"

"Construction."

Her eyes nearly popped out of her head. "Construction? Do you live around here?"

He shook his head. "South Boston."

She smiled. South Boston seemed to please her. Why? He didn't know.

"Can I get you a drink?" she asked.

"Wild Turkey."

"What's that?"

"Bourbon."

"Oh. Well, we have several bourbons. Follow me."

She guided him to the bar. "Hmm. Buffalo Trace. Eagle Rare. Kentucky Gold. No Wild Turkey. Sorry."

"Any of those is fine."

"Okay." She poured two fingers into a glass and handed it to him.

He took a drink. Nice. Smooth.

He could get used to this.

"Want to go to my room?" she asked.

He nearly spit out his mouthful of booze. "Excuse me?"

"You heard me. You're hot. Let's get busy."

"Exactly how old are you?" he asked.

"Oh, I'm legal. I'm eighteen. I'll even show you my ID if you want."

"It's not legal for you to drink what I'm drinking, then."

"No, it's not. But it's legal for me to have sex. That's what I'm after tonight."

He took another drink. Yeah, she was beautiful. And ready and willing. A quick fuck might be nice.

But a quick fuck had never been what Braden was after. He had more…exclusive tastes.

He finished his drink and set the empty glass back on the wooden bar. "That's a nice offer, but I have to pass."

Anger flashed in her eyes.

He got it. He was turning down an Ames hotel heiress, and she was pissed.

Well, she'd get over it.

"Thanks for the drink," he said. "If you see my brother, tell him I went home."

...

*B*raden had a small apartment near the rental where his dad lived. Ben still lived with their dad, but he spent a lot of time crashing at Braden's.

"Time you started chipping in for rent," Braden said.

"Aren't you going to ask me about my evening last night?"

"I already know how your evening was. You plucked an Ames twin. You got laid. That's why you have that dumbass smile on your face."

Ben kind of always had that dumbass smile on his face, but this morning it was more dumbass than usual.

Man, six o'clock in the morning came early.

Ben seemed raring to go, though. Getting his rocks off agreed with him. Of course it pretty much agreed with all men.

Braden poured himself a cup of coffee and took a drink. "Damn!"

"You burn your mouth every time," Ben said. "Think you'd learn by now."

"It's what gets me moving. Come on. We're going to be late."

Ben nodded.

One thing the Black boys had in abundance was work ethic. They both had their issues with their dad, but he'd taught them that much. He'd learned the hard way, burning their house to the ground when the boys were little. Their mother never fully recovered, but she'd saved both their lives.

...

"She saved you?" I ask.

Braden nods.

"There's so much you haven't told me about your mother."

"It's all related to the story I'm telling you," he says. "Be patient."

Patience isn't my strong suit, but I'm getting better. I nod.

...

No clouds at all that day. None. The sun was blistering hot, and by the end of the nearly ten-hour day, Braden was dehydrated, fatigued, and sunburnt. Ben had gone out for a beer with some of the guys, but Braden only wanted to get home and take a cool shower.

So he was more than a little surprised when someone was waiting for him at his truck.

Addison Ames. The heiress from the party last night. She wore denim cutoffs and a hot pink crop top. Her belly was flat and her navel sported a pink jeweled piercing.

"Hello there, Mr. Black," she said.

"It's Braden. What can I do for you?"

"I could use a ride."

"Yeah? How did you get here?"

"Just happened to be in the area."

Okay. That could be true. They were working on a mall near the Ames house. But she was lying. Braden could tell.

"Sorry, I have somewhere to be. I'll be happy to call you a cab."

"Don't be like that." She batted her long brown eyelashes. Then she went around to the passenger side and slid right into his truck.

Shit. Now what? He was tired and dirty and really didn't need this distraction.

He got in. "Fine. I'll drive you home."

He did, only to find her waiting for him again at the end of work the next day.

This went on for four days straight, until he finally said, "No dice today, Ms. Ames."

"Call me Addie."

"No dice, Addie. Find your own way home." Braden got in his truck and left her there, hands upon her hips.

He hadn't seen the last of her. He knew that. But he was tired of her games.

He hadn't given her any reason to think she had a chance, though he was close to losing control around her. She was beautiful, and she was offering.

His age, which he'd used the first night to keep himself in check, wasn't working anymore. He was still damned young with a damned strong libido.

So this had to stop now.

Unless…

Could she possibly give him what he wanted?

He wasn't looking for love, but he wouldn't mind a roll in the hay. Several rolls even, as long as they were on his terms.

The next day, she wasn't waiting for him after work.

Good enough. No roll in the hay, and that was okay, too. She'd finally gotten the message.

He drove home, and—

"Fuck," he said under his breath.

Addison Ames, this time dressed in a trench coat—yeah, a trench coat in this heat—was waiting outside the door to his apartment.

Braden's jeans were covered in sawdust, and what seemed like five layers of grime covered his body and lay beneath his fingernails.

"What are you doing here?" he demanded.

"What do you think?"

"I'm exhausted." He unlocked his door. "I don't have time for these games. Go slumming somewhere else."

She pushed out her lower lip, and he couldn't help himself. He thought about biting it.

Hard.

"You sure that's what you want?" she teased.

No, he wasn't sure at all. In fact, despite his fatigue, he was getting hard.

Fuck. Just what he didn't need.

"That's what I want," he said gruffly.

She opened her trench coat. "Still sure?"

Chapter Forty-Seven

"Seriously? She flashed you in the parking lot?"

"She did." Braden nods.

"And since you're a guy…"

"I was younger then," he says, as if that's a good excuse. "Hey, you wanted to know all this."

I sigh. "You're right. Go on."

. . .

Mother fuck.

She wore a leather bra with holes for her nipples. And those nipples were clamped. Already clamped. Fucking god damn.

She'd replaced the pink jewel in her navel with an onyx barbell, and the only thing covering the rest of her was a black leather thong.

She pulled a black riding crop out of her pocket.

"You'll never use that on me," he said.

"I know." She inched closer to him. "You're going to use it on me."

He was tired. So tired. And horny.

He didn't know this woman. Hell, she was barely a woman. But she was legal, and that was all that mattered.

"I need a shower," he said, more to himself than to her.

"Fine. Take one." She closed the distance between them, her clamped nipples nearly touching his chest. "And it doesn't have to be cold."

He was done fighting her. She wanted this? Fine. He'd give it to her. But on his terms.

"Let's get one thing straight," he said, meeting her horny gaze. "If I let you in, if we do this, we do it my way, got it?"

"Absolutely. I know what you like."

"How the hell would you know?"

"I've done my research, Mr. Black. Lots of research."

"What the hell kind of research would tell you what I like?"

"Trade secret." She smiled coyly. "But you like what I'm wearing, don't you?"

He couldn't deny it. She was a Dominant's wet dream. But he wasn't a Dominant. Not really. He liked bondage especially, and he wasn't averse to spanking and flogging, but to have total domination over someone? That wasn't him. He couldn't imagine it.

• • •

"You couldn't?" I ask.

"I've told you before," Braden says. "We were both young and inexperienced. Neither of us knew what we were doing."

"But—"

He places his fingers over my lips. "Shh. We'll get there."

• • •

*H*e had no idea how Addie knew his tastes, but somehow she did. "I need your consent," he said.

"You have it."

"And I'm going to give you a safe word."

"Whatever you want."

He opened the door and allowed her to enter his apartment. "Your safe word is black."

"Your name?"

"My last name, yeah."

"What if I call out your name in passion?"

"Then you'll call out my first name."

"No. I want to call out Mr. Black."

This was getting creepy now. "Do you have some kind of daddy fetish or something?"

"Don't be silly. You're way too young to be my daddy."

"I am, but I'm not into that. You will not call me Mr. Black. Understand?"

She smiled again. "Of course. Whatever you want, sir."

Sir. Hmm. He could live with that. "Good. Call me sir. And your safe word is black."

• • •

"**Y**ou never asked me to call you sir," I say. "And you've never given me a safe word."

"For God's sake, Skye, would you just let me finish? You've been pestering me for weeks to tell you all this. I'm not the same man I was then. Are you the same as you were eleven years ago?"

"Well, eleven years ago I was thirteen, so I'm going to say no."

His lips quirk. "I ought to bring you over my knee and give that cute ass of yours the spanking from hell."

My core throbs. "Okay," I say coyly.

"Sorry, babe. This is your one chance to hear this story. So choose. The spanking or this."

I could tell him I choose the story, that I know he'll spank me later. But that's not Braden. If I choose the story, he will intentionally *not* spank me later, no matter how much I crave it.

I'm caught between a rock and a hard place, my usual spot with Braden.

"Continue," I say. "I need to know, and I think maybe you need to tell me."

Chapter Forty-Eight

*S*he nodded.

"No, tell me in words."

"Yes, I agree to all that."

"All what?"

"I'll call you sir, and my safe word is black."

"And you'll do what I want."

"God, yes," she said breathlessly. *"I'll do whatever you want. Sir."*

Braden's cock was hard inside his jeans. *"I'm going to take a shower. I'm a mess."*

"I think you look great," she said. *"All dirty after a day of hard work. Work that gives you those amazing muscles."*

"Are you saying you don't want me to take a shower?"

"No," she said. *"I want you just as you are. You're so hot."*

Braden walked toward her, intentionally not touching her. *"Honey, this isn't about what you want."* He walked to his bathroom, stripped off his clothes, and got under the pelting water.

He scrubbed his body clean with lukewarm water, wondering what he'd find once he was done. Most likely, she'd realize what *she'd gotten into and turn tail and run. That'd be okay. He'd jack off and be done with it. Not like he'd never done that before. It was most of the sex he had these days.*

He stepped out of the shower, dried his hair and body, and then wrapped a towel around his waist.

Here goes nothing. *He opened the door and walked out into the living area.*

He'd gone over in his mind what he might find. Most likely she'd be gone. If not, she might have gone into the small kitchen area and gotten a couple beers out of the fridge. Maybe some bourbon. Maybe just some ice water. That sounded great right about now.

Or maybe she'd have discarded her trench coat and be lying spread eagle on his bed.

Those were the things he expected.

Not what he got.

Addison was kneeling by his bed.

Kneeling.

This woman knew something about submission. More than Braden knew at this point.

And he was more than slightly turned on.

He walked to her. "What's going on here?"

"May I look you in the eye, sir?"

She asked permission to look him in the eye? This was what she wanted? What she thought he wanted?

Fine. He'd give it a try. It was kinky. What the hell?

"You may."

She raised her head, meeting his gaze with her neck bent backward. "What can I do to please you?"

"Bring me your flogger and then get on the bed."

She walked to her trench coat, got the flogger out of the pocket, and then sat down on the bed. She held the flogger out to him as if in offering.

Okay, he could live with this.

"This is a two way street," Braden said to her. "I'm going to tell you what I want to do, and you have the choice to say no."

"I've already consented. I don't want that choice."

"I think I've told you before. This isn't about what you want."

"Yes, sir," she said. "But I want what you want."

"You may think that. I'm giving you the choice. Do you understand?"

"Yes, sir."

"Good. We understand each other. I will ask you each time we do something new whether I have your consent, and I want it verbally. No headshakes or nods, got it? I need a verbal yes or a verbal no."

"I understand, sir. But it will always be yes."

She certainly had a one-track mind. Great. Whatever. He'd see soon enough how far she was willing to go. Braden had wanted to experiment with some BDSM for a while now, but finding a willing partner had been an issue.

Now, one had walked right into his life. A fucking hotel heiress, for God's sake. But she was legal, so what the hell?

In the back of his mind, something nudged at his neck. That what he was about to do might be a huge mistake.

But he was erect, and a woman was on her knees in front of him.

He ignored the voice of his conscience.

It was the last time he'd do so.

· · ·

"Really?" I ask. "You knew you shouldn't be doing it?"

He nods. "It wasn't that I thought we were going to do anything wrong. You know my tastes. You share them. But I was inexperienced, and I was about to embark on something dark with someone I knew nothing about. She seemed to know much more about me than I did about her."

"It does seem unlike you."

"It does. Now. Then? I can't really tell you. I was young and horny, and she was offering."

I scoff. "Men are pigs."

He chuckles. "I suppose I should be offended by that."

"And you're not?"

He shakes his head. "I'm not. Men—especially young men— have the habit of thinking with the wrong head."

"You don't do that."

"No, I don't. Not anymore."

Not since that time in my life.

He doesn't say those words, but they're clear as day, buzzing in my head as if he actually uttered them.

"Go on," I say.

Chapter Forty-Nine

He didn't bind her that first time. He simply made her stay on her hands and knees while he flogged her ass until it was pink. Then he fucked her from behind.

. . .

"Skye?"

I exhale. "Yeah?"

"You okay?"

I wait a few seconds, gathering my thoughts. "Yes. It's just harder than I thought to hear you say you fucked her."

"I did fuck her. You already know that."

I inhale again. Exhale. "I know. But hearing you say it…"

"Would you prefer a little less detail?"

"Maybe. Let's keep it on a need-to-know basis, okay? Explain what happened and what the final result was."

"Without explaining how we got there?"

"Fuck." I bite my lower lip. "I don't know."

"I wasn't planning to paint a picture in your mind, Skye. All I said was I flogged her and then I fucked her. To me, that's not a lot of detail. I'm hardly painting a picture."

"But you *are* painting a picture. I'm an artist. I see pictures in everything. How do you think I figure out what to photograph?"

"Then you're creating the picture yourself."

He's not wrong. "I know."

"You want me to fast forward?"

"Maybe just a little."

"Good enough."

. . .

The affair went on for several weeks. They got together on Braden's days off and experimented with BDSM. He bound her wrists, her ankles, sometimes all four appendages. And he spanked her and flogged her. Braden was content to leave it there.

But Addison wanted more.

When he refused to go further, she began the stalking again. She showed up at his workplace and his apartment.

Braden did some reading up, and finally consented to go further.

They began with more elaborate bondage. Eventually he added some sensory deprivation and experimented with hot and cold.

It was Addison who brought up erotic asphyxiation.

. . .

"So that's why it's your hard limit," I say.

"Because she brought it up? No."

"Then why?"

"For God's sake, Skye. Be patient."

I sigh and nod. Patience will be the death of me.

"I did some research. I thought I could handle it."

"And you couldn't?"

"I've told you before. We were both inexperienced. Totally in over our heads."

• • •

After a lot of research, Braden was ready to bind Addie's neck and try some minimal choking. The scene started with getting them both worked up through a series of flogging and breast play and then going to oral. When Addie was good and turned on, Braden tied a loop around her neck, kind of like a doggie choke collar.

He gave it a yank right when the orgasm was imminent, and Addie came.

"That was incredible!" she exclaimed when it was over.

Braden admitted it was amazing to watch. Amazing to exert that amount of control over another person's pleasure.

He thought he'd found his calling. He was good at this. Good at taking control. At dominating. Perhaps he was a Dominant after all, though he disliked labels.

They practiced neck binding and breath control several more times, each time Braden taking more and more of her air to induce erotic asphyxiation.

Until the last time—

• • •

B raden stops talking mid-sentence.
"You can't stop now. I just got used to the image in my mind of you going down on her. This isn't fair."

"This isn't easy for me to talk about," he says.

"You've come this far."

He nods and continues.

. . .

B raden was hard, so hard, and he had Addie going. Her eyes were closed, and he'd teased her with a few small yanks.

"You want more?" he asked.

"Yes. Please, sir."

Another soft yank.

"More?"

"Yes, sir. Please." Her voice was breathy, airy.

He circled her clit with his fingers while, with his other hand, he pulled on the restraint around her neck. "Tell me you want it. Tell me you want me to choke you. Hard."

"Yes, sir," she said. "I want you to choke me hard. Harder, please, sir."

He gave the rope one last yank as he thrust his cock into her. It didn't take long for him to come, and when he withdrew...

She was limp. Addie had gone limp.

"Addie?"

No response.

He moved her onto her back. Her eyes were closed, her neck still bound. Quickly he removed the rope. "Addie! Wake up!"

He placed his fingers at her neck. Thank God. Her pulse was light, but it was there.

What the hell had he done?

911. Call 911. And tell them what? That he'd choked a woman

in his bed? Not the best idea.

He patted her cheek. Soft at first, and then harder. "Come on! Wake up, Addie! Come on!"

Time passed in a trance. Minutes ticked by like hours. After five minutes had passed, he grabbed his phone. Yeah, he'd probably go to prison, but he couldn't let her die.

He was ready to push in the numbers, when—

"Sir?"

Addie's voice. Soft and raspy, but still her voice. He heaved a sigh of relief. "Thank God!" He touched her cheek. "Are you okay? Can you breathe?"

"Yeah." She sucked in a breath and then let it out in a squeaky wheeze. "What happened?"

"You lost consciousness for a few minutes. Fuck. Are you all right?"

"I'm fine." Her voice was still a mess. "It was amazing, sir. Amazing."

"Amazing? You pass out and call it amazing?"

"Isn't that the point?"

"For fuck's sake, Addie, you could have died!"

"No, that's the point. Lose consciousness and the orgasm. God, sir, the orgasm…"

"I don't give a shit if it was the most amazing orgasm in the world and you flew to fucking Jupiter. We're never doing that again."

"But sir, I want—"

Braden's relief morphed into anger. "You're forgetting something. This has never been about what *you* want. It's about what *I* want. And I say we're done with this."

"Sir, if you only knew how it felt."

"I think I just said I don't care. I'm taking you to the ER to get you checked out."

"I'm fine."

"Your voice doesn't sound right."

"So I'm slightly hoarse. It'll heal."

"We're going to the ER."

Braden stood over her as she got dressed and then they drove to the nearest emergency room. Braden was honest with the doctor and told him exactly what happened.

"You're a lucky woman," the doctor said to Addie. "I recommend you never engage in this behavior again."

Afterward, Braden drove Addie home in his truck. "I think we need some time apart," he said to her.

"Time apart? Why, sir?"

"Because I'm not comfortable with what happened. I need to think about what we've been doing. Think about whether I want to be a part of it anymore."

"But, sir—"

"Do I need to remind you again? This has never been about what you *want."*

"Will you call me?" she asked.

"No," he said adamantly. "I won't."

A week went by, and then another.

Braden was relieved that she was out of his life. He'd discovered a lot that he liked in the bedroom, and one thing that he hated. Something he'd never do again, no matter what. No matter how careful you were with breath control, there was always a risk.

Braden was a risk taker. He always had been.

But he was not willing to risk a person's life.

He was relieved the relationship—if you could call it that— was over.

Turned out it wasn't.

The stalking began again.

Addie waited by his truck after work, this time wearing a black jumpsuit and a choker made of braided black velvet.

"Please, sir," she begged. "I need it. I need you.*"*

"I've told you it's over," he said. "This isn't about what you want."

"You miss me. You must. We were so in sync."

"We were in over our heads."

"But we've learned. We can do better."

"No," he said flatly. "It's over."

When the stalking didn't stop, he finally had no choice. He called the police.

. . .

"So you didn't dump her because she wouldn't get kinky."

"Of course I didn't. I was frightened, Skye. Wouldn't you be?"

"Yeah. Yeah, I would be. I can't believe she wanted to try it again."

"Apparently the climax was that good," he says.

"More likely she just didn't want to let you go. Did you consider getting back with her and just doing the other stuff?"

"Yeah, I considered it. But after she continued stalking me, I realized I wasn't dealing with a rational person. She was so used to getting what she wanted that she couldn't handle not having me. That wasn't a person I wanted any long-term involvement with."

"So you were never in love with her?"

"How can you ask me that?"

"It's a valid question."

"Valid, yes, but unnecessary. You already know the answer. I've told you I never loved a woman until you, Skye."

Chapter Fifty

My body warms all over and my heart nearly melts from the heat of his words.

Braden is a man who says so much by saying nothing. It's easy to forget that, but I promise myself that from now on I'll remember.

He never loved Addie.

"Was she in love with you?"

"She thought she was."

"She said that?"

"A couple of times, while she was stalking me after the incident. Contrary to popular belief, I *do* have feelings. I just don't wear them on my sleeve. I felt bad for her, but I wasn't in love with her. Besides, what she wanted to do was dangerous. It was easier for me to just nip it in the bud."

"Lesser men might have stayed with her for the money."

"Lesser men might have. I won't say it didn't occur to me, but if I was ever going to be rich, I wanted it to be on my own terms."

"And it is."

"It is," he echoes, though he doesn't sound completely convinced.

"Braden?"

He sighs. "The story's not over, Skye."

I swallow. "All right. Go on."

. . .

The day after Braden called the police, he got a visit from Addison's father, Brock Ames. Instead of Addie waiting by his pickup after work, Brock stood there, dressed to the nines in a tailored gray pinstripe and smoking a pipe. Braden inhaled the cherry bark fragrance. Nice, but smoking wasn't something he'd ever do.

"Mr. Black." Brock emptied the ashes from his pipe onto the ground and held out his hand. "I'm Brock Ames."

"I know who you are," Braden said.

"Then I suppose you know why I'm here."

"Can't say I do."

"I'd like you to drop the charges against my daughter."

"Mr. Ames, your daughter has been stalking me. She shows up here by my truck after work, not unlike you did today. She shows up at my home. She calls me at all hours of the day and night. It needs to stop."

"I don't think formal charges are the answer."

"Really? What is the answer, then?"

"Drop the charges, and I'll make it worth your while."

"What are you going to do? Ship her off to Europe or something? She's eighteen. She's an adult."

"In the eyes of the law, yes, but she's still a very young girl."

Braden met Brock's gaze. How did one tell a father what his daughter was capable of? "Don't try to tell me she doesn't know what she's doing. She knows exactly *what she's doing."*

"What if I told you"—Brock cleared his throat—"that I'd have you arrested for sexual assault."

"I'd tell you to fuck off." Braden hadn't assaulted Addie. Everything was consensual. Despite his words, though, his nerves skittered. Brock Ames was a powerful man.

"Addie will testify that you assaulted her, and she lost consciousness," Brock continued.

Braden's fingers curled into fists. "That never happened."

"Do you think that matters?"

Chills swept over the back of Braden's neck. "You fucking bastard…"

"Easy, Mr. Black. I can see you're an intelligent man."

"We went to the ER. She corroborated what I told the doctor."

"And she can easily say you coerced her into her corroboration."

"So you're saying you'll blackmail me if I don't drop the stalking charges? Is that what this is about?"

"Blackmail is such a negative term," he said, grinding his pipe ashes into the blacktop with his Italian leather–clad foot. "I prefer to think of this as two people making a deal."

"A deal where you have all the leverage," Braden said through clenched teeth.

"You may find it interesting to know that Addie thinks she's in love with you. She doesn't want to make any assault claims."

"Then why are we having this conversation?"

"Because she will make the claim…if I threaten to cut her off."

Money. Rage gripped Braden. It all came down to money. If he ever had money in his life, he would never use it to control others.

Fucking never.

"So we're back to blackmail, then," Braden said.

"Not necessarily. We're back to the drawing board where we'll make our deal."

• • •

"How did you not punch his lights out?" I ask.

"Trust me. It was difficult," he says, "but that would have only made things worse."

"I never found any record of any charges against you or against Addie."

"When you were nosing around," he says.

"Well…yeah. You know I was curious. But I haven't looked recently, Braden. Believe me. I made a decision to respect your right to tell me in your own time."

"I know." He smiles.

God, how I love that smile. He seems to smile more lately, now that the understanding between us has increased.

"So what ultimately happened?"

"We struck a deal," he says. "A deal that changed my life."

Chapter Fifty-One

"*Have you ever seen* The Godfather*?*" *Brock asked.*
Braden shook his head. They never had cable TV growing up, and now he didn't have time to watch TV or stream movies. He was either working or sleeping.

"*Too bad,*" *Brock said.*

"*Why?*"

"*Because I'm about to make you an offer you can't refuse.*"

Braden didn't respond. He simply lifted his eyebrows, waiting.

"*Here's what's going to happen,*" *Brock said.* "*You're going to drop the charges against my daughter and agree to never speak about what happened between the two of you again.*"

"*And she'll stop stalking me?*"

"*She'll attempt to stop.*"

Braden shook his head. "*No deal.*"

"*I know my daughter. She's just throwing a tantrum. She's not getting what she wants. It's her way.*"

"*Her way? I'm supposed to put up with her little fits?*"

Brock cleared his throat. "*In return, I'll finance your move to another place. She won't be able to find you.*"

"I have to leave Boston?"

"Yeah. But you can find work in construction anywhere."

"Maybe I don't want to leave Boston. My father and brother are here."

"So? I've done some research, Mr. Black. There's no love lost between you and your father. And your mother… Well, she's no longer an issue, is she?"

Rage, again. Reddish-purple rage. How dare this motherfucker speak about his family? About his mother?

Braden kept his mouth glued shut, though, as difficult as it was. No way was he going to let his temper dictate what happened next. No fucking way.

"I'm not moving," Braden finally said.

"That's your prerogative. But Addie knows where to find you. The stalking, as you like to call it, may continue."

"As I like to call it? What the fuck do you call it?"

"I call it simply an attempt to keep in touch."

Braden clenched his hands into fists once more. "I can't believe this. I don't want to move. I won't move." He was adamant. Boston was his home. He didn't want to live anywhere else.

"So you're rejecting my offer?"

"I'm rejecting your first offer. I'd like to make a counteroffer."

"I'm not entertaining any counteroffers, Mr. Black. This is my one and only offer."

"And if I refuse?"

"Addie will go to the police and allege assault."

Braden's skin tightened around him, his heart thundering. "You won't get away with this. The truth is on my side."

"Maybe so, but are you willing to take that chance? I'll have the best lawyers advising the prosecution, and you'll go down for a crime you didn't commit."

Fuck. Brock knew Braden hadn't assaulted Addie. He fucking knew. If only he had a tape recorder on him. A wire. Then he could prove that Brock had just admitted Braden hadn't committed any crime. He opened his mouth to call Brock out on his lie—

Then something hit him like a lightning bolt.

Money.

This all came down to money. Brock had it. Braden didn't.

"How much will that cost you?" Braden asked.

"What?"

"Those greedy lawyers who will advise the prosecution. Don't forget the judge. You may have to buy him off. How much will it ultimately cost you to bring me down?"

"Money doesn't matter."

"Not to you. So how much?"

Brock narrowed his eyes. "Six figures. Possibly seven."

"Here's your counteroffer," Braden said, "and you'd do well to entertain it. Keep your little darling out of the spotlight and your money out of lawyers' hands. Give it to me instead. I'll drop the charges, and you guarantee me that this is over. Fucking over."

"Meaning?"

"Meaning your daughter will never make false allegations against me. I want it in writing, signed by both you and her. I'll sign as well that I'll never talk about the incident that put her in the emergency room. I'll never talk to her again, if that's what it takes."

"Addie won't agree to that."

"Make her agree."

"As you said before, Mr. Black. She's an adult. She thinks she loves you."

"A million. That's what it would cost you to ruin my life. Give it to me instead, and I'll sign whatever you want."

Brock narrowed his gaze. He was considering it.

Good.

"A quarter million," he finally said. "And you never call the police on Addie again."

"No deal."

"Half a million."

Braden smiled. That was what he was after. Half a mill. He could get his new product off the ground with that.

"Half a million," he said, "and Addie stops stalking me."

"I've told her to stop, but I can't control what she ultimately does."

"Then I can't guarantee I'll never call the police on her again."

Brock met Braden's gaze, his own determined. "No wavering on that part of the deal. You cannot call the police on my daughter. Not ever. I'll write it into the agreement if I have to. Otherwise, you'll have my assurance that you won't be prosecuted on any false allegations. And there will be a non-disclosure agreement."

. . .

My eyes are dinner plates. "You agreed."

Braden clears his throat. "I did."

"And Addie…"

"Has been stalking me since."

My heart thuds. "Your business…"

"Was seeded with Brock Ames's money," he says, his voice monotone. "And I signed a document stating I'd never talk about what went on between Addie and me."

"So that's why…"

"That's why I couldn't tell you, Skye. Why I shouldn't be telling you now. Though it probably doesn't matter. I can now buy and sell the Ames business. If I crack, what can they do to me? Sue me, but then it all comes out anyway."

"Why wouldn't you tell me, then? At first, I mean."

"Because I'm a man of my word, Skye. A man is nothing without his word."

And now he's no longer a man of his word. He told me.

But not because I goaded him into it.

He told me because he loves me. Because he trusts me. And if we're going to have a relationship, there can be no big secrets between us.

"I learned some valuable things from Brock Ames that day," he continues. "First, never take the first offer, even if the other party says it's the only offer."

I nod.

"Second, I learned that a man is only as good as his word. Brock kept his word to me. Addie never made any false accusations, and she hasn't spoken of any details of our time together—"

"She hasn't? Then how does Apple know? Betsy?"

"She most likely told Betsy before the agreement. As for Apple, she's family and was there, so she probably witnessed a lot of what went on." Braden shoves his hands in his pockets. "Addie's still a spoiled brat at heart. The stalking never stopped, Skye. In fact, it continues to this day."

"So that's how…" My mind churns.

"It's no doubt how she knew about the nipple clamps. The anal plug. Our breakup. She's had me watched since then. What she doesn't know is that I've had her watched since I could afford to. If she steps out of line, I'll know it, and I'll stop it."

"You don't consider her knowing about an anal plug out of line?"

"My place is as secure as it gets. Yours isn't. At least not yet. I didn't feel it was right to have security installed in your home without telling you first."

"Good call," I say.

"Addie is virtually harmless. I ignore her, for the most part, but sometimes the devil on my shoulder gets the better of me. I can't be too upset about that, though. It is, after all, how you and I met."

I smile. "Your comment on her coffee post. Of course."

"The woman hates coffee. She always has. Sometimes it's something so small like that that sets me off."

"I get it. Honestly."

"I'm sure you do, after working for her."

"She knows I love coffee, and do you know she never once offered to give me the drink? She always threw it out."

"Not surprising," Braden says. "Everything's disposable to her."

"Except for you." I frown.

"Apparently. She never got over me. But it may be because of my money and status now."

I think for a moment. Sure, Braden has money and status now, but he didn't then. But he did have one thing.

Himself.

He was always Braden Black. Always a magnificent and amazing man.

"I don't think so," I tell him. "I think she'd still be after you no matter what. But we can't live like this, Braden. I can't live my life knowing she's watching every move I make."

"She might be watching you anyway," he says. "After all, you're in her territory now."

"Meaning I have you?"

He chuckles. "No, Skye. I was never her territory. I'm talking about social media influencing."

I scoff at myself. Of course, he's right. "I'll never be where she is."

"Don't sell yourself short. You have something she doesn't."

"You?" I giggle.

"You're incorrigible. No. You have *you*. You have Skye Manning, and Skye Manning is a real person. A person everyone relates to. Your gift is *you*."

Your gift is you.

With those words, I float on air.

I see myself in a new light.

Yes, I have Braden, and if Braden loves me, that must mean I'm something special.

But that's not what truly makes me special.

I'm me. I'm #*simplyskye*.

And that's something no one else has, not even Addison Ames.

Wouldn't the world be wonderful if personal people saw themselves as gifts?

This, right here, is the greatest thing anyone has ever done for me.

"I'll love you forever for saying that, Braden." I wrap my arms around his neck.

"I'll love you forever just because you're you," he says back.

Chapter Fifty-Two

"That's how I know Addie isn't over you. Because you're you. You're Braden. You're not a construction worker. You're not a billionaire. You're just Braden Black, and you're incredible."

He smiles. Really smiles. Maybe now I'll see that real smile more. But it lasts only a moment before he frowns.

"What's the matter?"

"You know my secret now."

"About you and Addie. Yeah. I'm sorry she got hurt."

"So am I, but that's not what I'm talking about. I always wanted to be rich on my own terms, but I'm not. You know I had help setting up my company."

"You mean Brock Ames's money?"

He nods.

I laugh. I seriously laugh almost uncontrollably.

"I don't see what's funny about that from where I'm standing."

"Aren't you the one who told me that opportunity is opportunity? That I should use all resources available to me as I build my career? My God, I spent weeks thinking I wasn't good enough. That I was only wanted because I was Braden Black's girlfriend. Even that the contacts I had were from Addie."

His lips quirk up slightly.

"And besides, it wasn't Brock Ames's money. It was *your* money. You and he made a deal."

"Which I just broke."

"For me. For us. And you have my word that the story won't leave this room. I swear on my mother's life. On my father's life. On my own life. On my love for you."

His lips quirk up farther.

"Besides," I go on, "you had an ironclad stalking case against Addison. You dropped it in exchange for half a million dollars and assurance that you wouldn't be prosecuted for something you didn't do. Brock Ames probably got off cheap. It would have cost him a lot more to fabricate a case against you and pay off everyone to see things his way."

"All true," Braden agrees.

"So it wasn't Brock's money. It was yours."

He chuckles then, shaking his head. "This right here. This is why I love you, Skye."

"*This* is why you love me? Because I helped you see something you already knew?"

"Well, this and about a thousand other reasons."

I melt into him and wrap my arms around his neck. "Better." I brush my lips across his.

He still hasn't told me about his mother, but we've had enough for one day. I won't push.

"I need to get ready for my dinner with Eugenie," I say.

He nods. "I'm sorry I can't join you."

"Are you sure? I really want you there."

"I wish I could, but there's something that needs my immediate attention."

I sigh. "Okay, but I have to tell you something first." I relay the story of the hashtags.

"Good for you. You shouldn't sell simplyskye. It's yours."

"And susieglow?"

"I'm okay with that. You wouldn't be using it for anything other than your work with Susanne anyway. Companies pay for creations all the time."

A bag of bricks falls from my shoulders. Braden agrees with me. I did the right thing. I knew it at the time, but I feel great knowing he agrees and would have advised me the same.

Maybe I'm ready to truly make my own business decisions. I'll love his input, of course, but I can make the final decisions myself.

For a minute, I'm wearing a tight Wonder Woman suit. I feel totally empowered.

And I like the feeling. I like it a lot.

Braden gives me a searing kiss. "I have to go. I'm sorry. The limo is downstairs and will take you to dinner when you're ready."

"I understand. And thanks."

"For what?"

"For trusting me."

He nods briefly and within a few seconds, he's in the elevator heading down. Away from me. To do what? Something about Addie? Something about Tessa? He was going to look into the ketamine situation, where Addie just happened to be that night.

It can't possibly all be related. Can it?

No time to think about that now. I dress for dinner in a pink camisole, black skinny pants, and a gray blazer. Businesslike yet sexy. I like the look.

I have a few minutes before I need to head down to the limo. A good time to check in on Tessa.

"Hey," she says into my ear.

"Hi. Just checking in. How are you feeling?"

"Good as new, to be honest. No aftereffects from the drug. I swear, Skye. I will never do any kind of drug again."

"Well, this one wasn't exactly your fault."

"I know that, but I did the ecstasy before. No man is worth this."

"True story," I say.

"Garrett and I are through, no matter what. Whether he gave me the ketamine or not. And I just talked to Betsy."

"About what?"

"About her and Peter. I told her what happened, and she agrees that she wasn't quite herself that first night."

My heart drops to my stomach. "Did she sleep with Peter that night?"

"Yeah, and a couple times after."

"Braden's looking into it," I say.

"I know. Tell him thanks again."

"I will. He's not here right now. I'm getting ready to leave for dinner with Eugenie."

"Without Braden?"

"Yeah, something came up for him."

"What was it?"

"He didn't say."

"Well," she says, "I hope everything's okay."

"Yeah, me too. I've got to run. I'll check in again tomorrow, okay?"

"Okay. Love you."

"Love you, too." I end the call and head to the elevator.

Eugenie, here I come.

Chapter Fifty-Three

A bourbon and one glass of wine. All I had to drink at dinner with Eugenie. I read every word of the new documents she drew up—they were fair, concise, and not too full of legalese—and then signed on the dotted line.

The limo drops me off at Braden's building and the driver walks me to the elevator. I slide the card through. "Thanks a lot for the ride." I smile.

He tips his hat. "At your service, Ms. Manning. Good evening to you."

The elevator doors open, and I step in. They close. I check my watch. Ten thirty. Is Braden home? I have no idea. He hasn't texted or called.

I thumb through some comments on my latest post, replying and deleting as necessary, when I realize something.

The elevator isn't moving. Odd. I don't press a button for the floor because there isn't one to press. This elevator goes straight to Braden's penthouse. There is, however, one marked "door open." I push it.

The doors open, and—

I jerk, nearly stumbling.

Peter Reardon stands in front of me with an older man.

"Hello, Skye," Peter says, his tone edgy.

Is he nervous? Maybe. I don't know him well enough to say.

"Peter. What are you doing here?"

More importantly, why isn't the elevator working? I keep the latter to myself.

"We came to see your boyfriend," the other man says.

"And you are?"

"My father," Peter says. "Beau Reardon."

I clear my throat. "He's not home yet."

"Oh, we know that," Beau remarks.

"Then why are you here? If you know he's not, I mean."

"Just waiting. Like you are."

"I prefer to wait upstairs." I walk back into the elevator and slide my card. "If you'll excuse me."

Again, the doors close, but again, the elevator stays still. What the hell?

I push the open button once more.

Peter and Beau still stand in front of the elevator doors. Did they have something to do with this?

"Something wrong?" Beau asks.

His tone is telling—icy with a sardonic edge. He knows exactly what's wrong with the elevator.

"What do you think you're doing?" I demand. "What did you do to the elevator?"

"Funny thing, being an architect," Beau says. "We have to understand building structure, how elevators work. All that kind of stuff. Things that don't concern most people."

"Braden has security cameras all around here," I say. "Whatever you're trying to do, you won't get away with it."

"We understand security, too," Peter offers. "Once you know where the cameras are, they're easily disabled."

I look toward the door of the building. Is the limo still out there? I can make a run for it. These two are giving me the creeps.

"What do you want?" I ask.

"Just to talk."

Icicles spear the back of my neck. *Breathe, Skye. Breathe. Don't show them you're scared shitless.*

"If that's all you want, you have a phone. You've disabled Braden's security and his elevator. What's going on here?"

But knowledge edges its way into my frightened mind. I know full well why they're here.

Braden was right.

Peter and Garrett gave Betsy and Tessa ketamine.

And they got it from Peter's daddy.

"You're not going to get away with this," I say to them.

"Little lady, I've gotten away with a lot worse, as your boyfriend knows."

"That's why he wouldn't give you the building contract," I say, whipping my hand to my hips. "He knows you play dirty."

"And he doesn't?" Beau shakes his head.

"No, he doesn't," I say.

"Maybe you'd like to know who financed his way to the top," Peter says.

Damn. They know. But how? There was an NDA. Except... Addie didn't hold up her part of the bargain. If she continued stalking Braden—in fact, is stalking him still—she may well have divulged the information about the settlement.

"He financed his company himself."

It's not an untruth. It was Braden's money, as I told him earlier. It was opportunity knocking. It was money for his cooperation and silence.

"There's a lot you don't know," Beau says.

Fine. Let them think I don't know. It only puts me in a stronger position. I won't give away the farm.

HELEN HARDT

"Really?" I say. "And I suppose you're going to enlighten me?"

"We'd be happy to," Beau says, "but there isn't time."

"Why not? Braden's not here yet. Seems we have time after all." I stride into the lobby, hoping I look less nervous than I feel. I take a seat on one of the leather wingbacks. "Care to join me, gentlemen?"

My heart is beating rapid-fire, and my mouth is dry. Still, I resist swallowing and licking my lips. I don't want them to know how they're affecting me.

I have no idea what I'm getting into. If they routinely drug women, they could be capable of anything. They could have guns.

My skin chills. I feel like a giant ice cube.

They each take a seat on the couch opposite me. Great. I'm right in their firing range.

I need to get a grip.

Braden, where are you?

Why didn't I text him while I was in the elevator?

"Your boyfriend is up to no good," Beau says.

"If you mean he's going to stop you people from drugging women, then I'd say he's up to a lot of good."

Peter's ears redden around the edge. Oh, he's trying to look calm and collected like his father, but I got to him.

"Those are unfounded accusations," Beau says.

"Interesting. Your friend Garrett drugged Tessa, and I'd be willing to bet you did the same thing to Betsy, Peter."

"More unfounded accusations," Beau says. "Your friend has a history of drug use."

"She's used drugs one time."

Crap. I wish I hadn't said that. I don't need to give them information.

"The allegations against Garrett and my son are fabricated," Beau says, his mouth a straight line.

The man is ice cold. Does anything rattle him?

"Are they? Because I'm pretty sure my friend was drugged."

"That's what she tells you, anyway," Beau says.

"I'm done talking." I grab my phone to text Braden.

Then I drop my jaw nearly to the floor.

Braden walks through the door swiftly, sailing past the unmanned reception desk. He comes directly to me, takes my hand, and pulls me off the chair and into the protection of his body. "Are you okay, Skye?"

I nod. "Yes." I will my voice not to shake.

"And I suppose there's a good reason why my doorman isn't at his post?" Braden eyes Beau and then Peter.

"He wasn't there when we arrived," Beau says.

"Nice try. I got a text from him after you threatened him. Knowing Skye would be home soon, I cut my meeting short."

"Mr. Black," Beau says, "I assure you that—"

"Stop it. Stop it right now. You thought you could get to me through Skye. You have no idea who you're dealing with. Skye has more intelligence in her right hand than the two of you have together."

A little warmth creeps up my neck. I love how much Braden believes in me. Still, I'm glad he showed up.

Really glad.

"She is formidable," Beau agrees, "but does she have this?"

I suck in a breath when Beau pulls out a pistol. Braden's body tenses, but only I notice, since I'm touching him.

Has he been held at gunpoint before?

I haven't, and the way my heart is beating and my skin prickling with fear, it's not something I ever want to repeat.

But Braden is in control. So very in control.

"Put that away, Beau," he says. "You and I both know you're not man enough to actually use it."

Oh God. Oh God. Oh God.

What if Braden's wrong? What if that gun goes off? Right

into our bodies?

God, Braden! Everything turns black and ugly all at once. The man I love could be gone with one pull of a trigger. I should step in front of Braden. Save him. But my feet won't move. They're mired in concrete. And then this maniac could turn on me next. I can't lose Braden. And I don't want to die. I'm too young. My life is just beginning. I have the most wonderful career in the world, the most wonderful man in the world, the most—

Quicker than a flash, Braden executes some kind of kick, sending the gun flying out of Beau's hand and sliding across the marble floor of the lobby until it stops against a wall.

"Don't even think about it," Braden says, as Peter eyes the gun. "We both know you don't have the balls."

Peter's face goes pale, and his eyes… Damn. Are those tears welling in the bottom of his eyes?

How was I ever attracted to this asshole?

"We don't want trouble," Beau says.

"You don't? You always threaten people with a gun when you don't want trouble? And by the way, my security has been back up since I arrived, so I've got you dead to rights for assault with a deadly weapon. Plus what you've done to Skye."

"We didn't hurt her," Beau says.

"You threatened her. You disabled the elevator so she couldn't get away from you. Believe me. I'll make charges stick."

"Fuck you," Peter says.

"Shut up, Peter," his father commands. "We'll just forget this happened."

"I'm afraid not," Braden says. "The cops are already on their way. You're both going to be arrested."

"We didn't hurt anyone," Peter says.

"You scared Skye. You threatened my doorman, and you held Skye and me at gunpoint. Plus, you've been drugging women for years."

"You can't prove that."

"I can. Ms. Logan and Ms. Davis are both willing to press charges against you"—he eyes Peter—"and Mr. Ramirez. But Mr. Ramirez will walk. You want to know why?"

Peter looks like he's about to hurl, but Beau remains calm. On the outside, at least.

"Probably because he hasn't done anything," Beau says.

"To the contrary. I approached him after Ms. Logan was hospitalized. All it took was a little prodding and he sang like a coloratura soprano. How he and your son drugged Ms. Logan and Ms. Davis with substances you provided them. How you've been drugging clients for years to get them to sign contracts with your firm."

"You can't prove any of that."

"I can," Braden says, "and I will."

"What do you even care?" Peter demands. "You have everything. Why don't you just stay out of our lives!"

"I did, for many years. I shouldn't have, but I did. Until it hit close to home. Tessa Logan and Betsy Davis are Skye's friends, and consequently they're important to me." He looks down at me. "I'm sorry it took me so long to put a stop to this. If I'd done it when I first suspected, Tessa and Betsy wouldn't have been in any position to be taken advantage of."

"It's not your fault," I tell him. "No one asked you to save the world."

"That's what I've always told myself. But I was wrong. What good is my fortune if I don't use it to help others?"

Peter drops to the floor. "Please. It's all my dad. I never wanted to do any of this. But he—"

"Get up, you sniveling piece of shit." Beau scoffs. "I'm embarrassed to have you for a son."

As angry as I am, I can't help feeling sorry for Peter in that moment. Being raised by Beau Reardon couldn't have been any kind of picnic.

Sirens blare in the distance, and two patrol cars pull up to the building. Five blues enter, and Beau and Peter are cuffed and charged, their Miranda rights read.

Everything passes in a blur as the cops take both Beau and Peter away.

Finally, when they're gone, I step out of Braden's arms, but then nearly fall. He steadies me quickly.

"You okay?"

"No," I say. "Not even a little bit."

"You seemed so calm."

"It was an act, Braden. They had me cornered. I didn't know what to do. I'm so glad you showed up."

"I had a feeling Beau wouldn't take this lying down. But I underestimated him. I figured he'd come directly to me."

"Why? He's obviously been exploiting women for years."

"Not just women. He uses the drugs to get what he wants in business as well."

"He's a coward."

"You're absolutely right," Braden says. "I won't make this mistake again. He found my Achilles' heel. I'm so sorry to put you through this, Skye."

"I'll be okay."

"I know you will. You're strong. The strongest woman I've ever known. Well, you're tied, anyway."

"Oh? Tied with whom."

He exhales slowly. "With my mother, Skye. You're tied with my mother."

Chapter Fifty-Four

Back at Braden's place, he pours a bourbon for each of us. I take a sip, letting the smoky liquor burn my throat. It's a good burn. A burn I need at the moment.

My heart is still thumping from having a gun pointed at me.

I always thought I could imagine what that might feel like. I was wrong. It's terror. Sheer terror. Your life doesn't flash before your eyes. All you see is fear. Fear with its ugly black-and-red head, laughing at you in a satanic, mocking way.

I don't want to experience that again any time soon. Like ever.

"I'll always protect you," Braden says.

"I know." And I believe him. I know he'll always try. And I know doubly that if he ever failed, he'd never forgive himself.

And with that thought, I know something about his mother.

"You blame yourself," I murmur. "Not just for feeling repulsed by her scars when you were a little boy. You blame yourself for her death."

"Yes. I do. I always will."

"It wasn't your fault." I don't know what happened, but already I know it wasn't his fault. Braden was six years old.

Braden could never be at fault. I know that as well as I know my own name, Skye Margaret Manning.

"She survived the fire," I say. "She was strong."

"She was. She made sure Ben and I got to safety."

"Any mother would save her child first."

"I know. But she was never the same. Even though she was still beautiful."

"I'm sure she was, if she was your mother."

He simply nods.

"You don't have to tell me, Braden."

"No. I want to. It's time." He shakes his head. "I've never told this story to anyone."

I smile. "Then I'm honored."

"I haven't even told my therapist."

"I'm doubly honored."

He draws in a deep breath. "She and my father stayed together, and he did get sober. He tried, but he wasn't cut out for marriage, really. In his way, my father loved her."

I nod.

"But she was never the same after the fire. She fell into depression."

Oh God. I know where this is heading, and I don't want to hear any more.

But as he continues, I widen my eyes. This path leads to an unexpected place.

"We kept her going. Ben and I."

"She loved you very much."

"She did. And she loved Dad, for all his faults."

"You love him, too, don't you?"

"In my way. But I've never forgiven him for what he cost me."

"Your mother?"

"Yes."

He stays silent as time seems to suspend itself. I don't push.

If he's done talking, that's okay. Oh, I'm wildly curious, but it can keep. Braden and I have all the time in the world.

"She got sick," he finally says. "One of the burn wounds never healed properly, and it got infected. She developed a bad strep bacterial strain. The one they call the flesh-eating bacteria."

"Oh my God. Streptococcus A."

"That's the one. I had just started high school, and Ben had just started middle school."

"And you lost your mother."

He nods, his eyes heavy-lidded. Still, no moisture pools in them. Braden doesn't cry. I have the feeling he hasn't cried since that day.

If he even did then.

"Why is this so difficult for you to talk about?" I ask. "It's not your fault."

"It is."

"Braden, it's not. Blame your father if you want. I at least get that. But not yourself."

"You don't understand, Skye. That day… That day of the fire…"

"What? What happened the day of the fire?"

"I didn't want to leave my room," he says. "I didn't want to leave my precious comic books to get burned into ashes. She's yelling at me to get out. She's got Ben in her arms, and she doesn't have an extra arm for me. So she finally leaves, gets Ben to safety, and then she comes back for me. She lifts me up and I drop the handful of comic books. I yelled at her, Skye. I told her…"

"It's all right. You told her what?"

"I told her I hated her for making me leave my comic books."

"Oh God…" I gulp.

"That's right. She got me to safety, and then she went back in to get the comic books. But they were already ablaze, and that's what…" He shakes his head.

"That's what burned her," I say monotonously. "The fire from your comic books."

He doesn't respond.

Finally, "Maybe. I don't know if it was the comic books or not. But she went back in, and she got dragged out by a fireman with third-degree burns on the left side of her body."

What can I say to him? It's a horrific story. But he was a kid. Just a kid. And kids have silly ideas about what's important. Surely he knows that.

Do I go to him? Take him in my arms? Kiss his lips? Embrace him?

"Tell me," I finally say. "Tell me what you need right now."

He takes a sip of his bourbon. "No one knows that story," he says. "Not even Ben or my dad. She told him she went back in to get our baby books."

"Have you considered that maybe that's the truth?"

"No. She was in my bedroom when the fireman dragged her out."

"So your father knows, then."

"He knows she was in my bedroom. He assumed that's where my baby book was. It wasn't. The baby books were in a cedar chest in the living room underneath some quilts."

"And Ben doesn't know?"

"He was only three. He had no idea where the baby books were."

"And you did."

"Yeah. Sometimes Mom and I would look at them together. I liked looking at my first lock of hair." He shakes his head. "I haven't let myself think about this in so long."

Again, I'm at a loss for what to do. But my hand, seemingly of its own accord, reaches out and touches Braden's cheek. "It's okay."

"It's not. It's never been okay, and it never will be."

Chapter Fifty-Five

"You now know more about me than anyone else," Braden says to me. "Anyone."

My shoulders weigh—in a good way—with the knowledge of his statement. "You can trust me, Braden. All of your secrets are safe with me."

He rakes his fingers through his hair. "I do trust you. More than you know."

"More than I know?" I lift my eyebrows. "How can—"

He shoots his bourbon down his throat and groans. Then he regards me. Sternly. "This can't continue."

My heart plummets. Whatever he's getting at, it can't be good. "What?" I ask softly, my voice cracking.

"Reardon found my weakness. I went to him, threatened him, and instead of going after me, he went after you, Skye. My Achilles' heel."

I rise to go toward him, but he stops me with a gesture.

I drop my ass back into my chair. "Everyone has an Achilles' heel, Braden."

"I don't." He pours himself another finger of bourbon. "I *can't*."

No. This isn't happening. Not after everything we've been through to be together. Not after he trusted me with his most guarded secrets.

No, damn it! No!

"Don't you see?" He slams his glass down on the table. "I can't keep you safe."

"But you *did* keep me safe."

"Because of circumstance. What if the doorman hadn't texted me?"

"But he did."

"Damn it, Skye!" He stands and hurls the glass against the wall.

I cower against the crash, against the tiny clear shards that rain onto the carpet. My heart is at once still yet beating thunderously. I feel... I feel...

I gather my will to say what needs to be said.

"You told me in the cornfield that there was only one master of control between us," I say, my lips trembling. "You. You, Braden. You're in control, and you protected me."

"What if I can't the next time?"

"Who says there'll be a next time?"

"I was wrong," he says. "I didn't think anything could touch you. Touch *us*. I didn't realize..."

"Didn't realize what?" I urge.

"Even now, it surprises me how much I love you. How much I need you in my life. To be without you will be torture."

I stand again, wanting—no, needing—to be near him. I tentatively reach forward. "You don't have to be without me."

"Don't you get it?" He rubs furiously at his temple, as if easing a throbbing ache. "I have to let you go. I can't take the chance—"

I close the distance between us and fall into him, resolving not to shed the tears that threaten. He thinks I'm the strongest woman he knows. Now is the time for me to prove him right.

"I won't let you go," I say against his chest. "I won't. I refuse."

"Oh, Skye…" He kisses the top of my head.

I ease back and meet his gaze. "We didn't work this hard to be together just to have it torn away from us. By Beau Reardon? By Peter and Garrett? No way, Braden. I don't accept this. Not for a fucking minute."

"You don't have a choice." He shakes his head. "Neither of us does."

"Bullshit." I pound my fist on his chest. "If it would truly be torture to live without me, why would you subject yourself to that?"

"For your safety."

"I can take care of myself."

"What if I hadn't come tonight?"

"You did."

"Damn it! Fight fair, Skye."

"Why should I? You're not."

He levels his gaze on me. "I always fight fair."

"Not with me. It's your way or the highway, always. Well, not tonight, Braden. We're not in the bedroom at the moment, and this time I'm getting *my* way."

My heart is beating like a hummingbird's. Fast and twittery. I'm ready to go to battle for the man I love, even if he's the one I'm fighting.

"I can't lose you," he says, his voice resigned. "Not like I lost her."

His eyes are sunken, as if he's resolved to his fate.

I curl my hands into fists, ready to win this war. "I'm *not* your mother, Braden."

He sighs. "I know."

"She made a choice. She chose you. I'm making that same choice. You want to condemn us both to torture without each other? I won't let you."

"I didn't keep her safe," he says into my hair. "I lost her."

I pull back and grip his strong shoulders. "You were six years old, for God's sake! Are you going to hold a child to some insurmountable standard?"

"Don't you?"

Fair question, and one I wasn't expecting. "No," I say. "Absolutely not. My parents' separation was *not* my fault."

For the first time, I believe the words with all my heart. My journey is far from complete, but I'm moving forward. And with each step, I understand myself a little better.

"And your mother's death was not your fault, Braden. It isn't. It never was."

He cups my cheek, then, running his thumb over my top lip.

"I won't give you up," I say. "You'll protect me. And I'll protect you. That's how it is when you love someone. We both have an equal obligation to each other." I cover his hand with my own.

What seems like an eternity passes between us, our gazes locked. Braden doesn't cry, but his eyes are glazed over with what I suspect are unshed tears.

I hold my own tears back—for him, and also for me.

Finally, he smiles. It's weak, but it's a smile. "I'll never truly control you, will I?"

I move forward and brush my lips against his stubbled cheek. "Braden, did you ever honestly believe you would?"

Chapter Fifty-Six

Black Rose Underground.

Braden's private suite.

I wear only platform stilettos and black-and-red lace panties.

"Lie down on the table," Braden says darkly.

A black sheet sits on top of the leather table. Braden has prepared for something. My nipples are hard and aching.

I know what's coming, and I know how much he's giving me.

I flash back to the last time we were in this room—that horrid evening when we almost ended for good because of something I wanted. Something he couldn't give me.

This lifestyle means as much—perhaps more—to me as it always has. But now, I see the play for what it is—play. It's not punishment for something either of us did in the past. It's simply part of our sex life, a part we both immensely enjoy.

And we both need to be comfortable with what happens.

I lie down as commanded, Braden's diamond choker heavy around my neck—a symbol of who I belong to when I'm here.

"Hold this." Braden places a black leather flogger next to my hip.

I grasp it in my hand, my body shivering. What will he do to me with the flogger? How will it feel against my hard nipples, my abdomen, my clit?

I can't wait to find out.

But Braden won't be rushed. He's always on his own time.

"I'm not going to bind you tonight," he says. "You have only your obedience to me in this room to hold yourself still as I do what I do. Do you understand?"

"Yes," I say.

"I've never given you a safe word. I give you one now."

"Okay, but I don't think I'll need it."

"Just in case," he says. "Your safe word is 'always.' Because you're mine. Always."

"Always," I repeat softly. "And you're mine. Always."

"I am. I never thought I'd want to belong to another person, but I'm yours. Always."

I can't help a smile, and I reach forward—

Braden grabs the flogger from me and whips my hand away.

I drop it back down to my side, the sting a lovely flame that probes straight to my clit.

"Stay still," he commands. "And stay quiet, as well. The only thing you're allowed to say is your safe word, if you need it."

I nod.

I understand.

I understand Braden so much better than the last time we were here together.

I understand myself so much better as well.

And I'm ready.

I'm ready for whatever he chooses to give me tonight. What goes on in this room is his choice, not mine. My choice is whether to consent.

He moves away from the table and out of my line of vision. When he returns, he picks up the flogger once more and whips it across my breasts.

I gasp at the sting.

He gasps as well. "I brought a blush to your tits. So beautiful."

My nipples are straining, having grown even harder from the flogger.

He brings it across my breasts again, and then once more. Then he whips my abdomen softly. Then harder. Harder still.

Until he comes to my clit.

It's hard and straining, and I want more than anything to lift my hips, offer myself to Braden on a silver platter.

But I'm bound.

Bound only by his command, but his will is stronger than the toughest rope.

He teases me with the flogger, trailing it ever so lightly over my clit.

I'm ready to explode. Seriously shatter like those glass shards from his glass on the carpet last night.

My flesh tingles, and I'm ready, so ready…

He flogs my clit then, and I jerk, the sparks flying through me out to my limbs and then arrowing back to my pussy.

Please, I beg inwardly. *Please, Braden. I need you!*

He turns from me for a moment, fidgets with something out of a drawer. Then he turns back to me, a red taper candle in his hand.

"Soy wax," he says. "It burns cooler than paraffin. I can't risk burning your beautiful skin."

He hands the candle to me then. I grasp it tightly.

He pulls out a match. "I could use a lighter, but I prefer matches." He strikes it and then lights the candle. "Watch the flame. Let it hypnotize you as you hold it."

I bring the candle in front of me, breathing in the aroma of the lit match, the sweetness of the burning wax. The small flame grows, flickering in a discordant rhythm. I stare at its orange warmth, at the red wax beginning to melt. Relaxation overtakes me, though my body still hums from the flogging.

After some time—I couldn't say how long—Braden takes the candle from me and tips it, so a drop of wax hits the inside of his forearm.

I open my mouth to ask him what he's doing, but he regards me sternly.

Right. I'm to stay quiet.

"I'm testing the wax, Skye. I'll never put something on your body that I wouldn't put on my own. It's my duty to protect you. Always."

Always.

My safe word.

Except it's so much more than a safe word.

Not just to me but also to him. Braden was so distraught when he thought he didn't protect me from the Reardons. So upset that he was ready to leave me rather than have me put in harm's way again.

Now, more than any other time, I understand his need to protect me. He'll never let me down, and I'll never let him down.

The wax hardens on his forearm, and he nods. "It's ready."

I tingle all over. Where will he drip the wax first? On my thighs? My chest? My nipples. Not knowing what to expect has me thrilled beyond measure.

Braden holds the candle over me, and the anticipation drives me wild. I don't dare close my eyes, though I'm tempted, just so I won't know where the hot wax is coming—

Until it's there. A drop on the top of one breast. I gasp. It burns, yes, but only for a split second. Then it's warmth, as it meanders for a few seconds before beginning to harden.

Braden tips the candle once more, and another drop drizzles onto my areola.

My nipple hardens as the areola shrinks around it. The red

hue of the wax makes my nipple look painted.

Painted red.

And it's fucking hot, in more ways than one.

My hips rise, seemingly of their own accord. Yes, Braden told me to stay still, but he doesn't admonish me.

He merely groans.

"You're so beautiful," he says, as he drips more wax over my breasts and nipples. "God, I didn't know how hot this would be."

I sigh, again tempted to close my eyes and surrender myself to the moment.

More drips, the flaming hotness melting against me, engulfing me in desire, and then cooling quickly into shapes, none the same.

He trails the candle lower, and I hold back a gasp. Will he drip wax onto my clit? Onto my pussy? Do I want him to?

I have my safe word.

But I won't use it. I know this already. Braden will never put me in harm's way.

I trust him.

I trust him with my body, my heart, my soul.

And I trust him with this candle.

He groans again. "I thought about binding you, but I decided against it, and I'm glad. You couldn't be more beautiful than you are now, bound only by my command." He drips wax on my abdomen, close to my mound, and I shiver at the burn and then the warmth and then the tingles as the wax cools and hardens.

Braden moves down to my thighs, dripping the wax into long rivers over my flesh. With each new burn, my excitement increases. My heart beats faster, and my pussy aches even more.

He spreads my legs. "You're glistening, Skye. So wet. Fuck." He blows out the candle.

I suck in a breath, part out of disappointment but more so out of anticipation. He's going to fuck me now. I know it in my bones. I'm in sync with Braden's passions and desires.

He disrobes quickly and within seconds he's hovering over me, ready to plunge inside.

"I love you, Skye. I fucking love you so much."

He thrusts into me.

The wax shapes bend slightly with each of his thrusts, and my nipples react to the friction. I meet Braden's fiery blue gaze. I haven't been told to speak, but I can't help it.

"I love you, too, Braden. So much."

He lifts his eyebrows slightly at my disobedience, but then he closes his eyes, squeezing them shut as he continues to fuck me hard and fast.

And with each thrust, I lift my hips, longing to grab his ass and force him farther and farther into me, but I hold back. I already disobeyed once. I will not do it again.

Instead, I rush. Inside my body I rush toward the peak I've only climbed with Braden. With this amazing man who I love so much.

And when I come, I undulate into him, take his body into my own with more passion than ever before.

I moan and cry out, shudder beneath him as my pussy explodes around his cock.

"Fuck," he groans.

When he releases, I feel every spurt, every contraction, every ounce of love he pours into me.

And I know.

I know this is the man I'll spend my life with.

Always.

Epilogue

Two days later, we're back in Boston. Penny runs toward me and I pepper her little face with kisses. Already she's nearly doubled in size. I give Sasha equal attention, while Braden hangs his suitcoat on the coatrack near the elevator door.

I take a quick look at my phone. Betsy never called me back, so I'll call her. I owe Kathy Harmon a call and dinner date, too. I have a therapist who is helping me. Tessa and I are great. Braden and I are great. I've forgiven my parents and myself, and I'm on a journey toward self-love and acceptance. It will take some time to get over the trauma with the Reardons, but I'll do it. I have to.

Addison is no longer a threat to either of us. Braden met with Brock Ames and a slew of attorneys this morning, paid back the half million dollars Brock gave him all those years ago, and they drew up a new agreement, nullifying the previous one. The statute of limitations for any allegations Addie could make against Braden has long expired. Now, if she comes near either of us again, we *will* file charges.

I smile to myself.

Christopher and the others seem to have disappeared, and I head to the kitchen for a drink of water. "You want anything?" I ask Braden.

"No, I'm good. Thanks."

I grab a glass, fill it with ice and water, and take a long drink. Flying dries me out, even a short flight like New York to Boston. I set the glass on the counter, and—

I gasp.

Braden is in the kitchen, and he cups my face and kisses me long and hard. I melt into him and return his kiss, already throbbing with want. I'll never get enough of Braden Black.

So I'm disappointed when he breaks the kiss.

"I love you, Skye," he says, his voice gruff.

"I love you, too."

Then he does something I don't expect, especially not from Braden Black.

He drops to one knee.

I gasp.

He pulls a ruby red velvet box out of his pocket, opens it, and hands it to me.

My heart nearly stops. It's a ring. A diamond ring, and it's large but not ostentatious. Braden knows me. He knows I wouldn't want anything over-the-top.

"I didn't want to do this in New York," he says. "I wanted to do it here. In our home."

"*Our* home?"

"Yes. I want you to move in with me, Skye."

I clasp my hand to my mouth.

"The diamond choker you wear at the club is yours now," he says. "It tells the world you're mine in the dark. But Skye, I want the world to know you're mine all the time. Everywhere we go."

"Oh my God, Braden."

"Will you accept this ring? Will you marry me? Will you be mine. Always?"

I drop to my knees in front of him, cup both his cheeks, and as a tear streams from my eye, I reply.

"Always, Braden. I'll follow you always."

Acknowledgments

This has been a blast! I hope you've enjoyed Braden and Skye's journey as much as I have.

Thanks so much to the incredible team at Entangled Amara for their belief in and dedication to this project. Liz, Jessica, Stacy, Heather, Bree, Riki, Lydia, Curtis, Toni, Meredith—you all had a huge hand in making the Follow Me series shine! These new covers are gorgeous!

Thanks to the women and men of my reader group, Hardt and Soul. Your endless and unwavering support keeps me going.

To my family and friends, thank you for your encouragement.

Thank you most of all to my readers. Without you, none of this would be possible. If you find yourself missing Braden and Skye, have no fear. We may see more of them in the future!

This erotic anthology has something for everyone and caters to many different tastes and proclivities. Discover what interests or excites you. Explore which is your perfect story. Return to it again and again. We dare you.

aphrodite

in bloom

a n o n y m o u s

Don't miss this extraordinary collection of twelve inventive and sophisticated stories guaranteed to awaken the forbidden desires of a new generation. From the sweetly romantic to the sublimely taboo, each provocative novella offers an opportunity to explore your most secret fantasies.

A virgin receives an especially satisfying gift at a masked ball...

A duke offers to settle a man's debt for one night with his wife...

As an introduction to a secret club, a viscount's heir is made over into a woman—and discovers her true self...

Plus nine more sensual stories of libidinous lust, catering to the tastes of varying sexual appetites. Whatever your fancy, *Aphrodite in Bloom* is ready and willing to serve...